TIME AND SPLACE

Omar Francis

Published in February 2024, by Ebookshelf Publishers, Kingston Jamaica, W.I.
ebookshelfpublishers@gmail.com.

Text copyright © 2024

All rights reserved.
No part of this publication may be reproduced, stored in a retrieval system or transmitted in any form or by any means, electronic, mechanical, photocopying, recording or otherwise without prior permission of the author or publisher.

Book design and layout by
Upper Echelon Jamaica
Ocho Rios, Kingston
Jamaica
upperechelonjamaica@gmail.com

Published by:
Ebookshelf Publishers
Kingston
Jamaica
W.I.
ebookshelfpublishers@gmail.com.

OMAR FRANCIS - *'Time and Splace'*

TIME AND SPLACE

Omar Francis

TABLE OF CONTENTS

CHAPTERS	PAGE
ONE	9
TWO	10
THREE	11
FOUR	12
FIVE	13
SIX	14
SEVEN	15
EIGHT	16
NINE	18
TEN	20
ELEVEN	22
TWELVE	24
THIRTEEN	27
FOURTEEN	30
FIFTEEN	33
SIXTEEN	35
SEVENTEEN	38
EIGHTEEN	41
NINETEEN	46
TWENTY	49

TABLE OF CONTENTS

CHAPTERS	PAGE
TWENTY-ONE	53
TWENTY-TWO	57
TWENTY-THREE	60
TWENTY-FOUR	64
TWENTY-FIVE	68
TWENTY-SIX	72
TWENTY-SEVEN	76
TWENTY-EIGHT	79
TWENTY-NINE	83
THIRTY	87
THIRTY-ONE	91
THIRTY-TWO	95
THIRTY-THREE	100
THIRTY-FOUR	104
THIRTY-FIVE	107
THIRTY-SIX	113
THIRTY-SEVEN	117
THIRTY-EIGHT	122
THIRTY-NINE	127
FORTY	131

TABLE OF CONTENTS

CHAPTERS	PAGE
FORTY-ONE	136
FORTY-TWO	141
FORTY-THREE	145
FORTY-FOUR	149
FORTY-FIVE	154
FORTY-SIX	159
FORTY-SEVEN	163
FORTY-EIGHT	169
FORTY-NINE	174
FIFTY	179
FIFTY-ONE	184
FIFTY-TWO	188
FIFTY-THREE	193
FIFTY-FOUR	198
FIFTY-FIVE	203
FIFTY-SIX	208
FIFTY-SEVEN	212
FIFTY-EIGHT	217
FIFTY-NINE	222
SIXTY	226

TABLE OF CONTENTS

CHAPTERS	PAGE
SIXTY-ONE	231
SIXTY-TWO	236
SIXTY-THREE	240
SIXTY-FOUR	245
SIXTY-FIVE	251
SIXTY-SIX	258
SIXTY-SEVEN	262
SIXTY-EIGHT	267
SIXTY-NINE	272
SEVENTY	278
SEVENTY-ONE	283
SEVENTY-TWO	289
SEVENTY-THREE	295
SEVENTY-FOUR	298
SEVENTY-FIVE	303
SEVENTY-SIX	309
SEVENTY-SEVEN	314
SEVENTY-EIGHT	319
SEVENTY-NINE	324
EIGHTY	330

TABLE OF CONTENTS

CHAPTERS	PAGE
EIGHTY-ONE	334
EIGHTY-TWO	339
EIGHTY-THREE	344
EIGHTY-FOUR	348
EIGHTY-FIVE	353
EIGHTY-SIX	358
EIGHTY-SEVEN	362
EIGHTY-EIGHT	367
EIGHTY-NINE	372
NINETY	376
NINETY-ONE	379
NINETY-TWO	384
NINETY-THREE	388
NINETY-FOUR	392
NINETY-FIVE	396
NINETY-SIX	401
NINETY-SEVEN	405
NINETY-EIGHT	410
NINETY-NINE	412
About the Author	415

ONE

Osha, the youngest of three sisters, came to the Caribbean in a slave ship. Being what she is, the journey didn't cause her much suffering. She spent most of the trip in *the place that's not a place* and the dreamtime, two of the many splaces she had access to. When she was here, in the fourth worlds (our splace) she mostly sang and played quiet songs to comfort and strengthen her fellow travelers, captive and captor alike.

In fact, it's not untrue to say that Osha came on every slave ship that crossed the Atlantic. Others came too, but no-one else went on ALL the ships.

She didn't suffer much, but since then she's certainly been a bit quieter and more pensive than she used to be.

TWO

Varoden and his twin brother would, when they were young, roam together across the vast stepped plain; forging a bond that would never disappear, despite their later divergence. They had always been different, of course; Varoden tall, thin and thoughtful, and his brother Thrango shorter, muscular and impulsive. No one who looked at them without knowing ever said to themselves "those two must be twins". But the resemblances were there: in the set of their jaw, their bright eyes, their determined gaze. Other stuff too.

Varoden had, at a certain point, decided to leave his home to seek wisdom and knowledge. His brother had decided to stay and steep himself in the ways of his own land.

So off went Varoden, to he knew not where, to find he knew not exactly what.

THREE

The sea was Ranga's home, and he knew it with most parts of his being. He knew the currents, and the winds, and the skies and the living beings and lots more besides. When someone knows something well enough to be called a master, as Ranga was a master of the sea, they often attain a kind of calm, which precludes the reckless questing after fame and gain which drives so much of the latter story of the fourth worlds. It is, thus, fair to assume that the epic journeys he took, having understood the sea, were not in search of glory; that he had some other purpose in mind.

He did.

FOUR

And then there's me. I'm just a regular human. Well, regular, except for one thing, which I'll get into later. I was born and have spent most of my life on the island of Jamaica, which is in the same Caribbean Sea that Osha sailed to on her slave ships. Most of my ancestors were slaves here, but some weren't. Thanks for sticking it out ancestors! Anyway, I'm a musician, and a writer (well, now I am) and a student. It was, actually, the student part that let me in on the stuff that I'm writing about. So thanks teachers!

FIVE

Ranga the Navigator was born in a beautiful land, between mountains and the sea. He could swim before he could walk, partly due to the fact that his mother birthed him in the salty water of the great ocean to the east of their land. There were some interesting events that accompanied Ranga's birthing; among which was the fact that a sea serpent swam up as soon as the newborn had left his mother, and put a small bit of plant in his hand, which Ranga reflexively clamped his hand on. There were multiple witnesses to this event, and so everyone knew from the beginning that he was, at very least, a little bit different from the average. His mother, once she was able, after much effort, to pry the plant from his insistent infant fingers, had a necklace made of it, and hung it around Ranga's neck, where it would stay for a long, long time.

Ranga's necklace grew with him, so that it fell around the same place on his upper chest whatever size he was, until he was his final size. He didn't take it off often, either. What did happen, though, is that his mother and he, when he was still a young boy, decided to cut a single leaf and a small bit of stem from Ranga's plant, to bury it, and see if it would grow.

Did it ever grow!

SIX

Osha and her two sisters were born and grew up in the shadow of the great Tree which interpenetrated, and in fact connected, many of the splaces close to the fourth worlds. The particular iteration of the tree that the three called home was in the splace called the dreamtime, which part of Osha would always remain connected to. Her sisters, on the whole, tended to be less sentimental, but we'll see about that later. The enormous tree, which Osha called Roko, was one of her first caregivers, and later one of her best friends. Their relationship was one of the ways that a young Osha learned patience: impatient people find it extremely difficult to hang out with trees at all, much less an iteration of the great Tree.

Roko lived right in the middle of the dreamtime, but then again, everything was right in the middle of the dreamtime. It is a splace made up of middles, in fact. This is in particular contrast to *the place that's not a place*, which does not, and probably cannot, have a middle. These two splaces- the dreamtime and *the place that's not a place* were, viewed in many ways, right on either side of the fourth worlds. They were, as a consequence, among the easiest splaces for us regular humans to perceive.

Keep it in mind.

SEVEN

I grew up in in the city of Kingston, which is a former refugee camp (after a big earthquake nearby) that became the capital of our country. It never really stopped feeling like (or being, really) a refugee camp; but there's a lot of beauty and possibility in that kind of place, so that's no insult.

When I was a child, Kingston became an overtly violent place, as opposed to the covertly violent place it had been for most of its modern history.

Its ancient history is less violent, but sometimes eventful, because it's a crossroads place, geologically, geographically, epistemologically and other "ly's" as well. It's equally true to say of modern Kingston, by the way, that it's a very peaceful place… that's one of the ways that crossroads work.

Anyway, I was born, went to school(s), learned to play sports and music and other things; until it became time to start doing my thing. It's certainly been interesting.

EIGHT

Varoden followed the sun at the beginning of his journey, encountering few others at first. "What is it", he thought to himself as he walked," that I want?" This was and is a difficult question to answer truthfully for anyone. He knew, for example he wasn't seeking comfort, because he'd left a very comfortable existence behind.

Varoden and Thrango were sons of The People, as they called themselves, the inheritors of a tradition that stretched past the imaginable past to the very beginnings, or so they said. The People had survived the great Cataclysm by the skin of their teeth, finding a cave near the top of a not so high mountain that provided protection for some (not close to all) of them. They had, as a group, made the rational decision that women, as child-bearers, were more central to their continued survival than men, so a sizeable percentage of those afforded refuge in the cave were women of an appropriate age. There were, wisely, representatives of all demographic groups present in their haven, to provide the balance that The People knew to be essential to life; but there was a definite and noticeable skew in the aforementioned fashion.

The other People went off in different directions, grouped in small bands. A few of them survived, as well.

Anyway, by Varoden's time, The People had learned the rhythms of nature well enough to achieve a fairly idyllic lifestyle. Their tradition involved movement, following the seasons, the stars, the herds, and other things as well. While many of the groups in their extended neighbourhood had started to form settlements, using the technologies that had accompanied the coming of agriculture; The People stayed with their way, which they, mostly, considered to be a lot freer and more *humane* (or maybe it should be human) than the backbreaking and monotonous lives of the farmers they would encounter on their movements.

After the necessities of life were accomplished, the people would gather and play music and games; make pottery and jewellery; swim and dance, and just enjoy themselves, really. It was, on the whole, quite a satisfying life. But Varoden knew there was more to life, and he was determined to find it.

NINE

The Caribbean Sea was named by some people after some other people. As things tend to be, these days. The people it was named after, the Caribs, are where we get the word "cannibal" from. Because they used to eat people, apparently.

Osha was never into the eating people thing, but she could appreciate the irony of the name that was given to the warm body of water with which she was to become so well acquainted.

This is because she knew, as few others did, that the Caribbean Sea was one of the middles of the earth (there are quite a few, to be fair). Like all middles of the earth, it was a kind of discontinuity in the regular running of time and space. Like other middles, it exerted a kind of pull on anything that came close enough to it. And like middles across this universe, it was a kind of door.

The Caribbean Sea didn't eat just anybody, though. It took a lot of work, effort and practice to even be considered for the process, and many a candidate spent years and years preparing, only to be summarily rejected, without so much as an explanation.

Osha, being who she was, didn't feel any need to pay too much attention to that whole business, at first; over time, though, she began to be more and more interested in what was really going on.

There was a lot going on.

Anyway, Osha arrived and arrived and arrived in the lands in and around the brilliantly shining sea. And from the first, the process was a form of ritual, the specifics of which were covered in a kind of mystery that was opaque to even her keen eye. The participants in the sacred dance were usually unaware, mostly, of the powerful consequences of their actions across time and space; they were tired or scared or distracted or greedy or something else. And so the movements were unself-conscious and archetypal, which works better.

She was bought and sold too. This had happened to her many times before, but it had never been like this. She keenly and analytically watched the type of binding that was done to her, and which was the ruling idea of the slave buyers and their country-people. She pondered the meaning of what she was seeing as deeply as she had ever pondered anything. And she remained open to life and death, which was a particular talent of hers...

    And so she learned.

TEN

Ranga was, despite the circumstances of his birth, quite an ordinary seeming child, at first. He didn't fuss or cry a lot, and he would stare at the people and things around with him with an inquisitive and almost amused seeming expression, but this didn't really garner much attention or comment.

When he was small, the thing he loved to do more than anything was to just float in thewater, especially sea water, and the let the various forces move him where they would.

Speaking of forces, it's a truth of the universe that beings explain things (and sometimes no-things) in terms that reflect more about themselves than any deep underlying nature. It's no co-incidence, I'm saying, that "modern" fourth-worlders tend to understand their surroundings in terms of "laws" of nature, and fundamental "forces". There's a lot more to it than that of course. A lot.

Anyway, at the time I'm writing this, (many) fourth-worlders say that there're four fundamental forces (the weak force, the strong force, electro-magnetism and gravity), while some are beginning to talk about a fifth fundamental force, that explains some of the stuff that isn't so clear right now.

There are an infinite number of forces. Also, there are no forces at all, and never have been or will be. Additionally, there are a lot of forces, but not an infinite number. Lastly, for now, there are six forces easily noticeable to fourth-worlders who pay attention... well maybe not "easily". They're definitely noticeable, though.

A young Ranga learned all this before puberty, just by floating in the sea. Good job Ranga!

Anyway, Ranga didn't only float all day long. He played with his friends, once he could, and learned the wisdom of his people, which was deep, if somewhat limited. Also, he tended to the tree that had grown out of his necklace, keeping it safe from the dangers which often faced young trees on their own. So it grew, and he grew.

ELEVEN

Our Sun, which is eight light minutes away from our planet, can sometimes seem like it's right next to us, close enough to touch, in fact. So it was for Varoden, one day not so long into his journey to the west. It wasn't actually that hot, and so he was able to continue at a steady pace, still following a path that his people knew well. If it hadn't been so bright, though, he might not have noticed that the animal tracks a little south of his way were unusual. They were signs of a herd, but the prints in the ground didn't look like anything he knew. So he followed them.

And followed them some more.
And still some more, until he was convinced that the animal was some kind of horse, but a bigger type than he had ever seen, or heard of; or imagined possible. His people had hunted and eaten equine animals for a long time, so he was quite familiar with their various species and types. He was following something outside his experience and knowledge.

The tracks, and thus Varoden, went mostly to the southwest, until, after not such a long time, he was in unknown lands, outside of his people's knowledge, lore or protection. And he was content.

And then there was a road, which, somehow, the giant horses seemed to be following. It was a well built road, as well, the liked of which our young hero had never seen. And so now he followed the road, which, at first, was still heading generally southwest, but which flattened its gradient until it was nearly back to west again; so that Varoden was following the Sun, the horses and the road.

Not long into its westward extent, the road met another road, which ran from south to north.And there, at the meeting point of the two ways, a tall, beautiful and exotically dressed man sat quietly beneath a tree, doing nothing.

He looked at an astonished Varoden, smiled, and said (in Varoden's language, which was also surprising) "Hello young man, I've been waiting for you"

To Varoden's gaping silence, the stranger said,

"Perhaps I should have introduced myself first" He bowed, and continued "I am Berondyas of the Ve, and whom do I have the pleasure of making the acquaintance of?"

"huh?" said Varoden

"Who are you?" asked Berondyas

"Oh... my name is Varoden, of the ... People, I guess?"

"You guess correctly" said the tall stranger "Now come along, there's much to do, and time's a going."

With that Berondyas of the Ve turned and walked westward down the road, leaving a bemused Varoden to follow quietly in his wake.

TWELVE

The library of time, which is another splace, is not so far from the fourth worlds. Viewed many ways, it was actually right next to the dreamtime. And so Osha and her two sisters would, when Osha was little, occasionally visit it.

It appeared to Osha as a long corridor, with many doors on both sides of it. Some of the doors were actually elevators, which she loved to take. The walls of the corridors were filled with books, in various languages and thought systems, on seemingly random topics- there was no arrangement that the sisters knew of.

Through the doors that weren't elevators were other long corridors, branching off perpendicular to the original one. The walls of these side corridors were seemingly transparent and translucent, and showed possibilities. There was also always music in the side corridors, of wildly variant types and agreeableness; thankfully (often) it was possible to change the music by touching different buttons on the wall.

There were about eight or so side doors for each elevator, off the main hallway. It wasn't easy to differentiate between the two types of door, until one knew what one was looking for. These weren't, as you might guess, regular elevators. Some were, taking you up to other levels of the main corridor, in which you could see, somehow, the whole library stretching out in all directions over sensibly high railings. There was every type of media in these halls, filled with all the information that ever was, will be or could be. It was a lot of stuff, in other words.

And then there were the special elevators, which could be used to travel in any direction at just about any speed, showing one different goings-on in a multitude of splaces. When I say "any speed" by the way, I mean "*any* speed"; light had nothing to hide here, and so enforced few boundaries or limitations.

It was, in other words, fairly easy to get a bit lost if you didn't know what you were about, and what was up. The sisters never did, though. They were wise enough to know their limitations, and cautious enough to mark their ways as a matter of course. Even on the special elevators. This meant that there was a lot of stuff they hadn't seen, but patience was one of the signal qualities of all three of them- they were very rarely in a rush to do anything.

Osha, in her early days in the Caribbean, would often think of the library, and one time there in particular. That day, she, the most daring of the three, had gone off by herself for a bit, into a special elevator that was, unusually, playing music. She listened to the music, which was strangely and complexly beautiful to her, filled with voices and ideas that sometimes ran quite counter to expectation and sensibility- but worked marvelously well together, in a way that they wouldn't have alone.

As the music continued, Osha took out her reed flute and played along, hesitantly at first, and then more confidently- until she unconsciously became part of a new and greater whole. At that point, the elevator began to move through time and space, startling her. She, as was customary, took the necessary precautions to mark her starting point and began the process of leaving a thread of consciousness behind her.

But the elevator didn't take her that far, only to the fourth worlds, where she saw the birth of the Caribbean Sea, as the great mass of land finally tore it itself apart, and left a space for new things to grow.

And so she knew she was going there, at some point; and that her music was part of why, what and how.

THIRTEEN

The Ve were, some say, born on the first true dawn, when creatures were finally wise enough to perceive. This isn't totally true.

Others say the Ve were older than the Earth, and only came to live there after many adventures in other places. This isn't exactly right, either.

It's perhaps most useful to say that the Ve came from different places, times and splaces, and were connected to the fourth worlds by two threads, love and envy.

They lived, mostly, in *the place that's not a place*, and had a country of their own there, which ran according to principles which they could accept, but which could be incredibly confusing to the uninitiated. Nevertheless, they roamed far and wide, especially on the Earth, which they perceived to be possessed of a surfeit of delights, diversions and challenges.

Berondyas was thought, by many non-Ve who knew about such things, to be one of the rulers of this country, alongside an equally powerful queen. This was definitely not true. The Ve didn't really do the whole "ruler" thing. Or the whole "government" thing. Or any "thing" at all, actually. Or any one shape/name/gender, I should add.

As a consequence of the above, they were a bit tricky to keep track of. I'm not really going to try.

There was someone or something, in other words that called it, him, her (or some other) self, "Berondyas of the Ve" that met and befriended Varoden of the People one fine summer day a long time ago.

Varoden wasn't very hard to make friends with, it should be said. He was possessed of an essentially compassionate and peaceful nature, a fact that was readily visible to the observer/interactor. He was also a fairly trusting sort, which made him even easier to get along with; and allowed him, in the first place, to go off to he knew not where, in the company of a strange person he'd just met.

Berondyas and Varoden did not stay on their westward road very long. Before they'd even had to break for rest or refreshment, Berondyas led them on a path that headed southward, toward a forest that rose tall before them. Varoden had never seen anything like it, and did his best not to gape too provincially.

The forest was, to be fair, quite an impressive sight.

The horse tracks had gone off in the same direction, though they must have been quite a ways ahead, based on what our young hero could tell from their leavings.

"So who are the Ve" Varoden had asked.

"We are a loose confederation of individuals co-operating towards a common purpose", replied the other.

"What purpose?"

"Well, that's part of the issue… We're not really sure. To be honest, we don't really even have a very good idea"

"Doesn't that make it harder to co-operate?"

"Yes. Yes it does."

After a little while Varoden had another question: "And how do you know your purpose is common, if you don't know what it is?"

"You," said Berondyas of the Ve "Ask good questions… Alas, this is another that I don't have any real answer for."

And so on.

FOURTEEN

Ranga could sing, too, I should mention. He had a natural ear for music, and was also able to quickly understand and play a variety of musical instruments.

So, as he grew, there were a variety of options available to him, in terms of disciplined learning and practice among his people. He could have delved deeper into the mysteries of being and becoming as a "Learned One"; or studied the music and songs that he so loved to play, and which were used to remember the ancient stories and ways; or done many other things besides.

But he chose to learn the ways of the sea, and of sailing; which his people were expert in.

Meanwhile, his tree had grown quite tall, and flourished in the fertile plain near to Ranga's home. It looked like a kind of fig tree, but it there weren't any others exactly like it anywhere near there, as far as anyone knew.

The fruit tasted good, too.

In fact, after eating it, one often felt a surge of... something... vitality, perhaps?

If it hasn't become clear to you, already, Ranga's people were a lot more accustomed to wonders of the sort so far described than modern folk are. There were a lot more of them, is why.

In fact, Ranga was not the only child given a kind of spirit gift at birth: there were quite a few others. That's part of why nobody went crazy about this tree.

Also, those people, and people everywhere and everywhen like them, were far less likely to be crazy at all. This is because they knew who they were, and are. They were connected to each other and their surroundings and their past and their future in a way that would be almost incomprehensible to us moderns.

There are advantages and disadvantages to this, of course.

Anyway, as Ranga studied with the teachers of the way of the Sea, he quickly became an adept the likes of which could not be remembered. And he knew it. And he became proud. And he began to feel a little separate from his people, a little higher perhaps. A little *special*

    You know how it goes.

His teachers noticed something was going on with the young man, but weren't sure what to do about it. They asked the Learned Ones, who, in turn, asked through the appropriate channels. "Let it be", was the response they got. So they did

Ranga never came close to losing his humility totally; he had real affection for his people and their ways, which were deeply peaceful. He also respected the traditions which had protected them through the long years of their stay at their beautiful home. It just wasn't enough for him.

He wanted more.

More of what he couldn't say, but he knew he wanted it; needed it, really.

And so, as the time came for him to make his first boat, he eschewed his people's regular way of going about it, asking through the appropriate channels, and accepting whatever answer they got. Instead, he went to his tree, and asked it to help him. After a while, it did what he asked for, and more.

FIFTEEN

Osha didn't just stay by the Caribbean Sea, by the way. She roamed the entirety of the Americas, virtually pole to pole and ocean to ocean- her favoured means of transport being the numerous rivers of the vast land. She had always loved the fresh water of lakes, rivers, springs and the like, finding them far more charming than the boundless and complicated seas. It was a kind of purity that she found in inland water, a purity that reflected some essential part of who she was.

This love of hers was, itself as pure as could be, affording her a relationship and connection to the object of her sentiment that was deep beyond explanation. Like all actual love, hers was free and undemanding, she sought not mastery but open understanding; not control, but compassion.

Like all actual love, her feeling for the waters blossomed beyond its immediate focus, to become a general love of all, without separation, boundary or category. This, in turn, opened her to the vast wisdom available to all true lovers; which wisdom was the fount of her deep patience.

She was and is super cool, in other words.

Anyway, there were special places that she visited more than others, and special waters that she came to know particularly well. Some of these waters already had people and/or settlements close to them, and she'd hang out with/at them, sometimes, doing a bit of this and a bit of that. Others grew settlements after she met them, and these she saw as her children, sort of. She loved children too, of course.

And everywhere she went, she played her music, learning all the different languages, perspectives and idioms of her fellow musicians. She learned a lot, and her music grew and grew and grew, until she almost didn't recognize it anymore. She saw that as her child too.

Keep it rolling Osha.

SIXTEEN

The tree that was almost, but not quite, a fig tree gave Ranga (quite specific and complicated) directions to another, much bigger, tree. If he showed this tree his necklace, and asked for help, it said, he could, if he was lucky, get a boat the likes of which the world had never seen. The young navigator thanked his tree, which he considered part of his family, and hastened off to follow its advice.

He journeyed for what must have been hours, until he saw, in the distance, what had to be the tree he had been told to find. It wasn't the tallest tree, or the widest, but it was possessed of a specificity that bordered on generality; as if it was *the* tree- that its neighbours had maybe been designed to complement, or even flatter, it.

He approached it respectfully and, taking his necklace in hand, told the tree his errand.

> Then he sat and waited.
>
> And waited.
>
> And fell asleep.
>
> At some point after this, he heard a voice saying "I have heard you, Navigator"

He attempted to raise his head, but was prevented from doing so by what felt like vines.

Looking down, he saw that he was bound to the tree by creepers around his legs, arms and torso. Loosely bound- he felt that he could break away if he really needed to, but bound nevertheless.

"Thank you for answering me, Uncle" said Ranga, once he had overcome his initial disorientationand fear, "Is there something I need to do to prove myself worthy of what I ask?"

"No" said the voice

"So... I can have the boat?"

"Perhaps"

Trees are not always the most forthcoming conversationalists

"What", asked Ranga after a time "must I do to get it?"

"Float"

At that, Ranga found himself far off the coast of his people's settlement, in the water and still bound by the vines around him- which had got much tighter. He began to sink under the water.

And he sank

Pretty sharpish, a sea serpent swam up and began to bite away the restraints keeping him from returning to the surface. Ranga could hold his breath for a very long time, and he saw, once the initial panic had subsided, that the serpent would succeed in more than enough time for him to escape and swim to shore.

Somehow, though, he also knew that this was not what the tree was asking of him. He closed his eyes, and then opened again, looking at the serpent, which had paused to look at him, and shaking his head. The serpent seemed to nod, and after giving the youth a long look, swam rapidly away.

Ranga immediately thought that he had made a horrible mistake, and had to use precious energy to calm the once again rising panic. He closed his eyes, and didn't move, opening himself to the sea and to whatever life remained to him.

And he sank a little further.

Long before mortality had any kind of real hold on him, Ranga felt a push in his back, and then another. And before he knew it, he was back at the surface, with two very large dolphins keeping him afloat between them.

"Thank you, cousins" he said, right before losing consciousness again.

SEVENTEEN

Varoden and Berondyas went quite a ways into the forest, always following the path, which had remained comfortably wide. Eventually, an unfamiliar sound reached the youth's ears, a kind of roaring, which only got louder as they continued forward. He glanced at Berondyas, to see if he was showing any sign of alarm. He wasn't. So Varoden decided not to worry. And he didn't.

Before too long, the forest thinned a little, until they came to a sight that stopped Varoden in his tracks. There was, first of all, a river straight ahead of him. The clear water seemed to dance in the sunlight, or maybe *with* the sunlight. To his right, the land rose gently, though increasingly steeply, until off in the distance there was an almost vertical incline rising up high. Down this, the river fell thunderously, accounting for some of the roar he had heard before.

       It was stunning. Beyond beautiful.

There was a kind of power to it which took Varoden's breath away.

In time, he recovered enough to look to his left. That way seemed almost flat, allowing the water to catch its breath too, until a steep drop created another waterfall, beyond which he couldn't see. That accounted for the rest of the roar.

Also that way was a charming wooden structure, perched on the edge of the cliff. How and why it stayed there was totally unclear to Varoden.

"I'm guessing" said Berondyas "that this is your first waterfall"

Varoden nodded mutely

"Not a bad way to start, then, I figure".

At that, Berondyas walked off to the left, along a wide path by the river.

The horses' tracks, which had been an ever-present through the forest, went that way too.

After a last look at the scene as he had first encountered it, Varoden followed.

"The horses stay here, sometimes" the Ve said, pointing off his left as he walked.

There, surrounded by huge and old looking trees, was a rolling, grassy and abundant seeming glade. Spaced out, individually and in small groups, there were the gigantic horses that the tracks had promised. What the tracks couldn't convey, however, was the sense of power and effortless grace that these beings exuded.

Already drunk with wonder, the youth from the steppes took a moment to appreciate what he saw.

What a moment!

The structure was yet another marvel. It seemed both straight and rounded, rising gracefully to a second level, which had huge windows made of a kind of transparent yet slightly reflective material that Varoden had never even heard of, much less seen.

"This is the house between the falls, and that's glass" Berondyas said, in response to his questions.

"The Ve built this place ourselves, but I'm not really sure exactly when... I wasn't or won't be involved in it"

"Won't be?" Varoden thought. But he said nothing, trusting that things would become clearer with time.

They did...

They do...S

Inside, the house between the falls was furnished in a manner so far beyond Varoden's understanding that it seemed to him to be past magic, and into some hitherto unimagined field of endeavour.He got accustomed to it fairly quickly, though, it should be said.The sound of the waterfall went from distracting to unnoticed fairly quickly as well; but he never got tired of going below the level they had entered on, to a space which was seemingly half built and half natural, though it wasn't always easy to tell where one or the other started, or even which was which. The water fell right through a space where you could sit and watch it, or even follow it down. That last, for Varoden, required learning to swim, which he did, with a minimum of fuss

He learned lots of other things too.

EIGHTEEN

The plantations that Osha frequented throughout her adopted lands were many and varied, growing sugar cane and tobacco and cotton and a lot of other things besides. They were in a wide range of ecosystems and took a variety of forms, but they all shared one characteristic. The sacred.

It was as if the people involved were coming together to enact the rites of a huge mystery religion- one that seemed, like most of that species, to be an apology for something.

Osha's memory was vast and profound, and she'd seen things like this before, but it had never been like this, exactly. There was a mechanistic quality to the process that spoke to a profoundly new understanding, one that interacted with space and time in ways that were both more and less predictable than what she had known.

It was, she thought one day long ago, while sitting underneath a huge tree beside the sea; as if everyone and everything wascollapsed to one of two states in this process, (like on or off, or up and down, for example). These states seemed to interact with each other to produce a more rounded and variable result, which was then immediately reconverted... recoded, really, into one of the two states- and on and on.

Knowing what she knew about the way things were (which was a lot), Osha could readily see some of the things that were likely to happen as a result of all this. First and foremost in her mind was the fact that the map of reality that it created had a tendency to the hyper-real- to becoming more real than reality, in other words. This alone gave her little or no pause, the hyper-real was endemic to consciousness, and had been a part of human endeavor for untold millennia, by this point.

No, the issue at hand was the fact that the machine that she was observing had (and inspired) a kind of sacred hunger... it seemed to always want more, and promise more; which had to come from somewhere, as is usually the case. And so it ate and ate and ate. It was just a machine though, and she had seen far more dangerous ones in her time. It was the seductiveness of this ritual which really caught her attention. It offered its participants rebirth into a kind of manufactured (and unachievable) utopia- the yearning for which few seemed able or willing to resist. When this last was combined with the previous two points, there was the potential for real trouble.

One of the dangers that Osha saw immediately was the way that the map of reality leading these bold explorers forward had already, by that point, *replaced* reality to a large extent. That, in itself, was danger enough; but this machine seemed not to want reality to exist at all. The map wasn't just the territory, in other words, it *consumed* the territory, and would not allow it to exist.

Osha got up from beneath the tree and went to the sea, watching the waves roll gently up onto the sandy shore. After a while, she took off her clothes and dived into the sea- the Caribbean Sea; her firm strokes taking her a long way out in a short period of time.

When she could no longer sea the land behind her, but had not yet reached into sight of the land that was ahead to the north, she dived down deep into the water, way past the sunlight, and the familiar creatures that lived in it; down and down and down until she reach an underwater ridge, filled with life that was very new to her.

She went still deeper, until she saw a glow that she swam towards, finally reaching a spot where reddish yellow lava spewed forth from a mound on the sea floor.

After a moment, she dived though the aperture, and into *the place that's not a place*

To the part of *the place that's not a place* called the shadow-world, to be exact.

She had been here before, but not through this particular entrance. So, she was cautious. Osha knew this splace well enough, given its usual proximity (viewed certain ways) to both the fourth worlds and the dreamtime. Her familiarity meant that she knew that it was easy for anyone, no matter who they were, to get lost in this splace, and that this was doubly true of the shadow-world. Getting lost wouldn't be particularly onerous for her, she knew, unlike the fourth-worlders one could occasionally find wandering the shadow-world in terror at being separated from themselves. It was damnably inconvenient, though, and Osha was in no mood to spend millennia meditating on the nature of this or that or whatever before having to find herself back to here and now, which was where this reality eating machine was. Which was why she was here.

So she turned herself into a river, and flowed to the place she wanted to get to, a lake on which there was a floating island. On this island lived Hampele the magnificent and terrible, eater of earth and shaper of lands.

Or Aunty Hammy, as Osha called her.

Aunty Hammy knew things, and was wise in a very different way from Osha. They both especially appreciated each other because of this fact, and they had been close for a very very very long time.

The lake was (deceptively calm) and inviting seeming, and Osha had no difficulty locating the floating island. She swam up to it, and as she approached saw a waving and smiling Aunt Hammy. Osha smiled herself, and ran out of the water, giving Hampele the magnificent and terrible, eater of earth and shaper of lands a big and all-encompassing hug.

"Hi Aunty" she said eventually "It's wonderful to see you"

"And you, my love", said Aunty Hammy "glad you've finally come to check out the new place"

"I was always coming"

"Yes, I know you've been busy, Osha, I've been paying attention"

NINETEEN

Ranga woke up gradually, and just lay there for a moment. Well, several moments, really. He tried to move his arms and legs, and felt them restrained still, but very loosely so. He broke his bonds with a minimum of effort, and then looked around him. He had no idea where he was, other than that he wasn't home.

It was morning, and he had woken up on a wide golden beach, fringed with tall thin coconut trees. He was in soft grass that lay between the sand and a more thickly wooded inland area. And he *really* had no idea where he was.

Getting up and walking along the beach, towards its closer southern end, Ranga reflected on (what he assumed was) the previous evening's goings on. It seemed that he had learned something important, and that it was about trust; but he was not quite ready to formulate it into a sentence or anything like that.

And, would he get his boat?

There was a promontory at the end of the beach, jutting out into the sea, and Ranga walked along it, seeing, after a few moments, some kind of cave dug into the rock up ahead. Her paused for a moment as he reached it, and then shrugged his shoulders and entered.

It was a kind of narrow passageway that lay before him, slanting gently downwards. He cautiously moved forward, and before long there was a glimmer of light at the end of the... natural corridor. It widened, too- so that Ranga moved more quickly and confidently, encountering nothing unusual on his way.And so, he emerged into a much larger cave, which opened out onto the sea. In there were two boats that looked like nothing else he had ever seen.

The smaller boat, which was pushed up on a little beach in the big cave, was still larger than the ones he had grown up with, and seemed to be carved out of a tree not totally dissimilar to the one that his not-quite-fig had sent him to: the one that(he assumed) had somehow tied him up and dropped him in the ocean. Unlike the boats he knew it had an extension to the side, which formed a kind of second hull. Also, it had a white sail, made out of some material he knew nothing about, and it was beautiful.

Absolutely beautiful.

The other boat was *enormous*.

It sat in the water like some kind of joke; also built on a double hulled design and too out of scale for his mind to deal withall in one go.

So he ignored it for a bit, and went to the smaller boat on the sand.

After appreciating the sleek and immaculate form of the smaller vessel for a while, Ranga climbed into it, at which point he noticed a bunch of coconuts under a thoughtfully provided (and comfortable looking) central seat. There was also an odd-shaped, and very large knife, and a big oar as well.

"Thank you!!" he said to whomever it applied to.

Using the oar, Ranga took the "little" boat out to the giant one sitting in the middle of the cave sea. He tied up, and carefully pulled himself up unto its flat deck. The sails were enough of a wonder, but there was even a *house* on it! Not a huge house, but a house, nonetheless.

"I'm going to need help with this one" said the navigator to himself.

TWENTY

"It's the natural conclusion of what they've been doing."

"I'm not sure natural is the right word."

"There's that, too."

Osha and Hampele were sitting by a small and beautiful natural pool, which was not far from the house where they were staying. The latter had only been there for a relatively short time, herself, before Osha had arrived, and hadn't changed all that much about the place, yet.

She'd built this pool, though

The two were talking about what Osha had been observing since her arrivals in the "New World", and the concerns that they shared about it.

"Do you remember when enslaving women first became a thing?" asked Hampele

"How could I forget?"

"Well there's a straight line from that to this"

Osha paused a bit before asking "You mean the whole property thing?"

"Yes, that; and this specific type of binding and bondagethat came from it"

"Yeah..."

Hampele continued before Osha could get her thoughts fully together, saying "It's really dangerous to bind anything at all the way they do, and they do it to themselves! It's like..."

"Sacrifice…" said Osha "… Except they're sacrificing themselves to themselves."

They were both silent for a time, pondering.

"To tell the truth" Hampele said "That's not even the most dangerous thing about it… This 'money' thing that they've started to get into…. It's a danger to the whole splace, and maybe others besides… Probably, others besides, as a matter of fact."

"Hmmmmm…" said Osha.

Hampele went on "It's bad enough to bind time down the way they've been trying to, and then to trade it is just… *perverse;* but now they want to *CREATE* it! I can't even…"

She paused and shook her head, her eyes, flashing brilliantly and terribly.

Time and space are not separate things. They are not even really things, in the truest sense of the word. They are a piece of the never before, always will be and nothing besides. They're what things are made out of, it's truer to say, but even that is just a crude approximation.

If they are going to be seen as two, nevertheless, then space is the hardier and more robust of the two, harder to break and easier to fix. Time is the elusive and more complicated one. And if you break it, you've bought it.

It's not that difficult, regardless of the above, to befriend time; or even tame it, if it's done gently and conscientiously. To capture it and enslave it is not good. It's never good. Even if it seems good, it's not. Having done this, to trade it willy-nilly, from wherever to whomever is even worse.

To use it to create more time now. That *really* dangerous. Dangerous is, in fact, not a strong enough word.

Why, you may ask?

Lots of reasons, I may answer. The most obvious thing is the strong likelihood of destroying yourself in the process. Worse, the destruction is of the rotting kind, leaving you a shell without meaning, beauty or realization.

If that's all that happens, count yourself lucky.

You're also likely to destroy everything around you, creating a desert of the real more total than is easily explained in language.

Even that's not close to the worst-case scenario. Without going on and on about it, splaces are relatively delicate things. They are liable (very very easily) to fall into slowly decaying time-space loops, in which the same things happen over and over, again, except worse each time- until they collapse.

Then you've got *real* problems.

You may have gathered, by this point, that Osha and Hampele *et al* are possessed of abilities beyond that of regular fourth worlders. This is so. Why then, you may ask, don't they do something violent and, possibly, final to the perpetrators of the crimes that they're speaking about?

Because it's a terrible idea, is why. And it doesn't work. And because the older had explained it to them.

It is a well-known first principle of this universe, they were told, that everything is interconnected; the particular *way* of our interconnection makes violence and coercion futile and foolish, the opposite of wisdom. Any real problem, they were also shown, is virtually guaranteed to be made worse by using these methods.The supporting examples and evidence were more than enough to convince them that this was probably so.

Hampele had, nevertheless, done a bit of violence, in her time. She had, in her youth, been somewhat... tempestuous, a bit of a hothead, in fact. And so, she had done some smiting.

She was, all this time later, still dealing with the consequences of her actions, and she had become an almost aggressive pacifist.

Also, there weren't *really* any perpetrators or crimes, as such

Anyway, all of this is to say that they both knew that was required was to work together to address the situation creatively. And not just them.

They would need a lot of help.

TWENTY-ONE

The first thing that Varoden started learning at the house between the falls was how to read and write. Berondyas of the Ve began these lessons the day after they arrived, and they would take up much of the first several months of their stay there.

Varoden was an eager and astute pupil, and he learned very fast. In fact, he seemed to surprise his teacher, and himself, with the speed of his uptake.

They had begun with the basic principles of writing, and the various philosophies and perspectives which could underlie it. They had then moved on to writing in Varoden's own language, and then to reading it. When he could read anything he was given, Berondyas moved him on to some other languages, including one of the languages of the way; which could be understood by anyone and anything.

    That took a bit longer.

Berondyas also taught Varoden many different types of meditation, with which he could begin to perceive more deeply.

    Varoden was good at that too.

The physical arts were a part of the way of Varoden's people. All children learned to wrestle and to run for long distances. So he was fit. Despite this, the lessons which gave him by far the most difficulty during his tutelage were the ways of the moving body, as Berondyas called them.

He had a lot to unlearn.

Berondyas had started these lessons by, one day early in their stay, suddenly grabbing and immobilizing Varoden, before he had even begun to react. He held him in position long enough for it to become distinctly uncomfortable, and then released him just as suddenly.

"Violence" the Ve said "Is the way of fools and children"

"..." said Varoden.

"I want to teach the way to impose your will without resorting to actual violence, do you want to learn it?"

The youth nodded his head thoughtfully, asking after a while "But isn't imposing your will a sort of violence, like when you were holding me a second ago? I couldn't get away, and I wanted to... your will... *dominated* mine in that moment didn't it? Isn't that violence?"

"If you had asked me to let you go, and I didn't; then maybe that would have been violence" said Berondyas, wearing an inscrutable expression.

"A bit of a fine distinction there, I would have said... and would you have let me go if I had asked?"

"You should have asked" replied the Ve "Then you would know."

Varoden accepted the need for physical training, nevertheless; and he began, first, to learn the way of the empty hand, as the Ve called it. Since he was quite a peaceful sort, he enjoyed the idea of overcoming physical force while attempting not to harm the attacker, and so was an attentive student.

It took a while, though.

Over time, he became even fitter than he had been: swimming (once he had learned) and running all around the neighbourhood, until he knew it almost as well as his old one; maybe better, even.

And then one day, they were sparring in the glade, both moving with a quickness and economy of motion that spoke to good understanding of the way. Berondyas was visibly the senior, his movements seeming to be both more solid and more fluid at the same time, but his student made up much of the difference with focus and determination. They flowed and danced and stood and played, until Berondyas said "Okay, I think you're ready"

So they moved on to the way of the gripping hand, and Varoden got his lasso. This way he learned very quickly, until he had outstripped his master in it, and begun to teach himself.

While the other lessons came and went, the reading and writing lessons didn't stop, and Varoden learned a bit about the fourth worlds, and the myriad seas, lands and people that made it up. It was totally engrossing to him, and he would always look back at this time at the house between the falls with a warmth that never failed to provide him succour when he needed it, and joy when he didn't.

One day, the Ve gave him a book that looked unlike any other he had seen.

"Take care of this" Berondyas said "It's from the library of time"

"The what?"

"Read it and it will help youunderstand."

TWENTY-TWO

Ranga spent the rest of that day familiarizing himself with the smaller boat, eventually taking it out of the cave, and introducing it to the wind and currents.

It sailed like a dream.

Exploring the waters around the beach he had found, Ranga convinced himself that he had never been before, or heard of this place, which was obviously (to him) far to the east of his home.

He returned to his cave in the evening, and ate a quite coconut-centric meal, before tying up next to the big boat, again and clambering up on its wide deck. He examined just about every inch of it, and began to develop an inkling of understanding.

To help digest the new knowledge (and the new food), Ranga took a walk back up through the cave and along the beach, occasionally heading a little inland. The stars above him provided further evidence to him that he was to the east of the familiar, but he got the sense from them that it wasn't ridiculously far.   Which was encouraging

Before too long, though, the day's exertions, not to mention to mention those of the evening before, caught up with him, and he fell into a deep sleep.

Lots of dreams though.

The next morning, after a fruity (and coconutty) breakfast, Ranga took the small boat out into the open sea again. He was going to try to get home. He knew, somehow, that the larger vessel would be waiting for him, and he felt a lot more comfortable taking the smaller one for this first journey.

Taking one last look at the cave and the beach beside it, Ranga headed west, with a strong wind behind him, and the generally favourable currents he had discovered yesterday. Before long, the eastern island (he had sailed to both ends of it the day before) disappeared behind him, and he was in open water.

When, close to his midday coconut, two very large dolphins appeared in front of him, and looked him in the eye, he wasn't really all that surprised. He smiled at them, and then bowed. In seeming response, they did a little flip thing, and swam ahead of him, their course a little south of due west. Any misgivings or doubts that Ranga had had were allayed by the appearance of the dolphins, and he relaxed and devoted his energy to paying attention to his surroundings, and enjoying the boat's almost miraculous speed, following them.

Soon, he had the sense that he was close to home, the conditions seeming very familiar. And he was. Land appeared on the horizon, and he saw the big bay where he had lived all his life. The dolphins allowed him to go a little ahead, but continued their escort until he had almost got to the shore, where a growing group of people, his mother among them, waited for him.

He had a lot of explaining to do.

So, explain he did, only omitting the "detail" of the bigger boat he had left in the island cave.

Everyone was impressed, not least by his boat. His teachers had eyed it throughout his tale, and wasted no time, on his conclusion, before rushing to examine it. They spoke amongst themselves in hushed but excited seeming tones, before one of them said: to Ranga and all the others; "we must inquire, through the appropriate channels, about this; but this one" she pointed at Ranga "has done well, and proved himself to be knowledgeable in the ways of the sea. He is no longer our student, and is free to use his knowledge as he sees fit"

The teachers all left then, leaving Ranga to the still growing crowd, which resumed peppering him with questions, offering congratulations, or just enjoying an impromptu party.

The Navigator answered as well as he could, but he grew increasingly distracted and often glanced out to the sea, where, if you squinted, it was just possible to make out the shapes of two dolphins playing in the waves.

TWENTY-THREE

They had swum for a bit, in Hampele's nice new pool, and then had lunch by the lake shore, watching the water move slowly by. Afterwards, over coffee, their talk returned to the pressing issue that faced them.

"I think we'll need to form new great bodies, Osha, both of us"

"Yes, I was thinking that too..."

There was a pause

"I haven't been in a new one since goodness knows when..."

"And I've never been in one, Aunt Hammy"

"Never?" Hampele looked at Osha for a moment before continuing "No I guess that makes sense..."

There was another pause.

Let me use this pause to tell you a little about great bodies. Simply put (too much so, probably), they are deep and profound combinations of conscious beings, all parts retaining their own selves, but also becoming something else, besides. It is a characteristic of great bodies that they are unstable, and tend towards dissolution, implosion or explosion. These last can be quite dramatic events, so most folks like Osha and Hampele tend to avoid them, all the while speaking of their power and beauty.

Sometimes they were necessary, though.

"You know how it's done, though?"

"Yes, I've actually read a lot about them, and I watched a bunch of how-to videos in the library of time once"

"Okay, that's more than good enough, I'm sure…"

"Yeah, it's not the formation part that would cause me any concern…"

Hampele smiled, and after a second, so did Osha.

"Well, maybe the stuff you read and watched wasn't so specific, so it's possible that I might be able to give you some pointers"

"That would be great, Aunty Hammy"

"Well" said Hampele after a pause "the main thing, I think, is putting together the right constituent parts… Only you will be able to know and then facilitate the right mix of beings, but for action in the fourth worlds and its environs, you'd definitely want at least one hell being, at least one animal, at least one numen, at *very* least one human…"

She stopped and looked at Osha, whose mouth hung a little open in surprise.

"And at least one hungry ghost…"

"A *hungry ghost* too!" cried Osha.

"Yep, I'm afraid so…"

They sat in silence for quite a while.

"I can see why we don't do it so often round here" said Osha at last.

"Yeah, that's a big part of why, I guess... But there's a little more, Osha.... Before doing this you should understand that you have to be totally open to all parts of your great body if you really want it to work properly... *totally* open..." Hampele caught and kept Osha's gaze before continuing "...And if you start it, you really need to complete it; for the good of you and everyone else involved."

"That last bit I knew, but when you say totally open..."

"I mean totally open."

"So I might end up making a god or a monster or something..."

"You might."

More silence.

In case you were wondering, by the way, Hampele the magnificent and terrible, eater of earth and shaper of lands, and Osha were not gods or monsters. They were **authorities**.

Eventually, Osha got up and went inside, after giving her Aunty Hammy a somewhat wistful smile. Hampele gave her own smile, which lingered, as she turned away from Osha's retreating back, and looked, again, at the lake. She felt a kind of complexly beautiful sadness mixed with pride, knowing what Osha would do, once the younger authority had recovered from her shock.

She would do it, of course.

And in forming the great body, her innocence, which Hampele had always found so charming, would no longer hold unchallenged sway over her being.

"Well that's the way of it, I suppose" she said to herself, before returning to the pool for one last swim before dinner.

TWENTY-FOUR

The book from the library of time was mostly about moving between different splaces, providing different approaches and their advantages and disadvantages. By this time, Berondyas had explained a little about splaces to an initially dubious Varoden; which disbelief was removed by the Ve performing a few dis- and re-appearances, one time coming back with a glass of some intoxicating beverage. One sip of this beverage, by the way, had ended Varoden's lessons for the day, but sent him on a deep and mysterious tour of the grass beneath him.

"Forgot how strong this thing is" sighed Berondyas to himself, before going inside and leaving Varoden to explore the wondrous new mindscapes he had suddenly encountered.

Anyway, some of the methods for inter-splace travel were clearly totally impractical for regular humans like him. He wasn't, he thought, likely to go diving twenty thousand feet under the sea any time soon; or to fly three times counterclockwise around the earth in the stratosphere, for that matter.

Some of them, though, were eminently achievable, ranging from ingesting certain flora (and fauna), to the many meditative techniques available to beings such as him. All of these ways of splace travel were very sensitive to the place that they were practiced, and his reading suggested it would be the work of several lifetimes to become anything close to an expert.

He loved it.

Like, a lot.

This was what he had been looking for, he felt; he would devote himself to learning these ways, and he would travel the splaces until he had achieved mastery, until he had real knowledge, until he was *wise*.Varoden had, since that first day on the crossroads, repeatedly asked Berondyas the whys, whats and hows of their meeting. Was it him in particular that the Ve was waiting on? Could it have been anyone?

And the questions had only increased, as the various wonders of the house between the falls and the horses, and the Ve himself, had revealed themselves.

There hadn't been many answers.

Berondyas had merely told him to wait until the right time, and to go on learning.

And so he had.

And the answers had begun to come, at first in a trickle, and then in a flood.

After having read the library book straight through from cover to cover two times in a row, Varoden took the book and went to look for

Berondyas. He found him in the kitchen, making some coffee for himself.

"Thisisamazingicandoitiknowhowandimgonnapracticeandwhydidntyoutellmeitwassoeasyithoughtitwasonlypossibleforoneslikeyou" he said.

Berondyas only smiled in response.

Varoden took a moment to compose himself, and then said "So anyone can do this?"

"More or less"

"So it really *could* have been anyone on the road that day that you took as your student?"

After a pause, the Ve said "Well... not really. I was told to wait there for one of promising characteristics, who could perceive beyond at least the first veil. A few came before you, but they did not see me, and they were not suitable candidates... You were a suitable candidate"

"Why was I able to see you when the others weren't?"

"I can't say I know that for sure, but if you ask me to guess, I'd say that it's mostly because you wanted to..."

And so on.

Varoden's lessons continued, but there was now a deeper focus on the meditative arts, which was supplemented by his own efforts, which occasionally took him deep into the night and morning.

And he learned.

Fast.

The sun appeared above the trees one morning, finding Varoden sitting cross legged beside the river. He perceived, and then heard, the Ve approaching and he said, without moving "Good morning to you teacher, your stride sounds particularly purposeful…"

"Get your lasso" said Berondyas "We're going to visit the Ve"

TWENTY-FIVE

The party ended up lasting all through the night, and well into the next day, and Ranga devoted himself to it with an energy born out of a seed of knowledge growing in his mind.

When, the day after the party had ended, and Ranga had woken up to a glorious sunny morning, his erstwhile teachers requested his presence, he wasn't all that surprised. He went to meet them by the boats, where they habitually gathered when they were on the land.

"We know of the island that you found yourself on, Ranga..." said one, after the niceties had been observed

"...and the boats that we build here could perhaps survive the voyage... perhaps. It is a place beyond the way of village, though. And we do not visit it. Your new boat is also beyond the way of this village, and we will not seek to replicate its marvelous design."

There was a pause

"We spoke to the Learned Ones, and together we asked the relevant powers for guidance"

There was another pause

"We have asked, and received an answer"

"And what is this answer?" Ranga asked, respectfully

"That our way cannot last forever, but that it is safe and right for this place that we inhabit now, and well into the future. That our way cannot survive the way of this boat of yours, or of the island to the east. That you must choose between these ways. That you will choose between these ways"

"You mean if I want to stay here, I have to give up my boat, and not return to the island?" asked Ranga

"Basically."

"Oh…."

"And if you choose to go, you must not, if you have any love for our ways, return more frequently than once every fiveyears"

Ranga had known, on some level, that something like this was coming, but the seed of knowledge had grown and blossomed before he was quite ready, and he walked away from the meeting troubled.

He spoke to his mother (his father had died many years ago, by the way). She counseled him to follow his own way, whether that meant to stay or to leave. The way they looked at each other, though, communicated the shared understanding that the decision had already been made, had perhaps been made a long time ago.

And then they hugged.

And hugged some more.

His next visit was to his tree, and they stayed together for hours, with very little being said. When it was time to go, Ranga hugged his friend, and smiled, with tears in his eyes.

"We're always together, anyway" he said, fingering his necklace.

With that, he turned and went off to look for his other (human) friends. He had decided to leave in two days, and once the news spread, he had a steady stream of people coming to his home, asking where he would go, and what he would do, or just spending a little time together. This was good, and would never forget the feeling of bittersweet love which was his constant companion during that time.

There was also a big surprise. Appa, the Learned One's most senior apprentice; and a woman of great presence and strength, came to visit Ranga the evening before he left. He had always admired her, in almost every way; but she was several years older, and possessed of a stillness and gravitas that had made him keep his distance.

"Ranga" she said, without too much preamble "I would like to come with you."

"What?"

She only looked and waited.

"But..." Ranga took a moment to gather himself "...You know I can only come back once every five years, right? And what about your studies? And you're sure you want to come with *me*? You've never shown all that much interest in me, to be honest..."

"Well," Appa said, in response "In order: yes; my teachers have given me their blessing; yes; and you interested me before, and you interest me now."

Ranga just looked at her, and Appa looked right back at him. Then she smiled, a sunrise smile at sunset.

And Ranga said "Alright, let's do it."

TWENTY-SIX

The home of the numen known as the Ve was also known as the Ve, or just Ve. One could expect, at any one time, just about anything to be happening there. That's just how those guys were, you know?

It seemed like night when Berondyas and Varoden arrived there, although the journey had seemed to take very little time, and it had still been early morning when they left the house between the falls. After Varoden had run to get his lasso, he had watched the Ve etch some words into the grass with the long stick he sometimes carried with him (and which Varoden had received many painful lessons from during their gripping hand lessons).

"Since it's both of us, it's probably better for me to write our passage" Berondyas said,

"Ahh okay"

Translated from the language of power they were written in, the words were these

Take the steppencub
With me to my home, the Ve
By the direct route.

Once he finished writing, he turned to Varoden, and said "Okay, so just stick with me, and everything will be cool. If we get separated, don't panic. You'll be fine. Either I or a friend of mine will find you before long... so you'd just keep your lasso with you, and chill until someone picks you up... Oh, and you're better off not eating or drinking anything while you're in Ve, It's not worth the trouble that it causes, usually."

By the end of his little speech, early morning had turned to a moony and moody dark, and Varoden could tell he was no longer in the splace that he'd grown up in.

He was so excited he could barely contain himself, but he did, looking around and seeing nothing except tree shapes on every side.

"Alright, let's go" said Berondyas.

"Right behind you."

"You're probably better to stay beside me."

With that last, the Ve started walking, his stick gradually becoming bright enough so that the "steppen cub" could confirm that they were, in fact surrounded by trees. Soon, the trees thinned, and there was a glow over a little rise straight ahead of them. The glow quickly became a glare, until, reaching the rise and looking down into a vast unwooded space, Varoden was virtually assaulted by a carnival of light and colour, much of which was being emitted by strange vehicles travelling at high speed along some kind of track that seemed to have more than the proper number of dimensions.

"The Great Race begins again today."

Varoden didn't respond, still trying to take in all that lay ahead of him. There were a multitude of brightly dressed (and lit) figures interspersed somewhat unnervingly with the vehicles, talking and watching and doing all kinds of things besides. There were also huge pavilions all over the place, shining brightest of all, and seeming to be also filled with "people."

"And on the day the Great Race begins, we all gather together. It's tradition, and everyone who can make it, does… and we're going that way" He pointed off to the right, to a slightly quieter part of the festivities, where there was a series of smaller tents, situated on another rise.

Seen close up, the Great Race was even more confusing, and Varoden willed himself to look away, and tried to pay attention to the people instead.

That was better.

Many of them wore little or nothing in the way of clothes, and the view was *wonderful*. Varoden didn't even try not to stare, and there were, additionally some folks doing things that made him, as at ease with the body and its goings on as any of his tribe, blush.

He could get used to this part quite easily, he thought.

But the walked right past the fun and reached their destination, entering a smallish tent with the front open to provide a good view of the goings on. There, at a table, sat two very different seeming women, arrayed in, and seemingly emitting, colours that changed so rapidly that they combined to form a very bright white, which hurt the eyes if looked at too long.

"These" said Berondyas "Are Friday and Atra, and I hope they'll be helping me with your teaching for a while"

"Hi there,"

"Hey,"

"Nice to meet you both,"

"Want a drink?"

"I better not."

TWENTY-SEVEN

By the time Hampele had finished swimming and got ready for dinner, Osha was sitting on the wide airy veranda that would serve as their dining room, looking somewhat less shell-shocked. The two authorities smiled at each other, and settled into a companionable silence, watching *the place that's not a place* settle into a soft seeming darkness.

They sipped at their drinks, until finally Osha said "you already know I'm going to go through with it, don't you"

"I thought you might,"

"It was just a lot to take in all at once, you know?"

"Yes, I thought you showed remarkable composure, actually"

More silence.

"So, Aunt Hammy, do you know who you'll include in your great body already?"

"Well, I have some ideas about the numen, and the animals are never usually a problem... The rest, not so much... The hell beings are actually easy enoughto deal with, once you've got the hang of it.... The humans and the hungry ghosts, though..." She shook her head

"You still have more of an idea than me..."

"I'm happy to help you, as I can... In fact, there are two numen that we should go and see first before we do anything else. They've both been a great help to me in the past, and I know where to find them..."

"That sounds like a plan."

"Yeah, they both have accumulated enough merit to shift phase already, but they both say the same thing, that the time is not yet right"

"Who are they?"

"They're called Sun Wu and the old man."

"Oh! I've heard of them,"

"Yes, they're quite well known, actually,"

"And you think they'd be willing to join great bodies?"

"Yes, I'm confident about it. Even if I'm wrong, they're both quite wise, and are likely to have good advice for us."

"Okay, that's great... I'd like to spend a couple more days with you here, but you think we could go and see them after that?"

"That sounds like a plan"

Feeling a bit rejuvenated, Osha turned her attention to the dinner that had appeared on the plates before them while they were talking.

"Mmmmm, I love pizza."

"I remember" said Aunt Hammy, smiling

They ate with a graceful gusto, until Osha wiped her mouth with the beautifully embroidered cloth set there for the purpose, and said "I'm going to ask my sisters whether they'd be willing to form great bodies, and I might even ask Roko, too. Between us, we should be able to deal with this thing"

"That's probably a good idea"

"Any other authorities you can think of that I should ask?"

"Not off the top of my head... I think a lot of the others went off with Nana on her long journey, some are off on their own, and of the few that are still around here..." She shook her head

"What about Madame, or Mister?"

"Definitely not their kind of thing..."

"Ahh, okay... Well, my sisters and Roko it is, then"

"Yeah let's do it like that."

TWENTY-EIGHT

Appa and Ranga headed east towards the boat cave island, the cries of farewell ringing in their ears, and small tears forming in their eyes. And they were happy.

Appa had been thoughtful and thorough in preparing for their voyage, and Ranga felt lucky to have her with him. She felt lucky too, actually.

She had been born to Learned One parents, and had been around the mysteries since she could remember. She had also had a birth gift, but hers was known only to her immediate family and, eventually, her teachers.

At Appa's birth, a little spider had, unseen, crawled up right behind her ear and whispered, in the language of the appropriate way.

You may have the chance
And so I give you a key
To a gateless gate

These words would never leave Appa, and by the time she was old enough to repeat them sensibly, her family realized exactly what she had been given. These were travelling words, which the Learned Ones had heard of, but not seen for generations. They would apply only to her, and could not be used by anyone else.

While it was possible, through extremely long study and practice, to discover one's own travelling words, and walk the ways; the Learned Ones deemed it unnecessary and, even unwise, to do so - the appropriate channels worked well enough, and the ways were fraught with danger.

Appa could not, however, reasonably be stopped from exercising her birth gift, and once she had learned to develop the focus required to enact them, she did so, and went to *the place that's not a place*. Where not much happened, to be honest.

Her family background and Learned One training had taught her extreme caution when dealing with the "outside", and she never went very far away from her starting point, even when; with age and practice, she had learned to go with her whole body, and not just her mind. Where she landed was a very quiet corner of the splace, with not much except trees for company.

    So she mostly talked to trees while she was there.

    Which was fine.

But they didn't say much different than the trees she knew in the fourth worlds.

    It was, in other words, a bit frustrating.

She had decided, when her Learned One training was complete, that she was going to explore *the place that's not a place* (or the outside) further, and damn the consequences, but the night Ranga had returned from his adventure, something had happened. She had been sitting by herself by the sea, a ways away from the noise and haste of his party. She had felt an odd sensation, and then heard a tiny voice from behind here ear say.

"I'm back"

She started in surprise, and then thought for a bit, before responding

"You're the one who gave me my gift, aren't you?"

"I am."

"Thank you very much… and who are you?"

"You can call me Anansi, but I have many names"

"Ahhh… okay"

"So listen, I don't have much time. If you really want to learn what's up, you have to leave here. If you stay, you'll be a great Learned One, maybe the greatest that ever was or will be; but you won't be able to use your gift to the fullest."

"But where can I go"

"The young man with the boat is probably not staying, you could go with him"

She examined this proposition for a moment, and found it somewhat surprisingly exciting.

"So you've decided then"

"I wouldn't say decided…"

"I would, here take this with you"

And just like that there was a feather in her hand, which seemed to be from some small bird she had never seen.

"Thanks... what's this for, now?"

"Luck"

And with that she knew he was gone.

As she saw the island appear on the eastern horizon, she thought about that conversation, and felt for the feather, which she had attached to a braided anklet.

"I think we've made the right choice" said Appa.

TWENTY-NINE

The rest of the time in Ve passed by in somewhat of a blur for Varoden. They stayed, for the most part in their tent, and they had no visitors. He asked about the Great Race, and was told that this was just the beginning, that the race had been known to last for years or, a few times, *centuries*. What he had seen was a sort of ceremonial parade that doubled as a grand festival for the Ve.

"And how do you win the race?"

"Well that's part of what you find out during the race"

"Hmmm... okay... So there's no goal? No path? No nothing?"

"I wouldn't say that, exactly... It's more like, each race is different, and each winner finds something new..."

"How do you know who wins, then?"

"It becomes known"

"Hmmm"

There was more like that until, suddenly, it was time to go. They all rose, and Varoden began to say goodbye to Friday and Atra

"No, they're coming with us."

"Oh! I didn't realize..."

"Yes, time's a going, and you can't stay in the house between the falls forever."

Friday and Atra volunteered to take them back to the falls, and they did so with a brief snippet of a haunting tune, which they hummed in harmony.

And just like that, they were back at the house.

The next day, Friday woke Varoden before sunrise, and said "It's time for our first class together"

"Mmmggrfhheeeeay"

"Meet me outside in 5 minutes, and bring your lasso", said she, turning and walking away.

"We will practice the gripping hand together" said Friday, once Varoden had come out into the pre-dawn quiet. She held what appeared to be a length of rope in her hand.

He settled into a comfortable stance, balancing himself and seeking to quiet his mind

"Not so bad"

"Thank you"

And then somehow, Varoden was on the ground, his leg wrapped in Friday's rope. He tried to kick out of it, and couldn't. After a few more efforts, he just lay there and looked up at here, the first rays of the new rising sun appearing behind her head.

"That was…. Impressive… I still haven't seen you move" he said

"Movement is possible in many directions, perhaps an infinite number of them. The eye is attuned to only a few. Our first lessons will be on unlearning the expertise of the bodily eye, and opening to myriad possibilities"

"Sounds... complicated"

"We'll see"

Wisely, Varoden didn't try to attack Friday with his lasso, in that first lesson. All his energies were devoted to defence.

And he did a lot of getting up off the ground.

They continued until almost midday, way past the point of frustration for the constantly falling and rising student.

"Time for a break" Friday finally said to a once again prone Varoden

"Mmph" said he

She turned and walked towards the house, and he got up and had started to follow her slightly dejectedly, when he jumped to the side and swung down his lasso, without even really realizing he had done so.

"Well!" Friday said, disentangling her rope from his lasso and turning back to the house "You really are a quick study... That took me weeks!"

Atra seemed older than Friday, though it wasn't really anything about her appearance that made it seem so to Varoden. Looking at her across the room where they both sat cross-legged, the evening after his first gripping hand class, it struck him that she had an air of sadness about her that Friday didn't.

Berondyas had given a text to translate from one of the languages of the way to his own language, which had taken up most of the afternoon. After a group swim, they had eaten dinner together, and then Varoden had gone to his room to relax. He was tired, and sleep had been circling above his head, when there was a knock on the door, and Atra had asked if he was up to a quick lesson.

He had quickly said yes, and she smiled, and led him into one of the meditation rooms, where she had, without saying a word; sat down, and arranged her hands into a simple folded position. After a second, he had sat across from her, and entered into one of the types of meditation that he had been taught: "the way of no way".

And that was that.... For a long time, too.

THIRTY

Osha and Hampele stood on the veranda of the house on the floating island in the shadow-world region of the *place that's not a place*. They were about to leave for the dreamtime, where Hampele thought Sun Wu and the old man would be. If they weren't there, she was confident someone would know where they had gone.

The past few days had been lovely and relaxing for both of them, their mutual joy in each other's presence never flagging. They had talked and swam and reminisced and philosophized and danced; and one memorable evening had seen them go to a party in a cave not that far away, where they had made some friends, and had some fun.

But now it was time to get started.

"We're just going to take a short route, right? I took a long one here, but…"

"Yes, I'm cool with that"

"Alright, let's do it"

Taking each other's hands, they both took a big step off the veranda, which landed on a grassy mountain plateau in the dreamtime. Behind them were high peaks stretching off into the distance, a breathtaking vista only enhanced by the dusky light playing on surrounding clouds. Ahead of them was a large, beautifully understated structure, which backed against a tall cliff face.

"The Mountain School" said Hampele "They're instructors here"

"Ahhh, okay... I've heard of it, never been here though"

As one of the Eight Great Schools of the dreamtime, the Mountain School was well known, and respected throughout the relevant realms. It taught all manner of lessons and classes, but it had a specific perspective (as did all the other Great Schools). The Mountain School's way was the way of wisdom.

As such, it was known to be the most welcoming and easy-going of the Eight, and no student had ever been turned away. Graduation, on the other hand, was said to be fiendishly difficult; for many different reasons. Not least of these was that the instructors and administrators wouldn't tell you when you were finished. You had to know for yourself.

So, some people stayed there for a very veryvery long time, while others left almost immediately. Neither of these approaches seemed to bother the school's administrators. They granted no diplomas or, actually, recognition of any kind. And you could stay as long as you wanted.

You had to know.

Osha had gone to the River School, and excelled there. Its focus was on diligent effort, and graduating involved achieving clearly pre-set and agreed upon objectives. While she had thoroughly enjoyed those days, and thought often of them, the idea of going to one of the other Schools for a while had crossed her mind several times; and seeing the Mountain school revived the idea.

Hampele had gone to the Island school, which had serenity in solitude as its way, and she was pretty done with that sort of thing.

"Shall we?" She asked

"Yep"

And so they entered.

There was a gate, but no visible fence. They walked through it.

There was a door, which was open, and they walked through that too, entering a vast hall, filled with people. A lot of these people were engaged in what appeared to be physical education classes, while others played a myriad of games and sports.

It was a *really* big hall. Way too big to fit in the structure as they had seen from outside.

One got accustomed to that sort of thing in the dreamtime, though.

Ringing the hall were lots of doors, some closed, some open. And, beneath the high roof, there were other too many other levels to count, all with a corridor overlooking the unfeasibly big hall

"There's Sun Wu" said Hampele, pointing at an almost aggressively regular looking man.

He stood, with one hand behind his back, in the middle of a circle of crouching students, seemingly explaining something calmly. One of the students asked a question, and Sun Wu beckoned her to rise, and then beckoned again, once she had done so.

At first, nothing happened. At second, too. And then the student said something, to which Sun Wu didn't respond in any way. Seeming to get a bit tense, the student said something else, and then suddenly moved in a way that was new to Osha, seeming to go in all directions at once, and into other splaces as well. Sun Wu was still.

And then the student was crouching with her fellows, looking a little confused.

Sun Wu said something else, and then smiled, and bowed, and walked towards Hampele and Osha

"She was an *authority*, the one who attacked him…" Osha said

"…And he's a numen"

"Wow, didn't know that could go like that"

"Wisdom is wisdom my dear"

And then Sun Wu arrived, with a big smile on his face.

THIRTY-ONE

Appa and Ranga were both surprised at how well they were getting along. They had talked well into their first night on the beach cave island, and had had to force themselves to stop and go to sleep.

The next morning, Ranga had woken to see Appa quietly sitting crossed legged, doing nothing. He had an almost overwhelming feeling of happiness to see her, and it struck him that she was beautiful beyond even what he had thought. There was stillness to her that seemed to erode the division between the outside and the in, and it drew the eye not just to her, but to the wonder of being. He lay there quietly, not wanting to disturb her, and just watched her.

The night before, Appa had taken longer to fall asleep than Ranga had, and she had seen him drifting off into unconsciousness. She had known, in those moments between waking and sleep; that they would be lovers, and more; and that they had some kind of deep connection beyond the explainable. How she knew wasn't immediately clear to her, but it was real knowledge, the type that can move and shift and change, without being effaced at all.

And so, they passed their first few days on the island getting to know each other, and also learning how to sail the big boat, which was a bit of a mission, to be honest. There was a lot to it. Steering was the biggest challenge, and they had some hairy moments before they got the hang of integrating the various forces at play.

Ranga was, of course, way ahead of Appa in nautical knowledge, a fact that they had both accepted from the beginning, without even having to mention it. Theirs was a true partnership, though; and the trust between them blossomed quickly. Power was never an issue between them, and it never would be.

The first time they made love was on the open sea, a week or so after their arrival. They had more or less got the steering thing under control, and they had been relaxing and playing music together on the big deck, Ranga playing his water drum, and Appa playing her thumb piano. Eventually, Appa had started to play an old old song about the love of the earth for the sky; and after a minute or two, she had started to sing too. Ranga had joined her, their voices creating a flowing harmony that seemed to match the wind's dance with the currents. They had looked at each other, and without hesitation, they had put down their instruments and embraced.

Their contact banished any ideas or stories or words from their conscious minds. Instead, they were filled with each other; from their first touch until slowly they pulled away from each other.

"That was…"

"I know"

"You're…."

"We are"

So that part went well, too.

In fact, their stay on the island was very encouraging on many levels. They were able to supplement their provisions with the various fruit and vegetables which they found, and they got better and better at sailing together, and being together.

As such, their talk began to turn more regularly to where they would go. They had idly speculated before, but the time, they both felt, was drawing near. It had become clear to them that their big boat could take them just about everywhere, as long as they could carry enough food. Even this last was less pressing than it might have been, because Appa knew the deep ways of fishing; which required the appropriate meditative state to be done well. They were unlikely ever to starve near the sea, in other words.

Ranga had thought to strike out to the south, where legend held there to be a huge beautiful island that was some kind of earthly paradise. Appa, on the other had the sense that they should follow the coast north and then northeast. She wasn't sure why she thought this, but her inquiries through the channels available to her seemed to support her idea, however vaguely.

And north was the way they would go, after much discussion. Ranga didn't really care all that much, to be perfectly honest, he just wanted to sail. There were, however, fewer stories about the north, and most of them weren't particularly nice ones. It was said there was some kind of magic barrier that prevented travel too far in that direction, but the stories were confused and often contradictory. None of these stories, however, referred to sea travel, so they both hoped that was a big enough loophole for them to fit through.

And then all of a sudden, it was time to go.

And they did.

THIRTY-TWO

It took a while for Varoden to figure out what Atra was instructing him in. At first, he had thought that it was just the way of no way, but over time, it became clear that there was a kind of shape to their discussions and practice, which immediately disqualified that option. The qualities of this shape remained vague until one day, while they were talking about the speed of light, he had a flash of understanding, which led to him blurting "You're teaching me about the law, aren't you?"

"Yes" she said, and smiled.

The law was a way of understanding a particular splace, based on clearly defined limits and boundaries, the breaking of which had consequences within that milieu. It was thought to be a somewhat dangerous practice, because it was easy to forget the limits and boundaries of the law itself while operating in this way. It could become to seem like reality, in other words, and you could get trapped in it. This was bad.

Anyway, once Varoden understood the overarching principle guiding his study, his already impressive pace of learning sped up further, seeming to surprise Atra, somewhat.

Oh, also, they had become lovers.

It had just seemed natural to both of them.

And it went well, while it went.

Moving back to the main thread, though, Varoden's grasp of the law quickly enough rivalled Atra's, at which point she called a house meeting.

"He is a master of the law" said Atra, without preamble

"A master? I knew he was moving fast, but...."

"Oh, we're here, then... Are his ways of the hand anywhere near that level?" Berondyas looked at Friday

"He's not far off, to be honest"

This last particularly surprised Varoden, who still ended up on his back in many of his gripping hand lessons, though he was able to defend himself far better than at the beginning.

"I'm not far off from mastery of the gripping hand? Really? Then how comes you always win?" he asked Friday.

"Well, I'm moving between splaces, and you're not... For you to defend yourself at all means you're doing very well"

"But I won't ever be able to move between splaces like you, you're a numen and I'm a human... so I'll never be a master, then?"

There was a silence

"You can move between splaces like her" Berondyas said, eventually

"I can? How?"

"Even if you've mastered the law, we haven't reached that point yet" Friday said. She looked at Berondyas and asked "Your part's pretty sorted now, isn't it?"

Berondyas nodded.

There was another silence.

"You will" Atra said "Have a choice to make... But not quite yet. We will leave this place, and you should, too; but meet us here in a year's time, and tell us what you choose"

"What! But...."

"If I were you, I would return home, and consolidate what you've learned, but you only you can choose your path"

"Yes, but..."

"Farewell" said she, and disappeared, smiling. Varoden turned his gaze to Friday and Berondyas, but they stayed solidly in place.

"One or two things to do before we go..." Berondyas said

"This is a bit sudden, isn't it, can't we wind down a bit slower?"

"Your year has started, and we can't guide you through it" Friday said, with a soft smile "Atra generally knows what she's doing, and if she thinks you're ready, so do I."

"Seconded" said Berondyas

It was, thus, the next morning, and Varoden had gathered his meagre possessions, and was thinking of taking a last plunge into the falls, when Berondyas and Friday knocked on his door and entered, holding, respectively, a dark cloak and a shining lasso.

"These are yours now, use them with wisdom" said Friday

Varoden took the gifts appreciatively, thanking his now former teachers at length.

"Just a word of warning, these items involve power far beyond what's available to most of the humans you will meet. It will be tempting to work with these powers. Do not do so unless it is absolutely necessary, and maybe not even then." Friday looked him in his eyes

"What can they do?" he responded eventually

"What can you do? Anyway, time's a going, let's go see the horses"

They all started moving towards the glade. Varoden, without really thinking about it, put on his new cloak, and took the lasso in hand. He hadn't taken five steps before he had an overwhelming burst of knowledge, coming from he knew not where. Immobilized, he understood the cloak, and the lasso, and their transcendent essence. He began to understand what he could possibly do with them, and he was suddenly a little afraid.

Quickly taking off the cloak, and resting the lasso over his shoulder, he hastened after the two Ve.

It was another fine day at the house between the falls, and the horses were at their leisure, in various parts of the grassy glade.

"We must go!" Shouted Berondyas

Nothing happened for a second. Gradually, though, Varoden saw that the horses were starting to coalesce into a circular form. This process took a minute or two, but at its conclusion, a deep stillness arose. The horses seemed to look at each other for several long seconds, before ten or so of them left the formation, and started to walk towards the numen and the human.

"So they will go him, after all" muttered Berondyas to himself, before turning towards Varoden and saying "These will be your companions. You are to take care of them, as they will take care of you" he paused before continuing "They will let you and those you designate be their riders, but do not ever forget that they are free, and that your relationship must always be based on respect"

Varoden was at a loss for words, and turned to look at the approaching horses. When he turned back towards Berondyas and Friday, there were gone.

THIRTY-THREE

"That was impressive"

"Thank you" said Sun Wu, "You're pretty impressive yourself." this last was accompanied by a little smile

Osha smiled back and glanced at Hampele, who also had a smile on her face

"As, of course, is Hampele the magnificent and terrible, eater of earth and shaper of lands."

"Of course" said Hampele, with a wink

"And to what do I owe the honour of a visit from two legendary personages such as yourselves?"

"You knew we were coming..."

"...But not necessarily why"

So Osha and her Aunt Hammy filled Sun Wu in on the matter that was facing them, and their determination to develop great bodies to respond to it.

"...And we'd like to know if you'd be interested in being part of a great body"

"It would be a privilege... will you both be making one big body?"

"No, we thought it was better to be more flexible, we'll both be part of one, and maybe there'll be a few more working with us.... You know how they'll need to be constituted, by the way? For real effectiveness in the fourth worlds?"

"Yes, I fear neither hell beings nor hungry ghosts… And of course, some of my best friends are animals and humans" he smiled at this last. "So who will I be joining?"

"Me" said Osha

"We both think the balance would be more favourable that way"

"Yes" Sun Wu said "I think you're probably right"

"Which leads" said Hampele "To the next thing… I want to ask your friend the old man to join with me. Is he here?"

"Ah, a potentially formidable partnership, which I think he'll readily agree to… Alas, he's not here…"

"Where is he?"

"Ironically, he's in the fourth worlds, at a meeting in the far western continents, that you have so recently made your home" he nodded at Osha

"You have a good enough idea of where for us to take the quick route?" Hampele asked

"I think so, yes."

"Okay, well we'll go now, then; will you join us, or should we return here afterwards?"

"I'll come, just give me a moment"

With that, Sun Wu was suddenly talking to his students again, and then, after a short discussion, nowhere to be seen.

And then he was back in front of them, a long staff in his hand.

"Alright, let's go on a trip to the west," he said, "I love these!" Aunty Hammy did the honours, and they found themselves in a beautifully rugged landscape, filled with mountains, valleys, and mesas.

"I know this place" said Hampele "The peaceful people live here! I spent some time with them a while ago, it was lovely, and I've been meaning to come back..."

"Here we are. I believe the peaceful people are the hosts of this particular meeting, and I think it's over there" Sun Wu pointed to the north, where there was a settlement integrated into a cliffside. The rock houses seemed to be natural, and had the same stark beauty the countryside did.

They started to walk towards the town, by unspoken agreement. Some environments and situations deserved the slow way.

"Can I ask you something?" Osha asked Sun Wu

"By all means"

"If you've accumulated enough merit to shift phase, why haven't you?"

There was a pause

"As the great Hampele knows" he smiled at her "My youth was characterized by some... *unfortunate* attitudes and decisions on my part. I do not feel that I have as yet achieved true peace with them, and have no desire to start a new way of being with that kind of... baggage."

Another pause, as both Osha and Aunt Hammy looked thoughtfully at the scenery, and Sun Wu smiled to himself.

"There is also" he said "The fact that I'm not really interested in becoming an *authority*."

One more pause, with even more thoughtfulness

"I just always assumed that was the path" Osha said eventually

"It's a path, certainly" Sun Wu said "But there are myriad paths and ways. I have been following the bodhisattva way."

Hampele and Osha had both heard of the bodhisattva thing, but neither had thought it applied to them, particularly, being *authorities* and all.

"Isn't a bodhisattva an *authority*, anyway?" asked Aunt Hammy

"Depends on how you look at it..."

"How do you look at it?"

"I'm learning to look at it with humility and patience, but it's taking a while. The bodhisattva way is good for that, though"

More thoughtful silence, and then they were at their destination.

THIRTY-FOUR

The first journeys of Ranga and Appa were filled with adventure, joy and discovery. Unfortunately, we've got lots to get through, so we'll have to come back to them if there's time. Suffice it to say, they generally followed the coast, north, and then northeast, and then again northwest, through a narrow strait until they came to its end, where some very interesting folk indeed made their home(s). Ranga and Appa stayed there a while, learning a little about the great sea overland to the north, and many many other things besides, but that, like I said, is a story for another time.

Their relationship had blossomed into something neither could have predicted. They trusted each other and life so completely that they lifted each other beyond the common run, and were able, from this solid foundation, to be open to whatever came. So, they learned a hell of a lot, very quickly.

Appa had taught Ranga the ways of the Learned Ones, and he taught her the ways of the seas. Eventually, their knowledge combined into something exponentially larger. Likewise, they had met and interacted with many different peoples, with many different cultures. These, they incorporated and studied, where appropriate, until they had their own culture, an amalgam of all they perceived to be wise from their experiences.

And the music had got super interesting, too.

Anyway, by the time they had sailed back down the gulf from the sea's northern end, and explored along the coastline of the land that lay to the east, several years had passed; and they realized that they could visit home again, without breaking the agreement they had made.

So they headed south, to their home.

By this time, their navigation skills, which had grown with the inclusion of local variations, were such that they didn't need to hug the coastline, once they had provisioned properly. So, they went due south, and then southwest, on the open sea; and were home before they knew it.

Mindful of the concerns of their teachers, they went, before returning to the village, to their cave island and left the big boat, taking the safely stowed little one.

They had a great time at home. Their families, which were all fine, were overjoyed to see them; and the Elders were deeply interested in the stories of their adventures. Ranga's tree had flourished, and they day they all spent together was lovely beyond words

But they had no urge at all to stay.

A few young people had wanted to go with them when they left again, and they might have considered it; but the combined forces of the elders and inertia, as well as a well-placed harbinger or two, put paid to that idea pretty sharpish.

Goodbyes were a little harder this time, too.

They weren't going back anytime soon.

Appa and Ranga thought this because Ranga's tree had had a message for them.

It had told them that the Great Tree had a task for them, for which they would be rewarded beyond human understanding, if they accepted. They were being asked to sail to a land not far away from where they had curtailed their exploration, and to help the people who lived there in a time of need which was to come.

The "catch" was that this mission, and their reward, would mean that they would not be able to return home for a long longlong time.

They had said yes.

THIRTY-FIVE

The horses made the journey home quick, once Varoden had got the hang of riding.

He loved it.

The feeling of speed, as well as communion with the powerful being beneath him, was absolutely intoxicating; and after a couple of shaky moments, and bruises, in the beginning; he felt like he had been born to ride.

So that went well.

Homecoming was, nevertheless, a gradual affair. He had a reasonable idea where his people would be at this time of year, and he headed in that direction. The terrain rapidly became more and more familiar, until he got within a few miles of his intended destination, and they stopped for the horses to graze and him to have a sandwich. Satisfied, he and the horses had set off again at a walking pace when he felt, rather than saw, that he was being watched. He had just turned his head, when he heard a voice shout "Varo?"

"Thrango!"

There, emerging from behind a rocky outcrop to Varoden's left, and running full speed towards him was his twin, who he had sorely missed. He felt a surge of joy, and leapt to the ground to run toward his brother, meeting him in a long embrace.

"It's so good to see you! I knew you weren't dead! And what's this you're wearing..."

Varoden maintained the hug a little longer, before saying "I missed you"

"I missed you too bro... You still gotta tell me where you got those clothes though"

Varoden hadn't thought about the impression that his shirt and trousers might make until right then.

"It's a long story" he said with a smile

"I bet it is, about as long as the story of how you came by that magnificent beast you were somehow.... riding?"

Just then, two more of his people arrived to join them, young men who Varoden had known his whole life, and counted as friends.

After greeting them effusively, Varoden suggested that they head back home, and promised that he would start telling him this tale on the way.

Thrango's face darkened, and he said "We can't, yet"

"Why not?" Varoden asked

"Raiders" said Thrango.

"We're keeping guard" Aren, one of the other youths said

"Raiders? Guard? What?"

And so Varoden learned that there had been, since his departure, two separate raids on his people. The attackers had killed six men, one of whom was a good friend of Varoden's; and taken three women, all of childbearing age, captive.

He wasn't happy about it, to say the least.

So, he stayed with Thrango, Aren and Heim, the third youth, the rest of their watch, giving them a synopsis of his experiences. They were suitably awed, and looked at him with a certain new wariness, as well, as if he might do something *Ve*like at any moment.

"Fair enough" thought Varoden

"Maybe your training can help deal with those raiding pieces of shit" Thrango said, when their watch was ended, and they were on their way to rejoin the group.

"It might… I'm pretty sure the horses will be willing to help, too" Varoden looked at his erstwhile mount, who he called Slider. The horse said nothing, unsurprisingly, but returned the youth's gaze steadily.

"I'll take that as yes"

Being among The People again had been almost overwhelming for Varoden, at first. He had told and retold his story so many times that it had occasionally begun to feel like it had happened to somebody else. He kept up his practice, though- regularly going off by himself and meditating, or flowing through the various forms of the ways of the empty and gripping hands.

His new lasso, which he kept hitched to his belt, made the gripping hand way seem like something else, entirely; and he, eventually, overcame his reticence, and donned the cloak as well- opening up forms and emptiness that simply hadn't been available before.

He also still had the book from the library of time, which he read carefully every day.

So, he continued to grow in and into his practice.

The People did not arrange (and apparently had never arranged) themselves hierarchically. Everyone is important to the whole, was their saying, and that was pretty much how they lived. Varoden's newfound presence was, thus, something to be dealt with. For the most part, they did this by making fun of him, which he supposed was good practice as well, even though it could get a bit old sometimes.

Which is not at all to say that his time with his people was all bad. Many of the young women, and some others besides, made it clear that were quite interested in him, and he occasionally reciprocated that interest, but he was already clever enough to not make anything too obvious, or to step on too many toes.

Thrango and a couple of others had taken interest in the horses, and once Varoden had impressed on them again and again the strictures that had been laid upon him by Berondyas, he showed them what he knew of riding. They all managed, with various degrees of proficiency, and riding quickly became a thing. In the end, virtually everybody wanted to learn, and did. The horses enjoyed it too, so all seemed to be well on that front.

Other fronts were not so positive, however. The raiders were a constant topic of conversation, and there were several different viewpoints about the best course of action to take in response. Some wanted to leave this area, or do nothing, some wanted to improve their defences and others wanted to go on the offensive. There were variations, but these were the main themes. A middle way had been followed, so far, and thus a watch had been maintained for the first time in recent memory.

Varoden'sthoughts, nevertheless, were haunted by the captive women, and, one night, he sought out one of the wise elders of the People, who had been a little bit away from the main group, looking at the stars.

"The Raiders take the women so that their group can grow faster, with more children, isn't that so?" he asked, with no preamble

"If you asked me to guess, that's what I would guess"

"And they could grow to be much more numerous than us, with their agriculture, isn't it so?"

"It is said that their way yields more numbers, yes"

"So, what can we do?"

"We are the People, we will find a way, as we always have"

There was a pause

"I think I can get our people back" Varoden said "Will you oppose this?"

There was another pause

"I think it doesn't matter that much what I think. Your new abilities, and the horses, will convince enough of the others, in all likelihood"

"Yes, but do you think that I'm wrong?"

"I don't know"

And that's how Varoden, Thrango, Aren and Heim came to be riding towards the Raiders' settlement in the middle of the night.

THIRTY-SIX

After a very hospitable reception at the town in the rocks, Hampele, Osha and Sun Wu had headed a little further along, where they had been told the meeting was being held.

"What kind of meeting is this, anyway?" Osha had asked

"Apparently, they're all followers of the wisdom way, from both this continent and the one to the south. They gather every few decades or so..." Sun Wu had replied

"Are there always numen there?"

"Usually, I think... I actually was a guest at one of these not all that long ago...Way down south .... Had a blast"

"Do **authorities** go too"

"Hmmm, not so sure about that one... There weren't any when I went, not that I noticed, anyway"

And so on.

They arrived to the plateau they had been directed to, and all took a moment to enjoy the view, before turning their attention(s) to the details of the gathering in front of them.

There were what looked like hundreds of people engaged in various activities. Some talked in small groups, some danced and some stood by themselves. There was music, and smoking and a big fire. There was also a larger group standing by a huge rock off to one side, listening to a very old, serene and stunningly beautiful woman speak.

"There's the old man" said Sun Wu, pointing to the group by the big rock.

They started to head in that direction, but before they could get too far there was a shout, and then another, then many

"Blessed ones!"

"Orisha!"

"Great Spirits!"

That sort of thing.

Within seconds, the attention of the whole gathering was turned on the three visitors, and just about everything else stopped.

And stayed stopped, as Osha, Hampele and Sun Wu continued towards the big rock.

"I guess we've been recognized"

"Well, we should have known that these types of folks would notice"

"To be fair, you didn't try to disguise ourselves all that much" Sun Wu, put in

"Don't usually have to all that much" Osha said

"Anyway, it's no big deal, I think we're all probably on the same team here"

"You're probably right"

And then they were at the rock, where the woman had stopped speaking to the group. She smiled her beautiful serene smile at them.

"Welcome, honoured ones, I am overjoyed and humbled to be in your presence" She used one of the languages of the way.

Hampele stepped forward, and said "And I'm sure I speak for my colleagues here when I say we're overjoyed and humbled to be in yours." She smiled widely, and it's to the credit of those nearby that hardly anyone flinched. Osha's Aunt Hammy was lovely and wonderful, but she could be a bit intimidating to the uninitiated, particularly when she smiled.

"We had come to speak to the old man, but we have no wish to interrupt the proceedings. Please carry on."

"Very well, Great Ones."

With that, the speaker took a second to compose herself, and then continued her presentation, which, it became clear, was about possible responses to the cataclysmic overseas invasion from the east which had already killed so many, and put so many more at risk. She even mentioned the reality eating machine that had so concerned Osha and Hampele, but she seemed not to have realized the full consequences and danger which it posed.

She was a good speaker, and when she had finished, she facilitated a somewhat brief but lively discussion, which was also very interesting for the three guests. They even added some input, here and there, where appropriate, but it's been said (and it's true) "those who know don't say, and those who say don't know". So they didn't say much.

Osha, Hampele, Sun Wu (and the old man, who Osha had eventually, but not right away, recognized) had learned, sometimes through hard experience; that beings had to find their own way to wisdom and awareness. This was true of all beings. It is also said that "When the student is ready, the teacher appears" (it's just as right to say "when the teacher is ready the student appears").

In other words, a lot of being wise is just chilling out, letting go of your ideas and paying attention.

    They were wise.

    "I can usually tell numen right away, but it wasn't so easy to pick you out" Osha had said to the old man; once they got a chance to speak to him alone, and introductions had been made.

    "Rivers rule the ten thousand valleys" he said with a friendly smile

    "I like rivers" Osha said, smiling back

He was in, by the way. He would join Hampele's great body, and aid the effort to correct the imbalance and ameliorate the destruction wrought by the machine.

THIRTY-SEVEN

Appa and Ranga's course, after leaving, was northeast, and favourable winds and currents took them away from home at a good speed. These conditions prevailed until, a week or two in, they sensed that the seascape had changed, and that if they just kept on, they'd end up too far east.

So they headed north, which they knew was safe.As if to endorse this decision, two dolphins showed up, and stayed with them until they sighted land.

As they approached the coast, they realized, with pleasure, that they had nearly got it exactly right. Familiar landmarks and conditions told themthat their destination, as per the tree's instructions, was a little to the northeast; and a few days sailing brought sight of a beautiful settlement nestled into hills just off a long sandy beach.

They beached a little bit away from the village, but soon saw an old woman and two younger men walking towards them.

They met them halfway.

"Welcome to Rasmu, travelers." One of the men said "We had heard of your coming, and would offer you hospitality"

They were speaking a dialect of one of the languages of the way, and even though Appa had taught Ranga this and other languages used by the Learned Ones, she was still far more proficient than he. As such, she did most of the talking

"We gladly receive it" she said slowly but smilingly

"Come" said the old woman, smiling in turn; and they all set off walking towards Rasmu

One of the things that had struck both Ranga and Appa on their travels was how *lovely* humans were, most of the time. This isn't to say they hadn't had some dodgy moments, they definitely had. In general, though, people were warm and welcoming, and each new place had its own genius, which was often challenging, but always interesting.

Rasmu was cool too.

It was even more charming close up, and the residents were of the relaxed smiley type which is the favourite of most travelers. They were greeted as long-lost friends by almost everyone they met, and treated to a wonderful spicy seafood lunch, accompanied by a calming brewed beverage and followed by a milky and very intoxicating wine which was apparently made from palm trees.

It was a glorious day, and marked the beginning of a long and beautiful relationship between them and Rasmu.

The day after their arrival, Ranga and Appa both woke up with headaches, a testament to the previous evening's festivities. Their morning meditations and ablutions eventually had them feeling ready to interact with other humans, if still a bit delicate.

They had been given a cozy little beach hut for their stay, and they were sitting on its veranda when they saw the three people who had come to meet them on the beach the day before walking down the path from the main village.

"I trust you are sufficiently recovered for breakfast" said one of the men with a little grin

"Breakfast sounds lovely" said Appa with a somewhat rueful smile

This meal was to be taken in a more private manner than yesterday's dinner, up on the cliff which lay above the village, and on which there was a massive tree growing by itself, surrounded by large rocks. The three locals bowed on arriving in the vicinity, and so Appa and Ranga did as well.

They laid a piece of fabric on the ground, put out the food and drink they had all carried up from the village, and started to eat. It was delicious again.

"We carried you up here to show you something" said the old lady after they were all finished "We are students of the great way, and this is one of its centers in our world…"

"The village or the tree?" Appa asked

"Yes" was the response

"Gotcha"

"Last moon we were in meditation around the tree" one of the men continued "when a bird, the like of which none of us had ever seen, landed right at the foot of the tree and proceeded to carve something in its bark."

He paused

"None of us know what it means, but it is probably not for us. It is probably for you"

With that he got up, and pointed to a point on the tree's trunk

Appa and Ranga also got up, and saw, written in a different language of the way

There will be a flood
In the lands to the northwest
All must not perish

Take Nana's children
To lands on the eastern shore
Where they will flourish

Take the ten young ones
To the great eastern river
Where they will flourish

"You can understand it, I can tell"

"Yes, I can…"

"Do not tell us what it says, we have faith in the way"

"As you wish"

When they had returned to their beach cottage, Appa told Ranga what she had read, and they agreed, somewhat reluctantly, that they should probably leave that same day, since they didn't know when the flood would be, exactly.

The villagers wouldn't let them leave without lunch, which was again glorious, and solicited from them promises to return at their earliest convenience, promises they intended to keep. It seemed like everyone came to wish them farewell, and as they walked along the beach towards their boat, they were both, independently, charged with a consciousness of the connectedness of all beings that would never really leave them.

They were going to need it.

THIRTY-EIGHT

Not wishing to interfere with the regular goings on of the meeting, Osha, Hampele and Sun Wu left not long after speaking to the old man. Sun Wu would return to the mountain school, until such time as the great body needed his active participation; Hampele had some business to take care of here in the fourth worlds, off to the east; the old man was staying for the end of his meeting; and Osha was going to hell.

Hell is more of a frame of mind than a specific place, but there are physical correspondents to every mental state, in one splace or another; so she headed to the *place that's not a place* which had a safe and reliable entrance. There were many other ingresses, but one usually wanted to take a known way to hell, if one could.

She had been, once, long ago.

That's another story for another time, though.

The spot she was headed for was in a very beautiful part of the *place that's not a place*, not actually all that far from the Ve. It was a wooded mountain side, with very tall trees poking their heads up here and there, and she took a moment to enjoy her surroundings, and exchange pleasantries. Presently, she turned towards the cave which provided access to hell, gathered herself, and walked in

The King and Queen of hell ruled with great dignity and compassion now, it was said, though Osha had had a somewhat different experience on her first trip there. The welcome she got this time around led her to believe that the current reports were at least not totally inaccurate.

She had been met, at the back of the cave, by a very polite demon, who had respectfully asked for her name and her business there. These, once given, had earned her even more deferential treatment; and after a short delay she had been shown to an elevator and wished a good day.

The walls floor and ceiling of the elevator were all made of glass, or some other transparent material, and she had very much enjoyed the ride. The scenic vistas, which stretched in all directions (literally) were many and varied, and one could easily have spent long periods of time just contemplating the way time and space played out in them. It reminded her a little of some of the elevators in the library of time, and she wondered idly if that's where they had got the idea.

The direction the elevator went in could be considered a descent, vis a vis the cave entrance, but that sensation was not borne out by (even) Osha's sensory experience; and the sense of movement without movement, and infinite regression as well, was deliciously tickling to her.

Eventually, the elevator door opened, and she stepped into a room that wasn't what one might have expected, given the previous view. It was large and airy, and almost empty, except for busy looking demons rushing here and there; and off to one corner, the King, and a being that she assumed to be the Queen, standing by a large picture window, and looking through it interestedly.

They noticed her immediately, and walked toward her with welcoming expressions, which got warmer with proximity.

"Welcome, your honour" said the Queen, bowing

"Lady Osha, please accept my deepest apologies for what happened last time, there's no way to make up for it, but if you could find it in your heart to allow me the privilege of being at your disposal, I would be profoundly grateful" the King said after bowing even deeper

"Thank you very much for your gracious welcome your Majesties" said Osha "And all is forgiven" she said this last with a smile at the King, before taking a step back and bowing to them both.

She meant it, too. Osha had learned, at some point or another, that forgiveness, understanding and love were all different versions of the same word, and she had worked hard to put her belief into practice. It had worked, after a shorter time than she thought might be the case; so by this time, long after her realization, grudges were truly alien to her.

She wasn't mad at the King for what had happened, in other words.

After the greeting process had been performed, Osha began to explain the situation as she perceived it, and the dangers of the reality eating machine to the fourth worlds and all the nearby splaces.

"It's funny" the King said "We've been seeing a HUGE increase in population here, both of the living and the dead... I haven't been keeping up with the goings on over there, but what you're telling me might explain what's happening"

"Yes, I guess it would, wouldn't it??"

"But why would that make them come here, necessarily?" asked the Queen

"Ah my dear, your grace and wisdom make me forget that you're relatively new to these things" The King responded "The attachment to hatred, anger and violence which brings beings here is based on a deep alienation from reality. If reality is being eaten, and replaced, then this result becomes far more likely..."

"Ohhhh"

Osha explained the plan about the great bodies, and the need for hell beings as part of it, before asking directly "Is this acceptable to you, King?"

"Oh of course, Lady Osha!" he said quickly "I would immediately volunteer myself, but my duties here..." he paused as he noticed a smile beginning to form around her eyes "... and of course the karma I created through my past actions.... Well, I'm maybe not the best candidate, is what I'm saying"

"I will participate if you will accept me" said the Queen simply.

"You would both be excellent candidates, but I wouldn't dream of taking you both from your important work here... I think my Aunty Hammy might find your offer quite interesting, though, Queen" said

Osha, the smile migrating from her eyes to her cheeks. "Can you think of anyone else who could go in the King's place, so we don't take both of you away?"

The King and Queen of hell both thought for a while, before the Queen looked at her husband and said "How about the First Owner?"

He looked thoughtful, and took a minute before slowly responding "You know... I think that's a very good idea". He turned to Osha and said "My lady, if you'd care to take a little walk, you can observe and then meet this person in his everyday existence... that might help you see if he's suitable for your purposes"

"Sounds good to me" said Osha.

THIRTY - NINE

They had left the horses once they had seen signs of habitation, and Heim had stayed with them, both as reserve and watchman. The other three had proceeded as stealthily as possible towards the Raiders' settlement; and they arrived unchallenged at their destination.

"What've they done there" whispered Thrango, pointing

"Those are walls, not very good walls, to be fair, but walls nonetheless" Varoden had whispered back.

He motioned to the other two to stay where they were, and, putting on his cloak, ran gracefully up the wall and jumped to the top of it, where he crouched, surveying the Raiders' town.

It was pretty big.

And there were a lot of people, too.

Interestingly, he noticed more women and children than men, which suggested to him that his was not the only tribe that had been raided.

There was a very large central structure, or series of structures, which seemed to contain several houses, entrance to which was through the roof. In fact, the roof seemed to be the main thoroughfare of this part of the town, as there were many people walking or standing around on it. Around this there were houses in a mishmash of styles, and more regular walking paths providing passage.

Varoden sat patiently on the wall and watched, knowing that his cloak would provide at least partial, and maybe total, camouflage. At last, his vigilance was rewarded, he saw two of the women from the People walking not far away from where he was, holding reed baskets and talking to each other. There was, inconveniently, a man walking beside them, holding a large and dangerous looking club.

Without consciously realizing it, Varoden had a plan, and started into motion, clambering down the acutely angled earthworks gracefully, and moving into the "East wind blows across the plain", one of the more dynamic of the gripping hand forms he had learned. His lasso became a blur of motion, and he seemed to float across the intervening distance, immobilizing the man with the club before anyone really knew what was happening.

"You are not wounded

But movement is forbidden

'til night has fallen"

These words of the way had the power to become law, if the person they were used against did not have the wherewithal to resist. Varoden's victim did not, and he disengaged his lasso, and slung it again at his waist.

His two tribeswomen watched in amazement, before one of them, Sarag, said "Varoden? Is that you?"

"In the flesh... But let's move quickly. Lela was with you too, no?"

"Yes" said the other woman, Gudra "She's over there, in our prison...." She spat that last word out, pointing

"Will she be coming out soon, or do I have to go in and get her?"

"She would have gone after we had returned, but if we do not, she will not, they will know something is wrong"

"Okay.... Look, let me take you out of here and then come back to get her, does that work for you?"

They both quickly nodded their assent, though Gudra asked "Won't you need help? There'll be at least two guards..."

"I'll be fine" he said

"I believe you" said Gudra, eying the still motionless man on the ground beside them...

Varoden moved the man behind a nearby hut, before they all scrambled up the steep gradient of the "wall" and ran back to the waiting Thrango and Aren. They decided that Aren would go with the two women to the waiting Heim and the horses, and that Thrango would wait there for Varoden and Lela to return.

Varoden retraced his steps, and headed, without incident, to the "prison" that Gudra had found. Once he caught sight of the two bored looking men standing outside, he moved into the "The Eastern gale scours the plain" a variant of his earlier form adapted to multiple opponents.

It was equally successful

Lela didn't require much prompting, once she had overcome her initial surprise. As befitted one of the People, she moved purposefully and readily, having quickly grasped the situation.

So, they left; but Varoden knew he would be returning.

This could not be allowed to continue.

FORTY

Flood was probably not a strong enough word for what happened. A vast land had been inundated by both river and sea water, connecting it to the ocean and creating a huge gulf. There had, apparently, been a little warning: the yearly river floods had got heavier and heavier every year, and the rivers had experienced a correspondent rise. Few expected the full fury of the cataclysmic deluge when it came, though; and it had been a disaster for the many people who had called that fertile confluence of rivers home.

Ranga and Appa had arrived not long after the flood did. They had heard it, in fact. And felt it, too.

Racing to find anyone or anything to assist, they had quickly encountered some survivors on two small islands. These people had, according to two elders who spoke the same language of the way that that Rasmusi did, been warned of the impending disaster in dreams. They had (wisely) listened, and immediately sought high ground, which had become these islands.

"Have you ever heard of someone called Nana?" Appa had asked the elders.

"The one who appeared to us in our dreams said her name was Nana!"

"Well…. We were asked to take the children of Nana to an eastern shore…"

"Then shorely we must go there" said the taller one, before quickly adding "See what I did there?"

"I believe I do" Appa said, with a slightly stunned smile

"You must excuse Lual" said the other elder quickly "He cannot help himself. EVEN IN IN THE MIDDLE OF THE BIGGEST DISASTER IN THE HISTORY OF THE WORLD… He is incorrigible, I'm afraid"

"Then don't incorrige me" said Lual with a bright smile

"Whooooo boy" said Appa.

It didn't stop either.

All the survivors were able to crowd aboard the boat without too much problem, and they set out in search of the appointed place. The course was west, at first, but the narrow strait they had entered through widened and turned to the northwest, providing candidate shores to the east.

None of them looked like it, or felt like it, either.

And then there was a bird, a large multi-coloured one that first circled their boat, and then flew on ahead, looking back to make sure they had noticed it.

They had, and they followed northwest, not far from the shore.

For two days.

And then they were there.

The bird had turned toward shore early in the morning, when everyone, expect Ranga, Appa and Lual, was asleep.

"I think that's it!" said Ranga, pointing at a grassy "beach", which was the end of a plain that gently ascended to fairly distant mountains, upon which dawn had just broken.

"Sun of a beach!" said Lual.

Appa, who had grown fond of the tragically punning elder, had, nevertheless, learned that a little smile was the safest response to his efforts.

"Cause the sun's shining on the beach, now, you see" explained Lual helpfully.

"Yes, Lual, yes it is."

The Children of Nana, had brought what food they could carry with them to their mountain (and then island) refuge; and they all shared a thanksgiving meal on the shore, before Appa and Ranga had to leave, promising to visit as soon as they could.

"Bye you guys" Lual shouted as they sailed away in search of the 'ten young ones' they were to take back east "I'll miss the boat of you."

"That one, I got" Ranga said, with a rueful smile and wave.

The bright beautiful bird stayed on the eastern shore, but new guides appeared within minutes of their departure, a pair of dolphins meeting them as they sailed to the northwest. The dolphins led them south, instead, and it wasn't long before they saw something bobbing in the distance. As they drew closer, it became clear that what they were seeing was a kind of small circular raft, on which little figures could be seen sitting.

Ten little figures.

None of the children spoke any of the languages of the way that Appa knew, but their dialect seemed to be a variant of one that was spoken on the other side of what the flood had made a great peninsula, by the people of the great river. Ranga and Appa had spent enough time there that they could, very generally, communicate with the children, and understand a little of their story.

The ten young ones varied in age, from about five to about fifteen; and there were four boys and six girls. As far as Ranga and Appa could make out, they were from a group of people who had lived right in the middle of the now flooded land. These particular children had all been apprentices to their people's Learned Ones, with the variant that their wisdom was specifically preserved, and used, in music and chanted poetry.

They had been taught a song by the oldest and probably wisest of their teachers which went something like.

The rushing waters
Will sing a song of rebirth

The end of this age

We the faithful ones
Will sing harmonies of hope
And trust the great way

We follow our song
To the place of the new sun
Where we will flourish

The raft which had saved them had been built according to specifications which had come to their old teacher during a long, improvised piece of music that he had performed, and enacted.
So, these kids were good musicians, even the littlest one, a shy and tiny girl.
    Very good musicians.
And they had, per their instructions, carried their instruments, as well as a little food, onto their raft.
    It was a great journey.

FORTY-ONE
(Shout out to Slartibartfast, Yo!)

Hell had changed since the last time Osha was there, that was for sure. The nature of hell beings was such that their painful and constant suffering emanated from within themselves, but the management of hell used to go in for the external trappings big time... Lakes of fire, torture dungeons, that kind of thing.

That had changed.

"We're actually pretty happy with the way things have been going" the King of hell said to Osha, as they walked through a pleasant looking garden "For the past while we've been thinking about really emphasizing the redemptive aspect of this place, and playing down the punishment side... It seems to work, too: we've been getting much quicker graduation..."

"Graduation?" Osha asked

"Oh yes" the King said with a slightly embarrassed smile "When a hell being has worked off the karma that brought them here, and/or accumulated enough merit to shift phase, we call it graduation... It's because we like to think of this place as a school, you see..."

"I like that" said Osha

Karma, it should be understood, does not refer to any kind of universal mechanism that judges beings and apportions reward or punishment accordingly. Karma is not separate from one's actions. Nor is it separate from cause and effect, I might add.

Keep it in mind.

Anyway, nobody could force anyone else to become a hell being (as the King had found to his deep chagrin, early on in his reign). Beings essentially chose that path for themselves. And then, through their efforts, they chose when they were ready to move on.

So, the school metaphor was, though not perfect, not a bad one, necessarily.

As Osha walked through hell with its King and Queen, she began to understand the nature of this new organization of hell. The beings they encountered seemed, still, to be in great torment, often (Hanging on in loud desperation is, was and is likely to remain, the hellish way). The difference was that there was no-one torturing them. Consequently, they had no-one to blame but themselves and each other. It being hell, the blaming each other route was definitely the most popular, and Osha could perceive war and strife in the distance.

That wasn't the whole thing, though.

For those that were ready, willing and able, hell had begun to actively encourage introspection and understanding: Osha walked past support groups and meditation classes, as well as a lot of organized (and other) sport.

She was impressed.

"I'm impressed" she said to the King and Queen

"Thank you, my lady" the Queen said with a smile, while the King looked almost overcome, for a moment.

"By the way, I meant to say it before, but feel free to call me whatever you want, Osha is fine, too…"

"I think I'll have to build up to that, lady Osha" the Queen said. The king nodded agreement, still seeming somewhat shy.

"We give up our names when we come here, as you know…."

"Well, nobody stays in hell forever" Osha said.

"No, it's true…"

They arrived, eventually, at an imposingly beautiful castle, which sat on top of a hill. There was, also, a picturesque river at the foot of the hill, over which a wooden bridge sat.

"The First Owner's Bastion" the King said, nodding towards the castle.

"So who is this guy, anyway?" Osha asked

"Well, it's as his name says, Lady Osha; this being was the first in the fourth worlds to take property for himself"

"Ah, I see… And just to be clear, what was the first property in the fourth worlds?"

"Women" said the King simply.

"Yes, that's what I thought you would say."

Osha remembered observing the fourth worlds when the process of property creation was happening. While groups had often had a concept of territory, there wasn't really any sense of ownership, as such. Humans hadn't seen much difference between themselves and their surroundings, in fact.

But there was a little advantage to be had. Any group which had more women could get bigger, faster. Innovations and changes, including but not restricted to, the blossoming of agriculture, had meant that it was possible for a lot more people to live as part of one group.

The more the merrier, they said.

And so, women's bodies, and their reproductive abilities, became a resource.

And then they became the first property.

Which was a horrible idea.

The worst ever, in fact.

"Welcome your Majesties, and my Lady" the First Owner said, after they had been met and brought inside by very respectful beings dressed in matching livery "I am at your service"

"Thank you, Owner" the King replied, before adding "This is Lady Osha"

The First Owner paled and immediately bowed his obeisance

"That's not necessary" Osha said simply.

"Great one, I have been in hell for a very long time. I have finally begun to understand what I did. Please believe me when I say that I had no idea what would happen… "

"You've seen some of the consequences, then?"

"Great one, part of my way of discharging my karma and gaining merit has been through learning… In fact, I am one of the architects of the new hell… But my studies have shown me the horror which I unleashed…" he had started crying "… All of the torturous punishment meted out to me when I was new here pale in comparison to starting to really see what I did, and who I have been…"

"I forgive you" Osha said, gently raising him up and giving him a hug.

He started crying even harder.

The First Owner, once he had begun to really learn, had devoted himself to the greater good, as best as he could. While his initial efforts had been more than a little tinged with selfishness and ignorance, over time he had grown into his self-appointed task; until by the time Osha met him, he was genuinely committed to being of service to the way.

He was still a hell being because he could not forgive himself.

FORTY-TWO

Varoden, Thrango, Aren, Heim, Lela, Gudra and Sarag talked virtually unceasingly on the way back to their people. The horses were able to manage the extra weight with no difficulty, and they were unconcerned about pursuit, so they did not rush.

In response to the women's questions about Varoden's newfound ability, Thrango had launched into a quite funny, though only occasionally accurate, retelling of the tale, complete with orgies in the Ve. His obvious pride in his brother was quite pure, though, andit added a touching element into what would otherwise have been farce.

"He's always been good at that" Varoden thought to himself with an inward smile, and a surge of affection.

Lela, Gudra and Sarag's stories had been less amusing. Lela had been taken in the first raid, caught unawares by the river with two of her friends. The two others, both men, and one of whom was Varoden's friend Bulda, had been killed after they had all been overcome by the force of numbers. Lela had been tied up and carried back to the village, where she had, she said matter of factly, been abused. Being of the people, she had not submitted easily, and the Raiders had, after a few injuries, decided to wait her out, and chosen easier targets. In the meantime, she had been put to work in the fields.

Gudra and Sarag had been taken in an ambush, on their way back home after a hunting expedition. There had been a little battle that time, since they had been armed, but eventually, their four male companions had been killed, and they had been taken back to the settlement. The Raiders had lost ten of their own people in the fighting, and had seemed to be on the verge of killing Gudra and Sarag; but after much discussion, which was just about intelligible, they had thrown the two young women into Lela's hut, and left.

Lela's resistance seemed to have been advantageous for the two later captives, because they had not been subsequently assaulted. Instead, they had joined her in the fields, and the three had developed a very close bond, as well as a taste for sabotage, whenever possible.

The Raiders were arranged hierarchically, as it turned out. At the bottom were the women taken captive in the raids of the surrounding countryside, a mélange of people with very different traditions and ideas, and often only a passing understanding of each other's languages. Above them were the regular people, the men and women who did the work that kept the settlement going.

Next up was a small but increasing class of skilled artisans, who were excused from much of the daily toil, but were expected to create beautiful jewellery, pots, songs, and the like. The class above them, the second highest, were the fighters, who were all men. This was because the main aim of their violence was the capture of women, with the view to increasing the female population. It seemed to the Raiders a foolish proposition to risk diminishing this population in the process. There was also the risk of women objecting to the brutalization and objectification of other women if it was right in their faces, as it tended to be, on raids.

At the top of the hierarchy was a small group of people, men and women both, who seemed to have access to the powers beyond the quotidian. They had created rituals and sacred places through which this power was made available, but over which they maintained a firm control.

This all seemed crazy to Varoden and his friends.

Like really crazy.

Its awful effectiveness could not be denied, though. The Raiders had grown and grown and grown, and showed no signs of stopping. Lela, who had been there the longest, had seen part of how and why this process worked. The captured women were often taken as wives by the men of the fighting class, and their children, who would have grown up as Raiders, cemented their new loyalties, eventually.

These captured wives formed a kind of special class, certainly above the unmarried captives, and probably above the regular people as well.

The divisions which this complicated social order created seemed to militate against any kind of organized resistance on the part of the classes that did all the work. On the contrary, the combination of the seeming efficacy of the Raiders methods, the control over knowledge of the "priestly" class, and harsh punishment for divergence from the given order created a very unfriendly environment for revolution.

As Varoden thought about it, he had to admire the cleverness of the methods, all the while abhorring the reality.

And then they were home, to a rapturous welcome.
The seven of them had forged a bond during their adventure, and homecoming seemed only to intensify it. Sarag, Gudra and Lela spent a lot of time with the horses, until they were clearly expert riders, with Lela the best of anyone. Varoden had also started to give lessons in both meditation and the way of the hands, and the six others were his most consistent students.

They all got good at that too.
They didn't speak about it often, but their little group had developed the intention of doing something about the Raiders, whatever that might be.

It was, then, no surprise that when the year was up, and Varoden was about to make his way back to the house between the falls, he invited Thrango, Lela, Gudra, Heim, Sarag and Aren to join him. They happily accepted.

FORTY-THREE

The "great eastern river" had not been hard to find, but they had had yet another guide to make absolutely sure of it. A huge manatee, solemnly beautiful, if a tad ungainly looking, had replaced the dolphins and led them out of the gulf, and then almost due east.

Ranga and Appa had realized, one afternoon, that they were fairly close to Rasmu, and thought it might be nice for the children to receive some of the same hospitality they had, before moving on to their new lives.

When, however, they had asked their young passengers if they wanted to stop, there'd been a unanimous no thank you.

They were eager to get on with things, in that manner peculiar to the young and innocent.

    So they got on with things.

    So will I.

They had been met by two tall and elegant looking people, a man and woman, who were clad in odd coloured robes. There, where the great river meets the sea, they had exchanged greetings and briefly made sure that everything was on the level. This was quickly proved beyond a reasonable doubt when the large multi-coloured bird, or one that looked just like it, showed up, and stared with meaningful intent at the gathering, before flying off towards the northeast.

"I guess that's our cue" said the woman in the robe, speaking in a language of the way

"So it would seem" Ranga said, with a smile

"Farewell and good luck" was Appa's response, before hugging the "ten young ones" and bowing respectfully to their new guardians

There was hugging and bowing all around, and then they were gone.

Back at sea, Appa and Ranga were able to relax in a way that hadn't been possible since they undertook their rescue mission. They made slow and deliberate love for most of that first day, but were able to decide, at some point in the process, that Rasmu was the winning answer to the question "where the hell we going now?"

They headed generally west, just following their sea-noses, and were delighted, and a bit surprised, when they made almost exactly the same land-fall they had the first time.

Good job guys!

They received an even more effusive welcome than their previous one, and spent a week or more in blissful (and enforced) idleness; before one afternoon, they were taken back up to the tree on the cliff by the same people who had taken them the last time.

They had a wonderful lunch, and interesting conversation, and then the old woman rose and said "We must leave you here, the great one wishes to commune with you alone"

"Alone?"

"This is what we have been told" one of the men said calmly

With that, the three Rasmusi rose and efficiently cleared away lunch, before disappearing down the path without another word.

Several smiles, though.

"Well" said Appa "I don't see any more writing, I wonder how we're going to communicate this time"

"Let's just sit in meditation"

"Works for me"

And they sat.

Before too long, Ranga's necklace and Appa's anklet began to glow, which light was increasingly visible in the deepening twilight.

They continued to sit quietly.

A little while after full night fell, the glow brightened, and brightened, and brightened some more, until they had to close their eyes against the glare.

"You have done well, thank you"

"You're welcome"

"You have earned a reward"

"It's not necessary, we were glad to help"

"You are free to refuse, but hear the offer first"

"Makes sense"

And then, with no sense of motion or elapsed time, they were on the boat at sea. It was immediately obvious to both of them, however, that this was no regular sea.

For one thing, it was glowing. There were other things, too

"This place, the dreamtime, is a place of centers, and a place of truth. Can you feel that?"

They both could, and said so

"This, then, is the truth. You are about to land on an island. If, when you land there, you plant the tree that you have around your neck, Ranga; and you the feather around your ankle, Appa; you will shift phase and become numen. Your lives will not naturally end before that of the world you were born on, and your abilities and capacities will likewise increase"

Ranga and Appa sat in stunned silence.

And then they felt their boat gently beach.

FORTY-FOUR

The First Owner had been almost pathetically grateful when Osha had offered him a place in the great body she was forming; his affirmative response had been accompanied by more tears (and hugs), and then an endearing eagerness.

They spent the evening at the great castle on the hill, sharing dinner, wine and empathy. The conversation was deep and wide ranging, and the First Owner proved himself to be deeply knowledgeable about the fourth worlds and its inhabitants.

"The humans are so interesting" The King of Hell had said at one point

"Indeed, their propensity to form these unintended great bodies is both brilliant and supremely dangerous..." the First Owner had replied

They had been talking about the reality eating machine

"Oh! I hadn't thought of it as a great body..." Osha had said with a little frown

"Well, it looks, sounds and smells like one to me, Lady Osha"

There was a pause

"I think you're probably right... well spotted" Osha had said thoughtfully

"Does it change the required response, at all, my lady?"

"It might..."

And so on.

Farewells and see you soons (and hugs) having been shared, and The Queen and the First Owner having been successfully recruited, Osha went home to the dreamtime, to talk to her sisters, and one or two others, as well.

Osha is the youngest of three sisters, you may or may not remember.

Her older sisters were Isha, the middle one, and Asha, the eldest.

They were cool too.

In fact, Osha's spirits rose at the prospect of seeing them, and she felt a palpable joy at their reunion, which sentiment only intensified as she approached her old home.

Her sisters were in, and seemed equally happy that she was there. The three spoke at length, in their intimate way, about their recent experiences, and other notable goings on, before Osha broached the topic of the machine, and her ideas about both its danger, and a possible response.

Isha and Asha had not been paying much attention to the fourth worlds, and were duly surprised, and then alarmed, at their sister's account. They would *absolutely* form great bodies to try to help, but it went without saying between them that everyone would have to go about it in their own way, and at their own pace. The sisters, you see, were extremely different from each other.

Having discharged her responsibility, Osha lapsed into her regular role in their triumvirate for the rest of her stay; enjoying the small dramas and adventures which she knew and loved.

It was great.

And then the time to go came, and Osha kissed her sisters, and headed to Roko, the Great Tree at the center of the dreamtime, her childhood friend.

"OSHA!"

"Hi Roko!" she hugged what she could of the tree's endless circumference, which was a lot. After a while, she raised her head a bit and asked "Will you form a great body to help sort out something in the fourth world?"

"WITH LOVE"

"Love" said Osha in Roko's slow language, which was not very easy for anyone other than a great tree to speak.

And that was that.

Not finished with the dreamtime yet, Osha next headed to the Forest Primeval, which wasn't far, and sat in a certain clearing.

And then there was a flapping sound, and an unfeasibly large owl landed on the other side of the clearing

"Greetings cousin" Osha said respectfully.

"And well met, Osha; your (good) reputation precedes you" said the Owl with a friendly lilt

"How would you like me to call you, cousin?"

"Owl is fine... and how can I help one of such legendary ability as yourself?"

"Legendary abilities, huh?" Osha smiled "Anyway, here's what's up"
She told owl the situation, and some of her plan.

"That is concerning" said Owl, slowly

"Do you think any of your brother and sister owls of the animal realm would be willing to join my great body?"

"I can think of several that would be thrilled to, just off the top of my head; but I think I can do you one better" Owl said "I am willing to provide you with my patronage, which would mean that all owls in the fourth world could take part in your great body, as needed; and which would also mean that I would have a stake in the proceedings, as well."

"Deal!" Osha said quickly, willing to sort out the details later

"I will also speak to some others of my kind, certainly Bear, Turtle and Beehive, at the very least; we are in this together, and must act together"

"Totally agreed"

"Very well, if that is all..."

"Wait! There's one more thing" Osha paused and peered into a certain dark corner of the clearing "Have you met Anansi, Owl?"

"The spiderman? Can't say that I have… certainly heard of him, too, though" This last was said with an owl grimace

"Well then come out and say hello, Anansi, don't be rude"

There was silence, and then a stirring in the shadows.

"Hi" said Anansi.

FORTY-FIVE

The journey to the house between the falls was great, anticipation and bonhomie making for a memorable experience. Five of the horses had come with them, and they had plenty of time, so there was no rush; they were able to really focus on enjoying themselves, and each other.

Of the five horses that had stayed with the People, three were pregnant, incidentally; which was cool, too

Varoden took the horses willingness to come on the journey as a portent of approval for his choice to bring Thrango et al back with him. He was just about able to convince himself that there wouldn't be any problem, and that he didn't need to worry. Certainly, there was need to worry about getting lost, he thought. He remembered the way well enough; and the horses didn't seem to be in any doubt about the path.

Pretty soon, they were at the crossroads where Berondyas had been waiting, and they duly followed the road west before turning off into the forest. And then they were at the house between the falls, which amazed the ones who hadn't seen it before; and filled the returnees with a pleasant warmth in their stomachs.

Friday, Berondyas and Atra were nowhere to be seen, so Varoden showed everyone around; sorted out sleeping arrangements, and then set up lunch.... which stretched into dinner. They kept up a lively enough conversation that Varoden didn't have much time to dwell on his teachers' absence. He was probably just early, anyway.

And then they slept.

The next morning saw them all up at dawn to begin their practice, which they had kept up. Thrango had just used brute force to overpower Gudra in their empty hand sparring session (again), and Varoden was just about to gently remind him that the way of the empty hand was about more than physicality (again) when he heard a familiar voice behind him say "Well, it looks like our student has become a teacher"

"Friday!" Varoden turned quickly "And Berondyas, and Atra" he added with an effusive, if somewhat uncertain, smile.

"Sorry we're late" Atra said, smiling back "It was just about unavoidable"

"Good to see you, lad" Berondyas said "aren't you going to introduce us to your friends?" he nodded at the six other young people, who had hurriedly arrayed themselves in a line behind Varoden

"Oh, yes, of course"

So, introductions were made, with no hint of reproach from the three Ve. Varoden decided to approach the matter headfirst

"I hope you don't mind that we all came; they've been practicing a lot, and we're basically a team at this point..."

"To the contrary, I think I can speak for all of us..." Friday looked around, and received nods of assent from the other two "...I think I can speak for all of us when I say that I'm actually happy you brought them... The more the merrier, and all that..."

"...So you'll train them too?" Varoden asked, somewhat breathlessly.

"Yes. We will."

There was, following this exchange, a period of quiet exultation, as seven young people tried their best to be extremely happy without losing too much gravitas.

"But your path is different from theirs" Atra said quietly, once a little calm had descended "At least for the moment"

"You won't train me, anymore?" Varoden responded, equally quietly.

"Your training was finished last year, now is the time for decision. Are you ready?"

"What right now?"

"Yes."

Varoden looked around at the now quiet gathering, before responding with a simple "Yes" of his own

Atra looked at him, and said

We go together

To the tree that's not a tree

So that he may choose

And then Varoden and she were no longer in the clearing.

"This is the *place that's not a place* isn't it?"

"Yes, it is"

He looked around him, and his eyes attempted to make sense of what had to be the tallest tree in the universe, which stretched up beyond visibility, and into ridiculousness. His eyes failed.

"There is always a cost" said Atra "You will have to decide if the benefits are enough to justify it"

"The benefits of what?"

"You will, if you choose to be, and if you survive, become a numen. You have achieved enough to make the transition possible." She said this simply, and continued without seeming to take notice of Varoden's shock "Once you start the process, however, it is *strongly* recommended that you don't stop until you achieve some kind of end. Do you understand this?"

Varoden shook his head dumbly

"Say, I understand"

"I understand" he said eventually.

"The process requires no instruction, but there are some things you should know" Atra paused and looked at Varoden to make sure he was following. He was "To be a numen is a fundamentally different thing than to be a human. You will feel differently, see differently, think differently, hear differently and have different abilities. In short, almost everything will be different. You will most likely live for a very very long time, and those you love may not do so. You will need to learn many things."

And so on.

"I've read about the numen at great length" Varoden said, when she had finished "I will become one if can"

"Why" asked Atra.

"For wisdom and knowledge, first of all... and to be able to do something about the wrongs that I have seen"

Atra just looked at him, with a sad little smile. And then she kissed him, as she never had before; a long deep and open kiss, which aroused in him a feeling of open possibility, and of boundlessness.

When it was over, she simply looked at him, and it was as if her face was an ocean.

"Are you sure?" she asked simply.

Varoden looked at her for a while, marveling at the sheer wonder of her, before saying "Yes, I think I am"

The next thing he knew, he was sitting with his back to the tree, bonds keeping him securely fast against the massive trunk. He heard a voice whisper "remember not to stop before it's finished" in his ear; and then there was silence.

FORTY-SIX

Night in the dreamtime has a disquietingly beautiful aspect, particularly to the uninitiated. It can seem as if there will be no following sunrise, and subsequent day; that there will always be night.

It being the dreamtime, that's true, in a way.

Truth is a tricky thing, though; particularly in the dreamtime, which, remember, is made of truth.

Ranga and Appa's first night there wasn't, as such, the full chillout scene. They had discussed the offer made to them calmly and clearly; and quickly.

They were in.

As soon as their discussion was ended, which was very shortly after they came off the boat, they planted the necklace and the anklet in the ground a little ways beyond the beach they had landed on.

And then they waited to feel something.

Very quickly, they did.

Appa noticed the sensation(s) first, and gasped. Ranga had just turned to ask her what was up when he noticed it, too. It was, they'd both decide when comparing notes later, as if they'd grown an extra limb, an extra sense and extra other stuff that it was hard to put a name to. What's more, they seemed to have lost a bit of something that was also hard to identify.

Later they would agree that it must have been human mortality leaving them.

Which is not to say that numen can't die. They can, and do. It's just a different kind of dying and is a whole different and more complicated process.

There was, anyway, a lot for them to take in, in that first little while as numen, and they went diligently about the process of learning about their new selves.

It was a great deal of fun, and they couldn't really believe their luck, truth be told. The wonder of the new lives stretching out in multiple directions was overwhelming, yes; but definitely in a good way.

They realized, quite quickly, that they had beached on an island, and that it was somehow floating. What's more, they recognized their surroundings: This place seemed to be identical to the island where Ranga had found his boat. The cave was different, though. It had all manner of accoutrements and gadgets and things they had never seen before. Luckily, there was an instruction booklet, which made things a lot clearer.

    And so on.

Their numenity seemed to mean that they didn't need to eat, sleep or respond to bodily imperatives in the way that they had had to as humans. They could if they wanted to, it seemed, but it wasn't necessary.

The numen way of sleeping, in particular, was interesting to them. They couldn't find any easy way to lose consciousness totally, in the way that had come naturally before. Instead, there was a kind of resting of different parts of their beings which took place at different times. Never all at the same time, it seemed.

    It seemed.

Of course, the sex was something else. There weren't, and aren't any words...

Anyway, that first little while on the floating island in the dreamtime was a kind of heaven, for which they remembered to be thankful to their benefactor(s). They created (and recorded, using some of the mind-blowing gear in the cave) a song of appreciation for life, which they loved; and which they set free to go where it would.

    And go it did.

The time, nevertheless, came when they realized that it was time for them to sail again. The island was definitely home, now, but so was the boat. They had decided that their first voyage would be all the way around the (fourth) world, because why not?

Afterwards, they would spend time exploring the dreamtime, and maybe the other splaces they could feel nearby.

Having got the boat back on the dreamtime sea, they used the ability that had become part of them, and moved themselves and the boat into the fourth worlds, appearing there in waters a little east of Rasmu, their agreed up upon first stop.

Landing on its familiar beach, they smilingly alit, and walked toward the town, only to notice that it looked very different.

To cut a long story short, the (still friendly) Rasmusi spoke a different language now. They also looked and dressed differently. This was because five thousand (or so) years seemed to have passed since their last visit.

This was a surprise.

FORTY-SEVEN

"Well, I must say it's lovely to be in the presence of two such august personages as yourselves" Anansi said, with a winning smile, having come into the clearing proper.

"Charmed" said Owl with a stare and tone of voice that would have led most observers to wonder just how charmed he really was. Certainly, Anansi wondered this, and edged a little closer to Osha

"Well Mr. Anansi Spiderman, to what do we owe the honour of your eavesdropping?" Osha asked gently, with a significantly less threatening expression than Owl's.

Anansi smiled even more winningly, and said "Eavesdropping is such an ugly word…"

"Nevertheless…"

"If you know anything at all about me, you know of my curiosity, and my affinity for stories… where in all the dreamtime could I possibly find anything more interesting and more likely to yield a great tale than a meeting between the famous Osha and the legendary Owl: two of the *authorities* that numen such as myself so admire and look up to"

There was a pause, during which Owl's stare somehow intensified, leading Anansi to smilingly move yet closer to Osha.

"Answer the question" Owl said, eventually.

"But I did"

Because they were in the dreamtime, Osha and Owl knew Anansi could not lie directly. Not even **authorities** can lie in the dreamtime.

"Answer the question fully" Owl said.

"Well! That's a tall order... let's see..." Anansi put his hand to his lips, and then said "There is a never before, always will be, and nothing besides. Out of this there are emergences, of which our universe can be said to be one. Ours is an interesting emergence, not least because of the nature of its construction..."

"I'm not asking you for the history of this universe "Owl said, his stare definitely having moved into glare territory "I'm asking why you, in particular, were listening to us, in particular, right now, in particular at this place in the dreamtime, in particular"

Anansi affected a look of wounded innocence "But that's what I was doing! Everything is interconnected!"

"Okay Anansi, well done. Let's just get on with it, though" Osha said calmly "If you don't want to tell us what's up, I can just go find out for myself. This will, of course, mean examining all your affairs very closely, as well as interviewing whatever associates and/or employers of yours that I find..."

"Ah... Well, maybe it's not impossible to find a more direct way to answer your questions, now that I think about it"

"Yes, I thought there might be..."

"Weeeeellll... besides what I said before, someone or someones might, potentially, have offered me a contract to spy on you, Osha, and before you ask me who, I don't know, and I've tried to find out, believe me..."

"Hmmm" said Osha.

"Spying is not good..."

"Said the Owl!" Anansi quickly rejoined, before quickly and totally interposing Osha between Owl and himself

Osha spoke before this exchange could continue.

"What were the terms of your contract?"

"Ah yes, the terms..." Anansi paused before stating, with a hint of defiance "I am to become an *authority*, at the end of the deal."

There was silence, before Osha thoughtfully said "So, it must have been someone that had the ability to deliver on such a promise- I assume you made sure the contract was binding and complete" she looked at Anansi.

"I have always been adept at the way of binding, Osha" he said simply.

"And a dangerous way that is, too, I hope you've been careful..." she said this last with a rare hint of disapproval, Owl's glare had become incandescent, and threatened to go supernova.

"Anyway," Osha continued "that does narrow the field down somewhat; most *authorities* wouldn't be able to deliver on that promise, I don't think…"

"I certainly could not and would not" Owl said fiercely.

"Not my kind of thing either, even if I have some idea how you'd go about it" Osha said, thoughtfully.

"And what have you discovered in the course of discharging your duties, Master Anansi Spiderman?" Osha asked after a pause.

"There's some others involved in this thing, besides even the ones who hired me… In fact, I'm involved it now, myself, I realize."

"You are?"

"The great Roko asked me to run a few errands for him, quite a while ago, actually… I've come to realize that his errands were somehow associated with your current concerns…"

"Yes, Roko, okay, who else?

"Well, me, like I said… I started to independently observe the humans' dealings around that time, and I intervened on more than a couple of occasions…"

"Intervened how?"

"Well, this machine that you were talking about was born out of the binding way, I'm sure of it; as I've already said, I'm quite good at this way… so I've just been doing a little loosening here, a little tightening there, and even some untying altogether, actually…"

"To what end" Owl asked flatly.

Anansi straightened a bit, and came out of Osha's shadow somewhat "I wish to be a worthy *authority*" he said "I wish to be of service"

"You?" Owl asked incredulously.

"Me" Anansi said, before offhandedly adding "The Ve are somehow involved too"

"Are they?" Osha asked "Well, that's interesting…"

"What shall we do with him Osha?" Owl asked, presently

"What shall we do with you, brother 'Nansi?" Osha asked, with a little twinkle in her eye.

"Let me help you" Anansi, said quickly "I genuinely want to help you"

Which had to be true.

"Is that so? Why?"

"Because tricks are just tricks" Anansi said "There has to be more to life…"

Osha smiled warmly, at that "How will you help? And what about your spying contract"

"I can help in many ways, Osha; I am older than is commonly known, and have learned much in that time" he said this with a dignified and open countenance, which made him look quite different. "And my contract is in no way betrayed by helping you. I never even promised to deliver any truths I discovered; whichever **_authority authorized_** that contract is an absolute novice at the deep ways of binding..."

"Hmmmm" said Osha.

FORTY-EIGHT

It wasn't even really uncomfortable, at first.

The bonds weren't painfully tight, or anything, despite their obvious fastness. It was certainly intense, though. He was totally alone in a way he hadn't been before, and there was total silence around him. His meditation practice had been thorough enough, nevertheless; and he had no particular problem with the intense solitude as he perceived it in that first little while.

Things began to get bad when the ambient light that had been keeping him company disappeared, and he could see nothing at all. Even that was okay for a bit; until slowly but surely it began to be less and less so.

Varoden felt trapped (which to be fair, he was), and the feeling that he wouldn't leave this situation alive got stronger and stronger as the time did whatever it did.

One by one, his other external senses ceased to register any input, until at last; there was just his mind and then events took a turn for the (much) worse.

Varoden could sense something nearby, but could not directly perceive it. This carried on, and he became more and more agitated, which didn't make anything better, of course. A deep terror of the unknown grew and grew within him, until he could take no more; and lost consciousness.

Waking up brought with it the return of light and sensation.

It was not an improvement.

He could now see what had been only indirectly perceived last night... and its bright horror nearly knocked him out again. Instead, he closed his eyes, and said to himself "it's just an illusion" over and over, before gathering himself and looking once more.

It was still there, of course.

And this time he passed out.

When he regained consciousness this time, it was dark again, but not completely so; and he could sense the horrifying apparition just outside his range of vision. Somehow, his bonds had got tighter, as well, and his body was one big undifferentiated miasma of pain.

He was slowly moving, too, up the tree.

By now, Varoden's fear had spread to all parts of his being, and he shouted and wriggled and cried until exhaustion left him hanging limply.

"Why are you doing this to me?" He gasped at the figure he could sense but not see.

There was no response

"Am I being punished? Did I do something wrong?"

Still no answer, and he began to gently cry.

When he opened his eyes again, it was much brighter, and he could feel that he was alone.

No, not alone, exactly, he realized. The nightmare figure was somewhere close by, his senses told him; but it was far enough that he didn't feel threatened by it, for the moment.

Everything else was worse, though.

His pain, which now characterized his existence, had been joined by hunger and thirst; as well as a maddening itch that was somehow worse than anything else, even the bizarre sensation of both freezing and burning at the same time which he had recently discovered.

None of this was made any better by the fact that he could see how high up the tree he had got, as a result of his incessant upward motion. The landscape was barely visible beneath him, and it seemed to mock him with its boundless expanse.

And then, at some point, the voices started.

These voices were always just below the level of audibility, and had no special malignance to them... but they kept going, and going and going; until Varoden passed out again, in protest.

Waking into darkness and silence was a profound relief, and his physical complaints seemed to have lost some of their edge. In fact, he could think coherent thoughts again; and he even smiled a little, thinking the worst had passed.

Ha!

There were experiences of which it is unwise to speak, and stories which cannot safely be disseminated in this manner.

Suffice it to say, the worst had not passed.

And so, it was a traumatized Varoden who woke up to what appeared to be a vast hall, at the centre of which were eight great chairs. Seated on these chairs were very brightly shining people, regarding him with a mix of expressions.

There was a white light suffusing everything, and it seemed to be expanding and intensifying, until Varoden's whole universe was whiteness.

No one said anything.

Then, after an indeterminate length of time, one of the bright people, who appeared to Varoden as a woman, pointed at him, with what he took to be a benevolent expression on her face.

He felt his first joy in what felt like lifetimes.

The next thing he knew, he was gone from there, and back on the tree. This time, though, he wasn't moving. In fact, he seemed to have reached the top. He could see, and perceive and sense and feel in ways that had not been possible in his old pre-tree life. It was overwhelming, particularly given the experiences which had marked his ascent.

The feeling that there was more than one way down arose in Varoden, and he was immediately tempted to take the quickest route back down.

He didn't.

The next idea which struck him was not to go back at all. He could sense there a myriad of worlds and splaces available to him now.

"Remember not to stop before it's finished" he said to himself. He would return the way he had come, was Varoden's decision, after some deliberation. He'd just go a little faster this time, and maybe loosen the bonds that secured him; as he now could.

The descent was still difficult, but nothing like what he had experienced in the other direction, and he was able to mostly ignore the abuse and indignities which seemed to be visited upon him again. He could still sense the figure that had so haunted him in his vicinity, but he could also sense that if he did not bother it, it would not bother him. So he didn't bother it.

When Varoden again touched the ground of the *place that's not a place,* His bodily complaints all disappeared immediately, though he had long since stopped really noticing them. His bonds fell away, and he rose gracefully.

"Welcome" said Atra, from somewhere behind him.

FORTY-NINE

"Five thousand years!" Ranga shouted

"Yes."

"What... the... fuck?" Appa asked, with a quite admirable calm

"One must be careful in the dreamtime, there is always the possibility of temporal incongruence"

"Five thousand years?" Ranga asked more quietly, having borrowed some of Appa's calm

"Yes."

"So you're saying that every time we're in the dreamtime for a while we run the risk of losing millennia here, just like that?" Appa looked at the tree above Rasmu with genuine curiosity.

"Now that you know about the effect, it can be guarded against"

"So why weren't we warned"

"Experience is the best teacher"

"Could we go back if we wanted to?"

"Probably not. Only the older would even think of trying, and even they don't do that sort of thing very often"

"Five *thousand* years" Ranga added.

The tree with which they spoke was a different one from the one that had been there on their earlier visits, but it was also exactly the same.

Once they had realized how far into what used to be the future they were, they had, with no concern for ceremony, rushed up to the cliffside, to find out what was going on.

"Our people are all dead now, and our village a memory, I take it" Appa asked.

"Yes. Though people still live in that place"

...*Silence*...

"Why didn't you tell us?"

"You were needed here, and it was better for you this way"

"Needed for what!"

"Balance"

As numen, they were able to perceive the tree more completely than they had before; and they also instinctually understood its way of being in a manner that was new to them.

This was as far as it made sense to go with it right now, they decided together with a glance. It was trust that had brought them this far, so they would maintain that way; as incomprehensible as it might be to them.

They would still keep their eyes open from now on, though.

Their previous plan was not really affected by the new time frame that they found themselves in, except for erasing any impulse to return home. They would sail around the world, and learn what they could.

They left Rasmu not long after speaking to the tree, heading east first, towards the great river where they had left the "young ones". Arriving there, they saw that a series of bustling communities had sprung up along the shoreline, and that they had adopted the circular boat design that had saved the kids from the flood. These charming round boats seemed to be used primarily for fishing, and there were a lot of them near the shore.

Their appearance caused a hubbub.

People thought they were gods.

And the "ten young ones" were now legendary fore-parents of the people of this land, so asking about them (numenity had given Ranga and Appa new abilities with language, apparently) didn't help to disabuse them of their divine ideas.

This was somewhat inconvenient, and they resolved to try to keep a lower profile when they could.

Anyway, they were told of huge cities in the north, both in the valley that the great river carved for itself, and off to the northwest as well. So, they sailed up the river, and were amazed by what they saw.

Another story for another time.

The "ten young ones" had, suffice it to say, done well for themselves, apparently.

Once they had returned to the sea, they decided to go and check on "Nana's children" to the northwest, having been so impressed by what their other passengers had bequeathed to this new age. Appa, at one point, thought of Lual's terrible jokes, and was sad for a moment. Everyone she had known was gone, except for Ranga. She went and hugged him tightly, and was rewarded with a somewhat quizzical, but still wide, smile.

"It's just us left"

"We're all we need" he said, and she hugged him again

They made good time to their destination, without resorting to many tricks, and had a similar experience; except Nana's children had left word to expect them, so they were treated to an even more lavish welcome than their last.

And Nana's children had given birth, in turn, to a whole new world.

Again, though, that's a story for a different time.

Their route around the world, they had decided, would be to the east, so they followed the land which lay to the southeast, finding it to be a gigantic peninsula. In fact, it was basically its own continent. They interacted with many different peoples, noticing that distance, language and appearance all seemed to be related variables among human populations.

They discussed this, at length

They taught the way of the sea, and other applicable ways, to any who wished to learn; and were taught much, in return. Often, these exchanges made them feel they were gaining more than their interlocutors, but this only encouraged them to be as open as they could be, which usually meant that they gained more than their interlocutors etc.

So it was cool.

I should add that the music, in particular, was wild in that part of the world, and they resolved to come back and study it when they were finished their journey. Even for numen, it would take a long time to master the ten million subtle variations which these people used to create vast tapestries of sound, the like of which, Ranga and Appa had never heard.

At last, though, they came to the southern end of this vast land, and discovered a large and beautiful island, which they quickly recognized as a place of power. The island was populated by different peoples, who had arrived at different times, but they all seemed to live in something resembling harmony, despite quite different habits and ideas, in some cases.

It was quite inspiring to Ranga and Appa; and during their time there they helped with the foundation of a school of wisdom, which was to become famous throughout the world, though it was often thought to be a legend in later times.

They kept themselves busy, in other words, it wasn't just vacation.

And then it was time to go, and they left.

FIFTY

It is a far greater shift for a numen to become an *authority* than it is for a human to become a numen. That's just how it works.

It's also true that there are regular paths through the vast domain of existence in this part of the all. One of these paths goes as follows: The life of sensation leads to the life of achievement, which leads to the life of duty, which leads, lastly, to the life of contemplation.

Usually, beings must understand the limits and boundaries of these lives before moving on.

>Not always, though.

Anyway, anyone or anything which was able to grasp (without grasping) the life of contemplation had almost always done enough to make the shift to *authority*. Not everyone who could did make this transition, of course; Sun Wu and the old man, for example, had chosen to remain as numen for the time being. There were other options, too.

I think it's fair to say that Anansi the Spiderman was not a master of contemplation. Nor had he been of wholly benevolent disposition. In fact, by most measures, he was not close to having earned enough merit to be thinking about becoming an *authority*. This was readily obvious to Osha and Owl, and it explained why they were surprised that someone had offered to make him one.

The amount of energy, and the precision of use, required to fulfil this promise was immense. They would have expected any being capable of doing anything like that to be more careful about the way it used binding magic, of which the contract (and all contracts) was an example- more careful about their choice of agent, too.

It didn't appear to be the way the older usually worked, and so seemed likely, to Osha and Owl, that they were either dealing with a new player that they were unfamiliar with, or that they were seriously mistaken in some of their understandings.

Neither was a comforting thought, particularly.

But to Osha, standing in that clearing in the dreamtime, something felt right about working with Anansi in this situation. She wasn't sure how, and she wasn't sure about the provenance of her intuition, and whether it should be trusted. It could not be ignored, though.

"What do you say Owl, should we trust him?"

"Definitely not" Owl said quickly and firmly, before adding "That doesn't mean he can't be worked with"

"If you're going to work with us, Anansi Spiderman, you must undertake to use as little binding magic as possible. In fact, even if you're *not* going to work with us, you shouldn't use it right now, for your own safety as much as anything else..."

"Oh yes, I promise on my true name, freely given, not to use binding magic again until you tell me it's safe..." Anansi spoke quickly, and with seeming sincerity.

"Your subconscious plays tricks, even when you can't lie" Osha said with a little smile "Oaths and promises are binding magic, too"

Owl smiled grimly, and said "In any event, what was just said became the truth, this being the dreamtime."

"But then it's true and not true at the same time" Anansi said slowly into the ensuing silence "As if I said 'this sentence is a lie'"

"Yes" Osha said "And that is where we will be, for now. I will ask you to perform a task for us, and I forgive you in advance if you betray us..."

"I won't, Osha"

"You are free to do what you will, Anansi. I ask you to watch over the islands currently called Jamaica and Cuba. Please try to keep some kind of balance, in these places; I have the sense they may be useful in our endeavour"

"Thank you, I will not disappoint you"

"I don't think you will. Shall we agree to meet again here in ten turns?"

"Works for me" Owl said.

"I'll be here!" said Anansi, and with that he bowed to Osha and Owl, and then disappeared.

"This should be interesting" Owl said, with a small smile

"He is capable, when focused"

"... when focused..."

Osha smiled, and then said "He also said that Roko had asked him to perform some related tasks a long time ago, right?"

"Yes, he did say that"

Well that's encouraging, if Roko's been on this for a while, then we're unlikely to be barking up the wrong tree... See what I did there?"

"I'm afraid I do, Osha" Owl said with a pained smile. "I should have company at our next meeting, in any event. I'm confident at least one of the others will want to act with us.

"Peace and love"

"And to you, Osha"

Osha sat by herself in the clearing after Owl had left. She thought about Anansi, and Owl; and then about the reality eating machine, along with the various rites and sacrifices which had brought it into being, and which continued to enact it. She thought about binding magic, and how it had become the most common magic in the fourth world, until it was no longer considered magic at all. Then she thought about its limits. She thought about the First Owner, who would soon know her as well as anyone else ever had, just like Sun Wu and the owlswould.

And then she thought about what her great body, in particular, would do.

"We will make music, and art, and we will dance" she said slowly "And we will learn, and be free"

She stood, exultant in her new understanding. Smiling radiantly, she headed to the library of time.

FIFTY-ONE

Varoden perceived Atra more clearly than had been possible before; and yet there seemed to be an even greater mystery to her.

They stood looking at each other.

"I'm glad you made it back" she said eventually.

"I wasn't sure I would. That was hard. Harder than I imagined possible" Varoden said this flatly, with little affect.

"You understand that everyone's initiation is different? That in a real way you designed your own trial?"

"Yes, I now have this knowledge"

They looked at each other some more

"One of your eyes has changed colour" said Atra

"Really? Which one?"

"Your right eye is now blue"

"Well, it still works, so that's alright"

...*Another pause*...

"I can *feel* the law now" Varoden said at last

"You have an aptitude for it, being a numen will have intensifiedthis"

"So that's it, I'm a full numen now, with all rights and privileges?"

"Yes" Atra said calmly.

"So what now?"

"Well, we can return to our friends, for one thing"

"Yes, that's a good idea... But Atra..."

"Yes?"

"You feel... different... than before"

"There is very little that is exactly as it seems" she said with a small, sad seeming smile

Moving between splaces by his own power for the first time gave Varoden a small thrill, and it really drove home his new reality.

He was a numen!

He exulted in the power and possibility that had just become part of his very nature, and he, there and then, resolved to be worthy of his newfound stature. The law would be his lodestone, and he would serve it and master it, all at once.

Varoden and Atra's return to the house between the falls was apparently unexpected, and there were joyous greetings exchanged. Thrango hugged his brother tightly, and Varoden hugged back, feeling no weakening of the connection that they had shared since birth.

Thrango, though, pulled back after a while, and said "Something's very different, you were gone a while, but it wasn't *that* long... and what happened to your *eye*"

"He's a numen, now" Berondyas said, shortly, having just come outside.

"What!!???"

And so Varoden was obliged to demonstrate some of his new (and untested) abilities. Friday volunteered for a bit of gripping hand sparring, and so they faced off against each other again, and for the first time."

It went on for a while.

Friday's attacking prowess was now matched my Varoden's defensive and counterattacking brilliance, and she no longer had the splatial movement advantage. So there was an impasse, and they cheerfully declared a draw. Varoden, though, knew deep down that it was possible to defeat her, and he could see how.

The law was the thing.

"That was amazing"

"I'm glad you guys are on our side"

"I didn't even see half of what was happening"

Thrango, Lela, Sarag, Heim Gudra and Aren crowded round Varoden, congratulating him. Friday had gone off for a swim, and Berondyasand Atrastood off by themselves, talking quietly.

Eventually Varoden was able to get a word in, and he asked "How's training going?" directing the question to all present.

"Great" Thrangosaid "Sorry, Varo, but these guys are much better teachers than you were, my gripping hand way has got*much*stronger"

"Your reading and writing, on the other hand..." Berondyas said

"Bah, Varo can deal with that stuff; we're a team, right?"

They had, it turned out, all shown different interests and aptitudes, with only Lela having displayed strength in all the various disciplines. It was also only Lela who expressed any interest in becoming a numen, when that topic came up. The rest found humanity perfectly acceptable, and Varoden's highly edited synopsis of his initiation wasn't encouraging to them, in the least.

At first Varoden found this surprising, but he grew to accept and understand their point of view

"I'm really happy for you Varo" Thrango had said "but I *like* our people's way. To die and become an even deeper part of who we are seems like the right way for me."

And so on.

FIFTY-TWO

Appa and Ranga were headed due east, instead of tracing the continental coastline back up to the north. The islanders had told them that there were fabled and mystical lands in the direction they were headed in, and that the people there were possessed of great wisdom and knowledge. They would visit the northern coast on their next trip, they had decided, and instead followed their piqued curiosity towards the rising sun.

Their voyage was eventful, with a big storm providing a good test of their maritime ability.

They passed.

In fact, they passed the examination without having to rely over much on their recently acquired extra-human abilities. In this, they shared a quiet pride; their connection to the sea transcended the specific circumstances of their lifestyles.

Appa and Ranga had ceased to separate themselves from the oceans they traversed. They felt like part of a big body, which might go hither or thither, but was, in general, working together in a manner that was not different from love.

They had never been so far from land as this journey took them, and they found the open ocean to have a peaceful quality unmatched in their experience, even in the middle of the storm.

It was wonderful, they would play music together with the waves and the wind, and whatever creatures felt like joining in. They had become proficient at many instruments, but Appa still gravitated towards her thumb piano, as did Ranga toward his water drum. Their singing, on the other hand, had incorporated elements of the many and various lands they had so far visited; and it was nothing like the simpler melodies and harmonies of their old home.

It was during one such musical interlude that they saw the island which their experience had told them was coming up. It was obviously quite large, and very hospitable looking, the many wide beaches providing them with their choice of landing spots.

The people of this island looked quite different from Appa and Ranga's previous norm, and they had quite a different, and quite sophisticated kind of lifestyle, as well. These people were, it turned out, the westernmost representatives of the Travellers, which seemed to be the culture whose fame had spread so far to the west. These particular folk humbly designated themselves to be the poor relations of a great family, but the welcome that Appa and Ranga received belied their words. They were really lovely, and interesting, as well.

They were generally acquainted with the *place that's not a place* and the dreamtime, but didn't seem to make a big deal about them, perceiving them to be unessential to a full human experience. There was, however, talk of the lands further to the east and southeast, where beings went between the splaces regularly, gathering knowledge and wisdom far beyond that of this western outpost.

The music they played was very percussive, and used tonalities and harmonies that Ranga and Appa had never experienced before, and even found a bit jarring before they were accustomed to it. It was intensely trancelike, though, and combined with certain plants gathered in the forest, provided a window to the neighboring splaces, or even a path, if one was so inclined.

They spoke of great festivals, in which Travellers from all around would gather to exchange knowledge, experiences and gifts, while also performing the sacred rites which kept the world in balance. There was lots of sex too, apparently.

This sounded like fun, but unfortunately the last one had just recently occurred, and there was none scheduled for a while to come.

Ranga and Appa were, though they were obviously the object of some curiosity, given room to explain as much or as little about themselves as they chose. They told the truth, only omitting the specifics of their becoming numenand skipping five thousand years forward in time. Their boat was also very interesting to the fisher folk among their hosts, whose craft were of a simpler design.

Finally, having been given a reasonable (and as it turned out, quite factual) account of the Travellers' geography; Ranga and Appa continued their voyage, sailing west until they reached the long peninsula they had been told about, where there was a great market, further to the south.

At this market, they were given a glimpse of the future turned present. It was situated on the southern tip of the peninsula, where another island lay just across a narrow strait. There were people and items from very far away, and there was a constant tumult, at all hours of the day. It was here that Ranga and Appa first saw currency, symbolic items of exchange with no particular intrinsic value.

This currency, which was the shell of a small sea animal, was only used in the market itself, and was subject to regulation. The people who ran the market, who were numen by the way, only allowed a certain amount of currency to be in the market at any time. Anyone attempting to carry currency from outside without authorization was permanently banned, which seemed to be an effective injunction.

Ranga and Appa had encountered no other numen since their shift (not counting the tree), and were gratified to realize that they could recognize their new kind immediately. The others didn't notice them, at first, so our voyagers were able to observe them for a while- there were three of them, and they seemed decent enough.

Their eventual meeting was very cordial and friendly, and they all retired to the three numen's house, which was a very fancy affair in one of the mountain forests to the north. In fact, the interior reminded

Ranga and Appa a little bit of their island cave in the dreamtime, just with wood instead of rock.

Over drinks and conversation, it turned out that these other beings were part of some group of numen known as the Ve, and they were very interested indeed to hear Ranga and Appa's story, sharing knowing looks when the trees were mentioned, and commiserating about the five thousand years that had been so carelessly misplaced.

FIFTY-THREE

Since we create the universe, we created the library of time, too.

    Good job us!

Osha walked along the main corridor of the library, looking for a particular door, through which she had never gone before. This door purportedly led to the office of the Librarian, a semi-mythical figure who was supposed to be one of the wisest and most knowledgeable of all beings, anywhere.

She found what she was looking for fairly quickly, helped greatly by a big sign which said **LIBRARIAN'S OFFICE**. Osha was fairly confident that that sign hadn't been there before, but she accepted the assistance with gratitude.

The Librarian, it was said, had been born a human in the fourth worlds, when humans were still quite new. Somehow, they had managed to attain a kind of status outside the normal categories of hell-being, hungry ghost, animal, human, numen and *authority*, and had been here ever since, curating the virtually infinite knowledge this splace held; and apparently helping visitors, as well, on occasion.

Osha knocked on the indicated door, and heard a pleasant voice say

    "Come in Osha".

Opening the door, Osha saw a very pleasant and friendly looking person, who appeared to be a human woman of middle years, walking towards her, having apparently just got up from a big and quite cluttered desk. The room itself incorporated a far greater number of dimensions than was usual in and round these parts: Osha counted six spatial ones and six time ones, and she could sense that there were more outside of her easy perception. The overall effect was quite charming, suggesting a cozy mountain cabin juxtaposed with a beach cabana and the office of the nicest teacher you've ever had.

"What a lovely office" Osha said, smiling

"What a lovely person" The Librarian said, smiling back "It's great to finally meet you, I've been following your progress with interest"

"I'm flattered" Osha said, and she was.

"Don't be, we're all in this together"

"I totally agree"

"So you want to know about this machine that's causing havoc in the fourth worlds, and what to do about it, I'd guess" The Librarian said, before adding "Oh, please make yourself comfortable, and would you like any refreshment? I get few visitors here, these days, and sometimes I forget my manners"

"Thank you, Librarian, I'd love a cup of coffee, actually" she said this while sitting down on a comfortable looking bean bag "And yes, your guess is correct."

"Coming right up" The librarian said, turning and beginning the coffee making process, while saying "I'm very glad you came, actually. There is much to discuss"

Osha said nothing, looking around the room, and attempting to open herself to more of its actuality.

"You're something beyond us *authorities*, aren't you?" Osha asked.

"Beyond? I wouldn't put it like that, personally; that could lead to misunderstanding. It's truer to say that I'm a person of no rank"

"A bodhisattva?"

"I could be called one of those, I suppose. It's still a bit misleading, but perhaps less so

"Hmmm" said Osha.

The coffee, when delivered, was very strong, but possessed, nevertheless, of an intriguing and deliciously subtle mix of flavours. The Librarian sat on another beanbag across from Osha, and they sipped in peaceful silence for a while.

"The machine could harm the fourth worlds beyond repair, if left to its own devices; we could have to start over from scratch" The Librarian eventually said

"Start over?"

"From scratch"

"So is my idea of forming great bodies the right response, you think?"

"I'd say it's definitely part of it, others will have to play their part as well... me included"

"You're planning to directly involve yourself?" Osha was surprised

"Directly or indirectly, I'm already involved."

"Well, that's good to hear" Osha smiled "I trust you implicitly, for some reason"

"I trust you, as well, Osha, and counted you as a friend even before we met"

"That's even better to hear... Do you have any specific tips for our action and interaction in and with the fourth worlds?"

"There is little that it makes sense for me to say to you, other than be yourself, be free, and pay attention. If you do this, everything else will fall into place"

Osha thought about this, before saying "To be myself, I must know myself, right?"

"Knowledge of self can't hurt"

"And my self is not separate from anything, is it?"

"The awakened person is one with cause and effect"

Osha thought about that, too, before saying "I'm going to spend the next little while getting to know myself better, I think"

"Me too" said the Librarian pleasantly, sipping her coffee.

FIFTY-FOUR

While the others continued their training, Varoden decided to go exploring.

"I think I've got all I'm going to get out of this book, I'd like to return it to the library of time, what's the easiest way to get there" Varoden asked Berondyas.

"The easiest way would be for one of us to take you... But I get the sense that you want to go on your own... I guess next best would be to go the dreamtime, and then use travelling words"

"I can just make them up, right?"

"Yes, that should be fine. But listen, it's very easy to get lost in the library of time, especially your first time there. And travelling is not always as straightforward there as in other places, so make sure you leave some kind of trail as you move... and watch out for the elevators"

"Elevators?"

"You'll see... Also, you won't be able to read a lot of the stuff there, but there's many ways to find what you're looking for, or even better, what you're not looking for"

Varoden smiled and said "Thanks, I appreciate the advice.
Which was how he found himself in the dreamtime, beside a mirror lake atop a mountain. Opting for effectiveness over prettiness, he said

> *First time visitor*
> *Respectfully seeks passage*
> *To the library*

And then he was in the great main hall.
He hadn't realized how excited he was until he looked around and saw all the information, in all its various forms, just waiting to meet him. A huge smile lit up his face, and he simply walked over to the closest shelf and picked a book at random.

> *It said: The moments of our life are not expendable, And the [possible] circumstances of death are beyond imagination. If you do not achieve an undaunted confident security now, What point is there in your being alive, O living creature?*

> *"Righteeo" Varoden said, putting the book back quickly.*

He wandered around in a kind of blissful fugue, picking up and replacing more books than he could keep track of. This section of the library seemed to be organized loosely around a theme that didn't interest him overmuch, as much as his he enjoyed his dabbling. He went, as such, further down the hall, stopping when the book titles were generally intelligible to him again.

This section seemed to be concerned with the beings of the fourth worlds and nearby splaces, which was a topic far more suited to his tastes. Looking through the titles, his attention was draw to one that was called, simply "The Ve". He took it, and put it in one of the many pockets of his cloak.

Berondyas had told him that there was no limit to the number of books that one could take at any one time, but that it was a good idea to return whatever one took. Remembering this, Varoden looked around, and found the "Returns" sign, that he had been told about. Walking over, he put his old book on the flat shiny surface underneath the sign, and was only moderately surprised when the book immediately disappeared.

Returning to his favoured section, he chose a general overview of the different types of existence most commonly associated with the fourth worlds, two books about numen, and one about humans.

This was almost enough for him, but he was looking for one more thing. He went across to one of the reference devices he had been told about, and spoke into it, as he had been advised to.

"Books about the law" Varoden said, somewhat sheepishly.

Immediately, there was a glow along the wall not far away from where he stood. Walking over to it, he found a whole shelf devoted to his desired topic. He quickly dismissed the higher shelves, which contained more basic texts, and the middle shelves, which had books that spoke of ideas and principles he was already familiar with.

On the lowest shelves, however, there was a lot more that he found interesting. Eventually, having perused and thumbed through multiple volumes, he settled on one called "The Law, Binding Magic and Power".

Varoden felt like he had enough books for right then, but he wasn't quite ready to leave the library yet. He opened a nearby door, and peered into darkness. Mindful of the warnings he had received, he trailed a thread of consciousness behind him, and entered the unlit space.

He could see nothing.

Shrugging, he closed the door behind him, at which point the "room" went from no light to a whole bunch at the speed of... well, anyway, it was fast. I say "room", but it was more like a long corridor than anything else. Interestingly, the walls were made of a translucent and transparent material, and, somehow, so was the door now.

There was someone outside the door.It was himself.

Quickly, Varoden reopened the door and looked around. There was no-one.

Re-entering the room, and reclosing the door, he could again see himself behind it. It wasn't a mirror effect, though. His double was unmoving, standing in a relaxed pose facing back the way he, or they, had come in.

This was a tad off-putting.

Recovery was swift, nevertheless, and Varoden decided there was nothing for it but to have a look around. So he did.

It is a testament to his intelligence and flexibility of mind that Varoden was able to figure what the hell was happening fairly quickly. This corridor was literally another dimension of time, perpendicular to the one he was accustomed to dealing with. Time did not move "forward" or "backward" while he was in here.

"It's sideways time" he said to himself.

He was able to perceive a great deal from this new perspective, and, fascinated, he decided to try and travel back to the dreamtime directly from here.

He could.

He could travel directly back to the sideways time corridor, too.

He had, he realized, just unlocked the ability to freeze time and look at things from multiple perspectives before acting.

"Damn" said Varoden to himself.

FIFTY-FIVE

The numen from the market were called Fausto, Eremes and Egoamaka; and they invited Ranga and Appa to stay with them for a few days, which invitation was gladly accepted. The house in the mountains was extremely comfortable and the views were stunning: Ranga and Appa spent much of their time there just appreciating nature in its glory.

The three Ve were quite young, for numen, having all been born within the past few centuries in various parts of the *place that's not a place.*

"So how'd you end up here?" Appa had asked

"We're taking part in the Great Race" Eremessaid

"What great race?"

"*THE* Great Race... you've never heard of it?"

"Never"

"Well, it's something we Ve take very seriously- winning it would make our names forever"

"How does one win?"

"By coming first"

"What does that mean?"

"It's hard to explain... sometimes it means literally returning the fastest, but that's not usually the case at all..."

"Almost never" Egoamaka had put in.

"Is there a course?"

"Not exactly... It's *really* hard to explain"

"So how could running this market make you win?"

"Sometimes winning is about the best idea... or about the most elegant execution of an old idea..."

"Who decides what's best?" Ranga asked

"There's a sort of vote among the participants, but it's a little more complicated than that makes it seem"

"Ah... I see."

For Ranga and Appa, learning about the Ve was quite illustrative of a broader point: there was a lot they didn't know.

This excited both of them.

They found the Ve's loose, amorphous, and seemingly chaotic confederacy to be an intriguing concept, although they had no urge whatsoever in joining it, as they tactfully made clear to their three new friends. They had the sea, and they had each other, which seemed to be them far enough past enough to approach paradise.

Eventually, it was time to move on, and after thanking the three Ve for their hospitality, they returned to their boat, happy to have made their first numen friends. Appa and Ranga set a leisurely coast to the east, where they had been told the central, and largest isle of the Traveller culture lay.

Apparently, word had preceded them, because their arrival saw an official and quite formal welcome at sea, followed by a stately procession to the well-appointed cave which would be their home during their stay here. Everyone was friendly enough, and they found the ordered and harmonious systems of governance in place quite impressive, but they shared a sense of slight boredom there- the official visits and guided tours weren't particularly their sort of thing.

There was quite a large and well run academy of higher learning there, and they were told of others on the island, so that was cool, but it was with a sense of relief that said thanks and farewell, heading northeast to the so-called "Happy" islands, which their hosts had spoken of with barely concealed disdain. Ranga and Appa took this as a recommendation.

They had been staying on a really big island, they discovered, while sailing along the coast. In fact, they would later discover that it was one of the biggest in the fourth worlds, just like the "Island That's Not an Island" to the west that they would later visit.

Anyway, the Happy islands were much more their speed, a sort of cheerful and indolent insouciance being the modus operandi there. There was a more or less constant party happening in multiple locations, so that Ranga and Appa began to wonder if the people there did anything else. They did, but nature's abundance, and the carefully curated culture of joy which the residents enacted meant that play was the thing.

It was great, if a bit tiring.

The next stop was far to the north, where the "Isle of the Magicians" lay, at the very edge of the travellers sphere of influence. This provided a total contrast to their last experience. The Magicians' Isle was sparsely populated, and its inhabitants tended to be older, quieter and more serious sorts of people than the determined hedonists to the south. It was, actually, misnamed: while there were many magicians of various types in residence, there were more ascetics, wisdom speakers and sages, by quite a margin.

These various students of the sublime were actively engaged in a great project, which underlay the Traveller culture in general. They sought to maintainbalance between the various beings, places, things and whatever else of the neighbouringsplaces, seeing themselves as custodians, of a sort.

It was their contention that the fourth worlds were a "middle realm", and that its goings on had a consequently heavier impact on the realms further from the centre.

They were not, in fact, wrong.

Ranga and Appa spent almost a year on the Isle of the Magicians, learning, teaching and sharing ideas. They left with a greater appreciation of the responsibility and freedom which their situation had afforded them, and knowing that they would certainly return.

Having stayed so long there, they decided to skip their previously intended visit to the "Timeless" islands which lay at the southern end of the travellers realm. They had heard much about them, and would visit them next time, but they wanted to up their pace, somewhat. The "Island That's Not an Island" would be their last quick stop within these lands, before they headed south to the great continent of the Dreamers.

It was super interesting, this island- whole parts of it seemed to exist in both the fourth worlds and the *"place that's not a place"* at the same time. There were many manymany different peoples and languages and ideas and cultures. They kept to their plan, though, and only stayed for a couple of days.

There was a whole world out there.

FIFTY-SIX

Osha had been born an *authority*, just as her sisters had. As such, the circumstances of her parentage had not been particularly relevant to her existence. She had woken up one day, and just found herself there, in the home where she and her sisters had always lived.

That had been good enough.

The beginning of Osha's self-examination told her that it still was.

The Librarian had directed her to a quiet and seldom used part of the library that she said was well suited to the introspective practices; and she was right, as she often was. It was another multi-dimensional room, but this time the effect was more felt than seen. There was a soft glow that slowly changed colour, illuminating the unbounded expanse which also ended in a large picture window, through which only the occasional shadow could be seen. There were chairs and couches and mats and cushions in abundance, but the room was uncrowded.

It felt to Osha like a kind of home arena, filled with a crowd of friends and supporters that would love you no matter what happened.

The room was also on one of the corridors at right angles to the main one, so that no time would elapse in the usual frame of reference.

Osha just sat for a while, feeling her body and her mind settle into relaxation. The thought arose, while she was there, that she hadn't felt this for a long time, and that she had missed it very much. This surprised her a little, and she could feel the wheels of her consciousness getting ready to drive her on a search mission, but she wasn't ready to do that yet- relaxation was too perfect right then.

That went on for a while.

At some point Osha began to feel her self being concentrated into one point. She immediately knew that trying to locate that point was... well pointless, but she did it anyway- accustomed to that kind of knowledge as she was. She found it, but profoundly lost it, as well.

Once she realized that, she returned to just sitting, without waiting or without anything. When the pointedness returned, as it did; she just continued to do nothing, not even observe.

This went on for a while

And the point became a multitude, all the various parts of her began to make themselves known, and she felt like she was a universe by herself. And that this universe was filled with other universes, which were, in turn, filled with other universes, and so on.

There multitude greeted each other, up and down, left and right and many other directions besides, and a feeling of deep connectedness arose in Osha, something unlike anything that had happened in all her time. She was tempted to sing, dance, celebrate, anything; but she remained still; allowing whatever would happen to happen as it would.

It did.

The multitude's celebration and joy grew louder and louder, until all spoke with one voice- and Osha disappeared.

When she returned to her more regular frame of reference, she continued just to sit, although there was now relative quiet within her, the pointedness remained, as did the multitude and the relaxation, but there was some kind of new consensus.

After a time, she got up, and returned to the Librarian's Office.

She knocked.

"Yes, come in"

Osha entered, and saw the Librarian seated cross legged in a "corner". "Am I disturbing you? I can go…"

"Stay"

The Librarian's voice rang in Osha's head as if it had been generated inside her.

After a moment's thought, Osha framed her question. "Is every being a great body?" she asked simply

"It depends on how you look at it" The Librarian said "But most answers I can think of are closer to yes than no"

"And when a being truly speaks with one voice, what happens?"

The Librarian's expression did not change at all, but her voice laughed on its own "I'm guessing you visited one of the formless realms." She paused "You will have to trust your own experience, and inhabit your own way, brilliant Osha."

"Thank you" Osha said, meaning it.

Osha left the library of time and returned to the fourth worlds, specifically to the far south of the American continents. She was going to work her way north, she had decided.

She took the first people she met as exemplars of human adaptability. It was *extremely* cold, and yet many of them went about virtually naked. Osha liked them, immediately, in other words. During her stay there, she learned some of their stories and songs, and left some of her own, as well. She also spoke frankly with those who were interested about the situation as she saw it, and what could possibly be done, asking only that they not speak of it or her to any representatives of the machine that they might encounter. They kept the faith.

Osha continued north, and had almost made it to the end of the great forest that dominated the top part of the southern continent when she realized it was nearly time for her meeting with Owl and Anansi. She had intended to invite Aunt Hammy, Sun Wu and all the others, so she had to get a move on.

She did.

FIFTY-SEVEN

Varoden did not return to the fourth worlds immediately after leaving the library. Instead, he spent some time exploring the dreamtime, getting involved in a number of interesting goings on which are outside the scope of our present focus. Suffice it to say, he enjoyed himself immensely, and learned a thing or two along the way, as well.

When he eventually got back to the house between the falls, only Berondyas was still there.

"Where'd everyone go?" Varoden had asked

"Well, we had finished teaching your friends the basics, so they went home; Atra had business to take care of in Ve, and Friday is off somewhere to the south, doing I'm not sure what"

"Finished? How long was I gone?"

"A year"

"What! I thought it was a few weeks at most"

"The dreamtime is funny that way: you have to pay attention, or time can really slip away from you"

"Yeah, really…. I'll keep that in mind"

Berondyas turned to face Varoden fully, and looked him in his unmatched eyes "I'm still here because I was waiting for you. I want to talk about your next moves."

"Moves?"

"Yes, what you're going to do with yourself"

"Oh… Well I've been thinking about that too, actually…"

"What have you been thinking?"

"Well we had originally planned to do something about those Raiders we told you about, but what I've been reading, and what I've seen is making me think bigger than that…"

"Bigger how?"

"The story of the strong and violent capturing or killing the peaceful and/or weak is bound to be repeated all over the world. I think I'm going to use the law and what I've learned about binding magic to do something about that."

"Something like what?"

"Well that I'm not so sure of…"

Berondyas looked thoughtfully at the sky for several moments, before speaking again. "The Ve are engaged in something not totally dissimilar to what you just spoke of, you'd be free to join us if you wished to"

"I won't say I haven't thought about it" Varoden said, after a pause "It'd be easier to make a decision if I knew what you were really up to"

"Of that I cannot speak to one uninitiated in our ways. I can say that you could do what you described while being one of us, certainly"

"Yeah, that's what I thought you'd say... and I really appreciate everything you've done for me and my friends... But I think it's better for me to do my own thing, at least for a little while... I could still join later, right?"

"Undoubtedly..." Berondyas smiled "And I name you friend of the Ve, Varoden, you have proven yourself beyond any reasonable expectation; and your abilities have surprised us all. I also consider you my friend personally, and I'll definitely keep in contact"

"I'm honoured to be your friend Berondyas, I'm always available to help you if you need it"

"Likewise, Varoden... Oh, and feel free to stay at this house whenever you want, as long as it's not being used for something official"

"Thanks! I certainly will"

And with that they parted.

Varoden went to say goodbye to the horses, and saw Slider there waiting for him. Having said their farewells, and noticing that more of the horses seemed to have left, they rode back to the People.

This journey was very quick, because Varoden was able to use splatial travelling to cover large distances very quickly, without the difficulties and dangers involved in full on teleportation. He had never tried this with Slider, or any horse, before- but found, to his gratification, that it came naturally to him. After a few efforts, he didn't even have to speak any words to achieve the effect.

The People seemed to be in general good cheer, when he got to them. There had been no more raids, and nature had shared even more abundantly than normal over the past year and a bit since his departure. Thrango, Gudra, Aren, Heim, Sarag and Lela seemed both relieved and happy to see him. They had begun to make plans of intervention in the Raiders parasitic lifestyle, not knowing when he would return, but they saw his inclusion as making any kind of success far more likely.

They had all advanced in their practice a lot, and could most probably have overcome the Raiders defences by themselves; but the question of what to do next had proved to be a major sticking point.

The People, in general, and the wise elders, in particular, had, as was their way, taken the group's departure and return very much in stride, and were even quite grateful for the protection that their new abilities had seemed to afford. This did not mean they were interested in taking over the Raider's settlement *en masse.* This was not their way.

Nor was killing the Raiders an acceptable option- their teachers had impressed on them the futility and stupidity of violence; and the People, anyway, didn't hold truck with that kind of thing. They would have been ostracized immediately if they had chosen that path.

Recapturing the stolen women and integrating them into the way of the People might have been plausible if every year was as bountiful as this last one had been, but that was not so. Only planting could support the numbers that would mean; and there was no way the People would stay in one place to protect their crops, as would be required. It was just too much of a departure, and seemed to lead to never-ending increase, anyway. So that wasn't going to happen.

As Varoden listened to them outline the situation as they saw it, he could feel the way forward developing in the back of his mind. When they had lapsed into frustrated silence, he spoke

"Did Atra teach you about the Law?"

There was a chorus of assent

"Do you understand how it works?"

This time, there was silence, except for Lela, who, after a moment, said "Kinda"

"It's the solution to this problem, I'm sure of it"

And he outlined his plan.

FIFTY-EIGHT

The dreaming continent was just a short trip south from the island that's not an island, and the shallow water told Ranga and Appa, now experienced navigators, that they had been one big land at some point. They saw a large number of very pleasant islands on their daylong sail, but didn't stop at any of them, cognizant of time as they were.

Having arrived at what they assumed to be their destination, they sailed east along the coast for a while, to make sure it wasn't another big island. Having seen landmarks that they'd been told to look out for, and satisfied themselves that they were in the right place; they landed on a wide beach. Since it was already evening, they settled in and had a leisurely dinner, making use of a charming and empty hut that they assumed was for that purpose.

The next morning brought with it visitors.

There were ten or so of them, who turned out to be representatives from several different neighbouring groups. These people had a certain gravitas and rootedness to them, which reminded Ranga and Appa a little bit of the people from their home. It's not that they weren't funny and lighthearted, when appropriate; it was more like they knew who they were.

The visitors suggested that they all go further down the coast, to a place that was special to all the nearby folk; which suggestion was readily accepted by our two intrepid navigators. They would all take the boat, which had been regarded with a kind of awed interest by their hosts- the quick trip seeming only to deepen that sentiment.

The tables were turned, somewhat, when they got close to their destination; there was a complexly beautiful reef ecosystem that seemed to go on forever. Appa and Ranga had never seen the like of it, and expressed their appreciation to their hosts, who only smiled.

They landed at another beach, which was already crowded; and there was a hell of a party for the next few days.

Over the course of staying in this area, Appa and Ranga learned a great deal about the dreaming peoples, and the continent, as well.

That the dreaming peoples of the dreaming continent had been there for a long time was obvious to the two travellers, who had already seen enough to understand human cultural development very well. It wasn't just a long time, though, they began to realize. It was *ages*. Over that immense period, these people had developed a beautifully peaceful relationship with space and time, which had resulted in their incorporation of the dreamtime into their everyday cultural practices. This incorporation had, in turn, deepened their relationship to their own home splace, so that they lived their environment in a very real sense.

The continent was filled with too many different peoples and cultures to easily keep track of, but their boundaries were deeply fluid, and they were able to keep close contact with each other through the dreamtime.

It was, in other words, a highly sophisticated civilization, the like of which Ranga and Appa would rarely encounter again.

This is not to say that there was never conflict, or even violence. There was. What there also was, however, was a well-tried means to deal with these disagreements, and their aftermath.

There were also, apparently a large number of numen, and even some *authorities*, living with or affiliated with the dreaming peoples. These beings apparently shared the Dreamers' philosophy, and were happy to contribute to the maintenance of their generally peaceful ways.

There were some similarities between the dreamers' self-expressed *raissond'etre* and that of the Isle of the Magicians in particular, and the Travellers in general. They both seemed to see their role as taking care of creation; but the Travellers did this through more or less instrumental means- whether that instrument was a drum, a party, magic or meditation. The Dreamers seemed to see their job as actually *living* their care.

Ranga and Appa were very impressed.

They stayed with these North-eastern Dreamers for much longer than they had intended; making several forays into the dreamtime during that period. While there, they met representatives from other dreaming nations, and some numen and even an *authority*, besides.

Eventually, though, they were able to drag themselves away, heading generally south along the coast to meet up with representatives of the Southeastern dreaming peoples at a pre-arranged point, before heading southeast to the Sanctuary islands, which had apparently been left as a human free safe place for animals since time immemorial.

The Southeasterners were also lovely, if occasionally more reserved and other-worldly than their previous hosts. They also seemed to be a little more clannish, and thus more prone to inter-ethnic disagreement; but they made up for it by even better hosts than their more northerly counterparts.

It was here that Appa and Ranga began to develop more insight into the history of the Dreamers, and why they were as they were.

The dreaming peoples had arrived at this continent not long after the great Cataclysm, apparently, which would put their residency so far back into the mists of time as to be almost unfathomable. They had found a fertile paradise, filled with food and all the other components of an easy life. The Dreamers had, by their own admission, deeply damaged this paradise, to the extent that vast tracts of it were now desert. But they had learned their lesson. They would never again take nature's generosity for granted. Instead, they had chosen to enact guardianship, and had learned to rely on the dreamtime for support. There were, also, hints of some role they had to play in a future crisis, when all their wisdom and knowledge would be needed to help humanity, and the fourth worlds, survive.

This future crisis had also been hinted at by the wise folk of the Travellers, and Ranga and Appa found themselves intrigued by it. There wasn't much more information forthcoming here, though, and they resolved to look into it at some future juncture.

Anyway, eventually the time came for Appa and Ranga to bid their farewells, and they did so with some regret. This had been the most interesting place they had ever been to, and they definitely wanted to find out more about it. The sea beckoned, though, so off they went, headed to the Sanctuary islands they had heard so much about.

FIFTY-NINE

The clearing in the Forest Primeval was suffused with a warm glow made of more than just light. Hampele, the old man, Sun Wu, the Queen of Hell, The First Owner, Owl, Bear, Bee-Hive, Dolphin, Bonobo, Anansi, Osha, and her sisters were all there, and Roko had sent an associate tree as well.

The meeting had been a total success.

They had agreed to work together for the good of the fourth worlds, neighbouring splaces and, in fact, all beings. A generally decentralized approach had been agreed, with each great body free to pursue its own path, with no oversight. There were to be regular meetings, so that news and counsel could be exchanged.

Not all the participants wanted to go the great body route. Dolphin and Bonobo had said that they felt that they'd be more useful as independent actors; and that it was good to have as many different approaches as possible, as long as they were willing to honestly appraise progress or the lack thereof. Everyone agreed.

Isha had asked how strictly they, as a group, wanted to stick to regular time protocol, and this had led to a great deal of discussion. It was generally known that the delicacy of time meant that one was usually best served to just go along with it, and not do too much messing around with one's subjective past. There were, however, a variety of ways to use time to your advantage, if you knew what you were doing. The problem with that, of course, is that almost no-one *really* knows what they're doing. Roko's representative, when they had got to this point, said that since Roko and Bee-Hive experienced time in a far less linear way than most other beings, their action was extremely likely to be un-sequential, and that it was better if everyone just used their own judgment.

Nevertheless, a consensus had emerged. They would mess with time as little as possible, particularly since the machine was already damaging it badly.

Everyone had differing ideas about how quickly the great bodies should be completed. Osha and her sisters, as well as Hampele, had all thought that it was best to finish them closer to the decisive moments, whereas Owl and the Queen had argued strongly in favour of completing them as soon as possible, so that all concerned would have had practice and developed their strength by the time it was need. The others had held various positions between those two poles. Eventually, a compromise was agreed. Since great bodies could be added to without harming their integrity, some could start now, and add more beings later, some could wait to start, and some could complete themselves from now, if they so desired.

The question of whether the machine could simply be destroyed non-violently had come up; but no-one could think of any way to effectively do that. The fact was that humans had the sometimes unfortunate virtue of being born deeply open and adaptable. This meant that that they were very sensitive to their initial and ongoing environment, which in this case was being shaped by their adversary. The machine was too deeply ingrained in too many people's selves to just destroy it without harming them. Added to that was the fact that, as the First Owner had pointed out, the machine could very well be a great body itself, which complicated things even further.

No, they would have to be creative.

Anansi had given his report on the latest going on in his protectorate, and he had seemed to be actually moved by the praise his detailed and well-thought analysis had received. He had declared himself available for any other tasks the group required, up to and including joining any great body that needed him. His offer was graciously received by all, and this seemed to move him even further.

Osha had also told everyone about the Librarian, and her most recent experiences in the Library, suggesting to everyone that self-knowledge could be an important aid to their collective efforts. Some had seemed interested, others not at all. The old man and Sun Wu had only looked at each other and smiled.

The Librarian's co-operation and tacit support had been generally seen as a big deal, though. Her reputation was immense, and beings tended to pay attention to her words and actions.

And so, the meeting had been adjourned, but only the old man, Roko's associate tree and Bear, who all had other places to be, had left. Everyone else had got involved in informal sub-groups discussing this and that, or just getting to know each other. Osha's sisters and Aunt Hammy were quietly catching up on old news; while Anansi, the queen of Hell and Sun Wu were having a deep and engrossing conversation in the corner. The rest just mingled and floated, enjoying the feeling of connection through shared purpose.

At some point, Osha had started to play her flute, and Bonobo had started to dance; and a party broke out. Not just any party, actually, this one would enter into legend. Others had been called, or just passed by, and they had, in turn, invited others.

It went on for a long time.

In fact, it hasn't really stopped.

The Party in the Clearing would become a permanent part of dreamtime society, and at any given moment, there were likely to be dozens of beings reveling in the continued glow, which had never left.

The meetings of the "temporary group to address the machine", as they unpoetically referred to it when they had to, would, henceforth, be held in various different locations.

We'll get to that, though.

SIXTY

The Raiders' settlement had grown noticeably since their last visit, and there were also now men with spears and/or clubs guarding the perimeter. This time, though, Varoden, Thrango, Lela, Gudra, Aren, Sarag and Heim- or the Seven against Thieves, as they had started calling themselves, did not attempt any subterfuge. Instead they rode straight up to the largest entrance and demanded to speak to the hierarchs immediately.

They had already drawn a crowd, and several more guards had also come to reinforce the five who had already been there. These guards had quickly and unsubtly surrounded the seemingly unwitting seven, and their apparent leader, confident in numerical superiority, had, by way of response, shouted "take 'em down, lads" and charged at Varoden and Slider, who had been at the vanguard.

This, as it turns out, was a poor idea.

They immobilized all the guards but one, the leader; and repeated their request. This time he complied willingly, at a run.

Varoden's plan had been agreed to by all, but Thrango and Saraghad insisted on okaying it with the elders first. Approval was, eventually, forthcoming, but there had clearly been some misgivings and debate about the topic. Yes was yes, though, and they had ridden off two mornings after, confident in the rightness of their course of action.

The Law, Varoden had told them, did not just have physical components. In fact, there were at least as many psychological, philosophical and epistemological (etc.) consequences to the shape of a splace as there were baldly material ones. The reason that this mattered was that understanding the Law had taught him that the inhabitants of the fourth worlds were particularly susceptible to binding magic. It was known that one had to be a bit careful in the employment of this kind of power, but it remained a viable resource, particularly given the dearth of other ideas.

He had proposed that they use a sort of mild binding magic on the Raiders' hierarchs, to mitigate their excesses, and stop them from preying so consistently on other people. This binding magic, Varoden had suggested, could be incorporated into their current system of ritual and social organization, so that the seven wouldn't be meddling too much in the affairs of others. Instead they'd merely be curbing the worst aspects of their nature.

This was a very intelligent plan.

Lela had had misgivings, at first, but she had given in to the weight of unanimity arrayed against her. To be fair, she was pretty right to have her doubts, but let's just see what happens, no?

Anyway, the leader of the guards had returned and led the Seven against Thieves into the "sacred halls" at the centre of the settlement, where the hierarchs lived in relative ease. The guard had stopped at the entrance gate, and motioned the Seven in, before heading back in the direction they had just come from.

"You must be pretty powerful" a female voice had offered, once they had gone through the gate.

There, to their right, were eight people dressed far more fancily than the regular folk they had encountered outside. There were four men, and four women, all human, as far as Varoden could tell.

Which was a relief. He had been confident in his abilities, but was far happier not to have to test them against another numen, at this point.

"Hi" Thrango said cheerfully "We're here to stop you abducting people"

"Ahhh" said the woman, with a little smile

"It will not continue" Gudra said with a level stare.

One of the well-dressed hierarchs, a man this time, asked "Have you come to kill us?"

"There'll be no killing" Varoden said quickly "But your options are these, you can willingly swear a vow to halt your antisocial practices; or I can force you to do what we say... I recommend the first option"

"So you're the driving force, are you?" The woman had asked, maintaining her smile.

"We're all in this together" Varoden had responded.

"And what would we have to do, exactly?" asked another hierarch, a tall woman.

"To cease the stealing of women, and to work in favour of the balance of life, to the best of your ability" Lela said.

"The balance of life? What is that, exactly? As far as I can tell, this life means the strong devouring the weak, and the powerful doing what they will" A male hierarch had said, with a sneer

"The balance of life is enacted by following the peaceful way" Lela said simply "The strong must use their strength for the collective good…"

"And the weak must do what they can" Varoden had added

"What's a vow, anyway?" asked the first woman, with actual seeming curiosity.

"A kind of… sacred promise" Varoden had responded, before adding "Speaking of sacred, how'd you all set up this system anyway? What's the source of your power? And why aren't you trying to use it against us?"

"We've never had anything to compare with what you apparently can do" said the tall woman slowly, after several exchanged glances "We were given some objects of power, to create a good show at the beginning, but after that it's been mostly intelligence, frankly"

"And why so much violence?" Lela had asked

"We had to protect ourselves, there's a new world coming, and those who don't adapt will die" the tall woman said.

"Protect yourselves by being evil?" Sarag had asked incredulously.

"Protect ourselves by being effective. We're not the only ones who do this, if we don't and they do, they'll overpower us, the same we we've been overpowering the followers of the old way"

"I can understand that" Lela said "but it can't go on"

"Well, we're all dead then; us, your people and the other old-fashioned types around here." This was said by a man at the back of the group who hadn't said anything up to that point

"We will offer protection to those who take the vow" Varoden said.

"We will?" Thrango asked, looking at his twin

"We will"

And so it began.

SIXTY-ONE

The Sanctuary islands were filled with birds. Not just any old birds, either; Ranga and Appa saw many species they had never seen before, as well as giant versions of more familiar avians.

"I guess being out here by themselves with lots of space and food means that they can grow as big as they want" Appa had said

"I guess so" Ranga had replied.

They also encountered some new ecosystems on their trip, including a few that were far too cold for their comfort. In fact, they realized that these islands were fairly close to the frozen southern continent they had heard of, and which they definitely weren't going to visit until they had learned to appreciate the cold more.

Ever curious, Appa had returned to the dreamtime to do a little research one day, while Ranga was off floating in the sea. She had discovered that not only had these islands once been part of a bigger continent which included the one to the south, but that all the land on earth had been joined into one big landmass at some point in the distant past.

This was very interesting to her.

Anyway, Ranga and Appa stayed on the islands for a week or so, before embarking on what they already knew was going to be a very long voyage. They were headed generally north-northeast, to the fabled lands that lay across a vast ocean, which was said to be the largest in the world.

They were psyched.

It was, in fact, to be one of their most memorable voyages. They discovered a *lot* of uninhabited island paradises, and, nearer to the end of their journey than the beginning, came across the home of an **authority**, on some (again stunningly beautiful) islands that were pretty much in the middle of nowhere.

This **authority** whose name, they learned, was Hampele the magnificent and terrible, eater of earth and shaper of lands; was super friendly, and hosted Ranga and Appa for a particularly lovely couple of weeks. She clearly loved the islands, and explained to them that she had made them herself, over the course of her existence.

Appa and Ranga hadn't realized that this was possible, and had asked if all **authorities** were capable of this kind of thing.

"I wouldn't say that, no" Hampele had responded "Just like anyone else, we'll tend to have things we're good at, and things we're not so good at"

"I guess that's why working together is so important" Appa had responded thoughtfully, before looking at Ranga with open appreciation

"Yes, I guess you're right…" Hampele had responded "… although co-operation has maybe been one of the things I've historically been not so strong at…"

"You?" Ranga had asked "I'm surprised to hear you say that, you seem so lovely and sociable"

"Thanks, that's nice of you to say… but I've had anger management issues in the past, as well as a slight tendency to be jealous… I'm working on it… That's actually why I'm here by myself, right now… "

At this, Hampele had looked so sad that Ranga had, without thinking, just gone over and hugged her. She had looked surprised, at first, and then had returned the hug with appreciation.

Appa had smiled at them, and then looked around their beautiful surroundings. "What a joy it is, to be alive" she thought to herself "And how lucky I am to be here with these people". Her smile had widened, and she'd felt a wave of glorious connection rise from within her, and then wash over everything at once.

"Why don't you come with us?" Appa asked Hampele, once the hug had ended

"Come with you?"

"That's a great idea!" Ranga had said, with real enthusiasm "You should definitely come!"

"Hmmm" said Hampele

She went with them, and found herself healed by the time they had reached the continent to the east. The addition of a third person is, in many cases, the largest change possible to a group. Hampele's addition had certainly changed the dynamic aboard the boat, and it had taken a little while for everyone to get used to the situation. But the subsequent consensus had been truly harmonious, in every sense of the word.

They had deeply enjoyed each other's company; so much so that Hampele had asked if she could stay with them as they explored the new lands they had arrived at, instead of returning to her islands as she had originally planned. Appa and Ranga had been delighted to say yes.

They had landed in a lovely sheltered bay, which their nautical arts had directed them to. The people who lived there were, obviously, very surprised to see them, but invited them to stay for a while; and the idyllic scenery and easy, relaxed vibe convinced Appa, Ranga and Hampele to do so.

These people, the newly arrived sailors learned, were the descendants of intrepid travelers who had themselves come from the east. These ancient peoples had come by land, though, across a frozen land and then south to prosperity. Their cousins had peopled this whole land, from north to south, but their hosts counted themselves lucky to have found a home so perfect as this.

To be fair, they were quite right, it was a wonderful place to live, having a relaxed island vibe combined with continental access and sophistication.

Their culture was very interesting: they were very focused on the fourth worlds, and seemed content to leave the dreamtime, the *place that's not a place*, or any other splaces, to their own devices. This is not to say that they didn't know that other splaces existed; they did. They just didn't really make a big deal about them. Their wise people were just as knowledgeable, in their way, as those of the Travellers, or the Dreamers, or any they had encountered. It seemed to be their choice to focus on the here and now, and the ways of making life beautiful and meaningful.

As such, they had developed many sophisticated social technologies, and seemed to be very open to changing their lifestyle, if a better idea occurred to them, or was seen to have worked somewhere else. Appa, Hampele and Ranga were told that this was a characteristic of the whole continent spanning family of "Descendants", as they called themselves; as was an affinity with the lands they lived on.

It was impressive.

SIXTY-TWO

Osha returned to the Americas, picking up where she had left off. Her long travels are for another story, but suffice it to say, she was more encouraged at the end of them than she was at the beginning.

There was real possibility here.

Danger too, of course.

Having completed her self-assigned survey, she was somewhat at a loss about how to proceed. It would be centuries before it was time to act, and the seeds of revolution that she and others had planted would take a while to grow. Too much interference before then was likely to do more harm than good.

In the end, she decided she would follow up on the second part of the Librarian's suggestion to her: she would try to be free.

Now *authorities* are often assumed to be the most free of beings, being subject to no-one, having huge capacities and abilities, and living almost unfathomably long lives.

This is not totally accurate.

Nor is it how they experience themselves, for the most part.

Most *authorities* lived lives of indolent (and wonderful, to be fair) pleasure, not bothering to concern themselves with anything other than the happiness of their existence. They didn't think of themselves as free, because they didn't really think of themselves.

Until they did, which was often a huge and unpleasant shock.

The ones who did take part in the goings on of their neighbourhood splaces found themselves to remain subject to the shape and nature of wherever they were, which meant that they would not, if asked, have usually described themselves as free. "Nothing is free" is the kind of answer you were likely to get.

Osha's recent experiences in the Library of Time had led her to question many assumptions which she had always made, and also to believe in the possibility of liberation for herself.

The problem was that she didn't really know what that meant, or how one would go about it, particularly.

"The journey of a thousand miles begins with a single step" she said to herself, and went off to the Mountain school in the dreamtime, to talk to the old man and Sun Wu.

Reaching her destination, and entering its gateless gate, Osha quickly found Sun Wu in the main hall, practicing with his long staff by himself in a corner. Well, not really by himself, his grace and skill had drawn a little crowd. Osha joined them, and waited for him to finish.

"Is it super urgent Osha? I've just got a little while left..." Sun Wu asked calmly, having seen and smiled at her approach

"Not at all, my friend, there's no rush at all"

He was true to his word, though, and it was a short while later that he and Osha were walking towards the old man's rooms.

"How do I go about being free?" Osha had asked, once the niceties had been observed.

Sun Wu and the old man looked at each other, before the old man looked at her, and said,

> *"There is something formed of chaos,*
> *Born before heaven and earth.*
> *Silent and void, it is not renewed,*
> *It goes on forever without failing"*

He held her gaze and asked "Are you sure you're not free already?"

"I have no idea" Osha responded

"A wise response" the old man said with a smile. "There are some that could probably help you, there is no quick way to get to them, though"

"I'm in" Osha said immediately "Just tell me where they are"

There was silence for a while, and then Sun Wu quietly said "people don't always come back from this place Osha"

"It's dangerous?"

"I wouldn't say that, no... it's more like..." he sighed, and then said "There's no way to explain it, really, you'd have to see for yourself..." before adding, brightly "I'm pretty sure, you'll return , though, it would really be more a matter of when..."

"Well if I miss any meetings, please apologize and explain for me" Osha said with one of her charming grins "You still would need to tell me where it is, though"

"I'm confident you'll be fine, actually" the old man said "And the way is this:

> *Go through the gateless gate*
> *And past the ancestors' wisdom*
> *Across the ten thousand seas*
> *And the pure land of tranquility*
>
> *There is a second gate*
> *Which is both unlocked and secure*
> *Only enter with humility*
> *To learn the way of true unfolding"*

"In other words," he continued "three splaces over and then take a left"

"Got it" Osha said.

SIXTY-THREE

The Seven against Thieves quickly made a name for themselves, roaming far and wide and addressing injustice to the best of their abilities. Their original interaction with the hierarchs of the Raider village had provided a template for them, and before too long they had effected a kind of revolution in their neighbourhood.

The hierarchs had agreed to take their vow, and had immediately announced the end of raiding, and the freedom of the captured women. Interestingly, many of the former captives had chosen to stay, and the Raiders growth seemed likely to continue, at least partly because of the high-quality public relations and symbolic marketing which were their new method of population expansion.

The previously vague allusions to the sacred that had characterized the old way of doing business had been systemized and concretized into narrative form. They made a religion, in other words.

They were actually pretty clever about it, too.

Even the People had heard talk about the children of Nana, a near mythical civilization to the south, who were said to worship a very powerful goddess. This goddess was said to grant her followers wonders, magic and knowledge beyond the grasp of even the wisest and most learned of elders here to the north.

The hierarchs had included Nana in their new ideology, suggesting that she had sent powerful representatives (the Seven against Thieves) to them, to tell them of the coming of a new age. The Raiders, and anyone who joined them, would be part of the vanguard of this movement, which would lead to a golden age of peace and understanding.

    It worked.

    Boy, did it work.

Not all groups that behaved badly had leadership as creative as the Raiders did. When the Seven encountered such groups, they usually just suggested that they adopt the methods that they had seen work so well.

    Most did.

The ones that didn't tended to either break apart quite quickly, or to move as far away as possible, in all directions. The general trend, however, was to coalesce in larger and larger settlements, powered by the twin engines of agriculture and religion. The protection of the Seven easily withstood the few attempts at organized violence that threatened the increasingly coherent region, until there was something resembling a prosperous and reasonably united nation.

The Seven had, in the meantime, become six, for a while; as Lela had returned to the house between the falls to complete her training. She would return a couple of years later, as a numen, which only reinforced the strength of their group.

They had never had any real disagreements, and they shared a sense of both pride in their achievements, and of purpose and duty. Even better, their People had retained their freedom to move and live as they would, even though the Elders could often be seen sharing somewhat sad and plaintive smiles.

Their world had changed, they knew; and they could do nothing but change with it.

Lela's return freed up Varoden to roam further and further afield, exploring the gigantic landmass that was their home. He would dress in a variety of guises, always seeking to redress any wrong that he found; and learning much about the seemingly infinite faces of humanity.

It was during one of these periods of wandering, far off in the frozen northeast of the continent, that he would meet Raven, another numen with whom he clicked immediately. They would go on to become close and famous friends, and it might not be an exaggeration to say that it was this friendship which would give Varoden a chance to save himself, when the time came.

That we'll almost definitely get back to, though.

When Varoden returned to his homeland, after that particular journey, quite a bit had changed. In the few years he had been gone, a new ritual had been added to the developing religion, this time by a group at the southern edge of the region. It was called a "sacred marriage" and was supposed to represent the instantiation and enactment of the new age. This ritual involved the binding together, through magic and sex, of a human and the goddess. The human, called a hero, had to prove themselves worthy of this honour by either performing some great service for their neighbours, or, as was increasingly the case, by winning some (also sacred) competition.

This idea spread like wildfire.

Another thing that had changed was that Heim had gone to see if he could be a numen too.

He would be gone a long time.

None of the others had shown any greater interest in walking that road; to the contrary, they seemed to increasingly delight in the idea of joining their ancestors, and sharing and merging their achievements with all the People that ever would be.

They were definitely proud to have effected change, and to have become as strong as they had been, but their identity remained strongly tied to the group they had been born into- to the extent that they would return "home" at every opportunity.

Varoden would occasionally feel a pang of regret for what he had lost. Neither he nor Lela could really hope to be one with the People in the same way; and their numenity proved to be a subtle barrier to total comfort back with their kin. No-one treated them differently, particularly- although there might have been slightly more jokes made about them than before. No, the difference was in them, they did not and could not see or feel things the way they used to- the way the People did.

So Lela and Varoden returned less frequently, and didn't stay as long. They didn't spend that much time alone with each other, either. They were very different, and Lela had never lost her misgivings about their activities, although she rarely voiced them. She preferred to spend her off-duty hours at the Library of Time, having gone once with Varoden to get her bearings. He didn't get around to showing her his trick with the sideways time door, but he meant to.

There were, by the way, a lot more of the big horses that had befriended Varoden and his People around. They had bred and bred, and the Seven had used access to the horses to bribe recalcitrant groups. Berondyas's injunctions against mistreatment or disrespect had not been forgotten, but it was certainly the case that the horses brought up amongst humans had generally not had the same strong-willed temperaments that their parents had. In fact, Varoden had even heard humans talking about "owning" horses, a lapse he always quickly addressed; but which was a clear indication that things were a bit different than they used to be.

One last change to tell you about was that Friday had come to join the group a little while after Varoden had returned from his journey to the northeast. Which was nice.

SIXTY-FOUR

The Descendants played a ball game, which involved a lot of running and yelling; and Ranga and Hampele had taken to it like gangbusters. Suitably tuning down their abilities to roughly match those of their fellow players, they spent hour after joyous hour at it, becoming very good in a short time. It wasn't really Appa's kind of thing, but she watched it with interest, seeking to understand the tactics, strategies and philosophies underlying the game.

What she found drew her even further in, because the game was well designed to provide insight into the splace in which it had been created. It could be played in many ways, and the tactics one gravitated to functioned as a sort of personality test and philosophical manifesto, rolled into one.

One could, for example, play the game individualistically, and for those with certain talents, this appeared to be the easiest path to success and glory. Taking the team-centred collective approach was much harder, and required more work- but it was, for some, the only path to winning. This second approach, additionally seemed to be the path to the highest levels of play. At its best, though, the game seemed to make the distinction between individual and collective disappear- so that both perspectives became equally valid and effective. This, however, seemed to be rare and difficult to maintain.

And this was just one of the axes of analysis that Appa considered, there were several others.

So she learned quite a bit.

It was after one such game, while everyone was relaxing on the beach, that talk turned to the Twins that were said to have used the game to make the world what it is. They were still around, apparently, never staying in one place too long, but always looking out for the Descendants.

This was extremely intriguing to the three newcomers, and they asked for more information. As luck would have it, the Twins were said to have been not ridiculously far away up till fairly recently, in some lands to the northeast, which could be traveled to in a couple of weeks.

They were definitely going.

Having got general directions, they entrusted the boat to their hosts, warning them that they probably shouldn't try to sail it, but if they did to be very careful, because it wasn't always a very straightforward proposition. They could have used other means to secure it, but preferred not to use binding ways if it wasn't absolutely necessary.

The countryside was starkly beautiful as they set off, browns and greens seeming to combine into some strange colour that didn't really look like either. They had no intention of walking the whole way, of course, they'd take a shortcut through the surrounding splaces once they got a bit further on. For that moment, though, it was nice to take in the scenery and to just enjoy each other's company.

It was, then, a day or two later that they arrived at the rocky highlands they'd been directed to. The land was austere, but seemed to emit a sense of welcome, as well. Which was nice.

Following a path that led east, they came to a pass, on either side of which stood steep escarpments. They decided to check out the view, and so climbed up to the wide summit of the western rise.

Below them was a wide valley, bustling with settlements, and which had dwellings built into the rock itself.

"That's super cool" Ranga said

"Isn't it?" Appa said

Hampele smiled her agreement.

Heading back down, and through the path, Hampele seemed to be lost in her thoughts

"What's up, Ham? You're far away from here..." Appa asked, after a while.

"I feel presences that must be the Twins, but it's weird, they don't feel like **authorities** exactly, but I don't think they're numen either, they're definitely not human..."

"Well they have to be something, right?" Ranga said with a smile "Let's just go find out what"

So they did.

The Twins were living in a very large apartment which was off by itself on an otherwise empty cliff-face. They were tall and identical looking, but seemed to be very different in several other ways. Having graciously greeted the three of them as guests, and offered refreshments, the more snazzily dressed Twin had asked how they'd ended up there.

They'd told their tale

The other Twin, who was quieter and dressed in animal pelts had said nothing, but seemed to be engrossed in their tale, muttering to himself occasionally.

"It begins" Animal Pelt Twin had said simply

"You might be right" Sophisticated Twin had responded

"What begins?" Appa asked

"We must perform certain tasks to ensure the continuation of this world" S.T. (as they started to call him, A.P.T. being the other... they didn't seem to mind) had explained "These tasks form concentric, yet overlapping, circles, and with much smaller and much larger diameters... This appears to be the beginning of one of the biggest circles..."

"I know what you're talking about" Hampele had said simply

"You do?" Ranga asked

"I wouldn't have put it like that, exactly, but there is definitely something coalescing which is both part of larger cycles and something completely new... and big"

"That makes sense..." Appa said slowly "And I think we're wrapped up in it too" She looked at Hampele and, after a second, asked "Is it really so easy for numen to lose track of five thousand years in the dreamtime?"

"For numen?" Hampele wrinkled her brow, and then, after a second, said "I wouldn't have said so, no. Maybe a year or two but I feel like you'd definitely notice even a hundred, much less five thousand"

"I see what you're getting at" Ranga said, thoughtfully

"The tree must have moved us forward in time for its own purposes while we were still human, it's the only thing that makes sense, and I've thought so for a while. He said we were needed here, too, remember?"

Ranga nodded

"That fits with what these guys are saying about the cycles, and with what Ham is saying too." Appa looked at the Twins "Are your tasks anything to do with balance?" she asked.

"They are everything to do with balance" S.T. said

"Balance is exactly what I've been working on in my own existence, too" Hampele said quietly "This is definitely not coincidence" And so they resolved to trust and help each other and existence, and to work together to maintain balance in the fourth worlds and the neighbouring splaces

"We have some friends you should meet" S.T. had said, after having hosted Hampele, Ranga and Appa for a few days.

"Sounds good, where are they?"

I'm not actually sure... I know Raven was going back to the old continent for a while, I don't know if he's back yet, but we can definitely find him one way or another. Coyote will almost definitely be in the dreamtime, he spends most of his time there these days; and Bird-Snake will most likely be on one of those southern mountain-tops he likes so much"

"You think they'll want to help?"

"Coyote and Raven definitely. Bird-Snake can be a little funny, but he's very helpful sometimes- if only for his way of looking at things"

"Well, let's go"

Raven and Coyote were both balance incarnate. As such, they had enthusiastically agreed to do what they could to help, when they had been found in their respective corners of the world.

Bird-Snake, now, was a different proposition.

SIXTY-FIVE

Leaving the mountain school through the same gate that she'd entered through, Osha travelled to the Library of Time, which she was pretty confident was the "ancestors' wisdom" that the old man had spoken of. She entered the main corridor and thought about the next step in her journey.

The "ten thousand seas" was probably the Great Ocean, a splace that Osha had heard about, but never had any particular reason to visit. She also would not have said it was next to the Library of Time, but she trusted her directions, and resolved to make them work. Direct travelling wouldn't have been too much of a big deal for her, and there was almost definitely away to get there using one of the elevators; but those didn't feel like routes that were in the spirit of what she had been told.

So, she walked.

The main corridor of the Library of Time is very rarely the same twice. There were always changes, little or large, that made each visit the first. As Osha made her way down the wide (and widening) hall, she found herself paying attention in a way that she never had before. She could see, feel and otherwise sense patterns that just eluded conscious definition, and cycles that repeated in small, medium, large and infinite sizes. And these weren't just external perceptions, either.

She walked and didn't seek to collapse the waveforms that danced within and without. Untrammeled, the possibilities called their friends from the surrounding halls, and they called theirs, until, all around her, there was a carnival of unexpressed energy that felt like a kind of soup; making walking more challenging than it had previously been.

It's not that collapsing waveform is bad, as such, by the way. It just creates a whole bunch of stuff to deal with, is all.

Still, she walked, until the carnival had ended, and a kind of deep quiet emerged, arose, descended and met in the middle, speeding up her progress. And then she disappeared again.

When she returned, she found herself still walking.

At some point, she saw a clearly marked exit. And she walked through the door.

Osha had, as I may have pointed out before, always loved rivers and springs and other sweet waters. The ten thousand seas- The Ocean- was not like that.

And she loved it, too.

The door had opened to somewhere just below the surface, and she was obliged to swim. She could have walked too, in actuality, or made a vehicle for herself; but those options didn't feel right.

So she swam. At first, she headed towards the pale and huge rising moon of this splace; but she caught it, eventually; and figured she'd just go wherever.

Osha did not tire, at all; and there came a point when she realized that she felt as wonderful as she ever had. There was so much joy in every moment that it didn't quite fit, and the overflow became as profound as its source.

"I could do this forever" Osha thought to herself "But I won't" And then she entered the Pure Land of tranquility, which seemed to be contained in the Ocean, to contain the Ocean and also to be a whole different splace.

"Well! We don't get a lot of *authorities* here these days…" a voice said.
Osha looked in the direction that it seemed to have come from, but saw no-one.

"Oh! Sorry, forgot the right frame of reference…"

With that there stood before her a bright and beautiful being, whose luminescence was accompanied by a deep gentleness that made Osha smile.

"Hi" She said "I'm Osha"

"Yes, you are, aren't you? Why don't you call me Ami?"

"Why don't I?" she said with an even bigger smile.

Osha looked around, and found herself slightly dazzled by her surroundings. Everything seemed to be emitting the same kind of light as Ami, but there were varying degrees of subtlety and intricacy, which suggested the possibilities that lay beyond possibility.

"This place is super cool" Osha said "How comes I haven't heard of it?"

"Can't say for sure... We definitely don't get a lot of **authorities**, though"

"You feel very welcoming, but I guess I should make sure that I actually *am* welcome here... You don't mind my presence?"

"To the contrary, Osha. I'm extremely pleased to see you, and you will always be welcome here. Consider it a refuge for you, should you ever need one" Ami replied.

"Thank you, that's nice of you. I'll keep it in mind" Osha said, and smiled her biggest smile yet.

"I think you're probably" Ami said "Looking for the second gateless gate"

"How'd you know"

"Call it a lucky guess... In any case, the quickest route is that way" He pointed "And you can't get lost, so don't worry. If there's any problem, just call my name, and I'll come help"

"Thank you, Ami, I'll come back to visit if it's no issue"

"Consider this a second home" said Ami, who pointed again, and then disappeared.

Osha headed in the indicated direction, taking care not to get lost in the deeply fascinating topographies surrounding her. Not too lost, anyway.

And then there was a sign.

On this sign was written the following:

This gate is no gate

This gate is unlocked

<u>This gate has no lock</u>

THIS LOCK HAS NO GATE

This has locked no gates

No has unlocked gates

Osha smiled, cleared her mind, and entered the second gateless gate.

It seemed as if she was back at the Mountain school.

It didn't feel like it, necessarily, but her surroundings certainly *looked* like her starting point.

Osha entered the main hall, and saw Sun Wu practicing with his staff in the same corner as before. She thought for a second, before turning the other way, and heading towards one of the classrooms on the far side. Passing and smiling at several unfamiliar faces on the way, she reached her destination, opened the door, and entered.

"The supreme way is not difficult" Said a man sitting with a book in his hand "It simply dislikes choosing"

"Choosing what?" Osha responded.

"What's your name?" a woman sitting nearby asked.

"I'm Osha"

"I'm Sana and that's Chou" she pointed at the man with the book.

"Nice to meet you both" Osha smiled.

"And nice to meet you, Osha"

There was a little pause

"So how can we help you" !Sana asked, at the end of it.

"I came to find out how to be free" Osha said simply.

"Are you not free already?"

"I'm not really sure what it means, to be honest"

"Then why do you want to become it?"

"The Librarian suggested it would aid my efforts to help the fourth worlds not be destroyed, probably seriously damaging at least the dreamtime and the *place that's not a place* as well"

"Is that all?"

Osha thought about that, and realized that it was not, in fact, all. "I'm realizing that there's more to my existence than I thought" she said slowly.

"More like what?" !Sana asked.

"More like openness, like types of awareness I hadn't really even heard of, like...." Osha stopped there, at a loss for words.

"Freedom is just a word, a concept, an idea... It's conditioned, and impermanent" Chou said "The way to be free is to not be free, that's why it's called being free. And the way to not be free is to be free, that's why it's called not being free."

Osha felt his words hit her like the front edge of a storm. She smiled, bowed to !Sana and Chou, and left the room, the School, and the splace.

"Well done" !Sana said, bowing to Chou

"A good horse runs at the shadow of a whip" he said, with a wink.

SIXTY-SIX

The years went by, and the lands under the protection of the Seven grew and grew, so that their names and stories, or reasonable facsimiles thereof, were known across the huge landmass on which they lived. The general peace which had arisen around them provided testament to their greatness, and to their benevolence; but they all retained enough natural humility to not care overmuch for fame or the possibility of gain.

Friday had seemed to enjoy the camaraderie and *esprit de corps* the Seven shared, and had, without much comment, ended up staying much longer than she or anyone else thought she would. That might, in fairness, have had something to do with the relationship she and Varoden had struck up, as well.

Varoden and Friday made a good team, in fact. He might have caught up with her in the ways of the gripping and empty hand, and far surpassed her in the binding ways, but she outshone him in the tactical and strategic arts. Her genius was such that he would sometimes find himself just admiring her as she spoke, learning what he could, but acknowledging her singularity.

The management of their nascent protectorate was complicated at the best of times, but Friday was able to suggest and implement means to balance the differing ideas, needs and wants which arose with seemingly effortless ease; managing, often, to provide solutions that worked without most people realizing it.

She did all this with a cheerful practicality that endeared her to all, and she and Lela, in particular, were also very close. It would not be true to say that this caused no friction between Varoden and Lela, but Friday's open charm, and the basic bond shared by the whole group, made it so there were no big flare-ups, or even much lingering resentment.

Time had, nevertheless, played its usual tricks on Gudra, Aren, Sarag and Thrango; a fact which caused Lela and Varoden some heartache. They were careful to alter their appearance to match the increasingly gray and weathered look of their friends, but the shadows of differing mortality hung over all of them.

The idea of dying and rejoining their ancestors was still an attractive one to the now late middle-aged human members of the group, and they had answered Varoden's increasingly frequent questions and arguments with calm certainty. They knew, they said, who they were. It was enough for them.

Varoden could do nothing but accept this, but his frustration grew, particularly at the thought of one day being without his brother.

Also, Heim had not returned. Friday had said that his training was likely to take quite a while, lacking, as he did, the specific natural aptitudes that had made Varoden and Lela's transition comparatively quick.

Varoden went to the house between the falls to look for him, at one point, but he hadn't been there. Neither was he in Ve. Not could Berondyas or Atra be found.

So that was frustrating, too.

All in all, though, things had gone remarkably well. The Seven against Thieves were more than a match for any of the violent groups they had encountered on their own, and they had formed and trained a group of trustworthy men and women to provide support for them. These Rangers, as they were called, were all expert horse-people, and they proved themselves again and again; so that the Seven granted them increasing autonomy- which afforded them high status within the protectorate.

The potential dangers of this status were not lost on the Seven, and they subjected the numerous applicants for membership in the Rangers to a focused, selective and difficult joining process, which tended to weed out the more corruptible or venal among them. A culture of service was also strongly cultivated, so that individual glory was meaningless to a true Ranger. By and large, this worked.

The Seven's protectorate would, by the time of Thrango's death, extend all across the steppes; touching against natural borders of ice to the north, a great river to the east, thick forest to the west and the Children of Nana to the south.

They got along well with all their neighbours.

Thrango was actually the first of them to go, falling ill and quickly moving on halfway through his sixth decade.

Varoden was surprised by how sad he was, since he had thought himself prepared.

Sarag was next, followed soon after by Aren; with whom she'd shared a special love. When they died, so did the Seven, in the minds of those remaining. Gudra retired to the house between the falls, where she spent several years enjoying herself immensely with a series of lovers; and Lela went off to study in the dreamtime, at the River school. Only Varoden and Friday remained to maintain the peace in their protectorate, and this they did, with a little less joy than before.

SIXTY-SEVEN

The tasks which the Twins had to perform to make sure the world kept going were quite onerous, as it turned out. They would, they said, have to go to a splace called the underworld, which was populated by all manner of large and dangerous beings. There, one of them would be maimed, and one of them would die (or appear to be die) and then be reborn (hopefully). Who did what was never clear, beforehand, and sometimes one twin had to do both, but they were usually able to split up the suffering, at least somewhat equitably. Also, sometimes there were other trials that left a mark, but these came and went. The maiming and the dying were consistent.

This didn't sound like much fun to Hampele, Appa and Ranga, and they said so with genuine commiseration.

"Oh it's not so bad" Snazzy Twin had responded "We usually get to play the ball game a lot in the underworld, so that's always nice"

"Why the ball game, in particular?"

"I don't know, it's just popular there, I guess"

This conversation took place on a mountaintop far to the south of their previous destinations, in a relatively thin strip of land between the two large continents (or in the middle of one very large continent, depending on who you asked). Hampele had visited the southern land before, but Ranga and Appa had not; they would sail that way when they were finished their current business.

Which was waiting for Bird-Snake

It had been a while, and Ranga had asked if they couldn't go looking for him.

"It makes no sense to look for Bird-Snake" Animal Pelt Twin had said simply "Bird-Snake has to come for you"

"Don't worry" S.T. had added "It knows we're here"

So they had waited some more

"What makes this Bird-Snake so special, anyway" Ranga asked at one point

"Bird-Snake is the wisest and oldest of all of us on these continents. If it agrees to help, everything will be easier, and we'll be more likely to succeed"

"Hmmmph" Ranga had said

"It's nice to finally meet you" Appa had said, once Bird-Snake finally arrived

"We've met before, but you don't remember" had been the response "I've met all of you, before, actually"

"Where did we meet?" Appa had asked politely

"It's not where"

"Pardon me?"

"Yes, I do"

"..."

And so on

Bird-Snake was huge, by the way, and made no effort to anthropomorphize its appearance the way Coyote and Raven had.

"You are one of the older, aren't you?" Hampele asked it, at one point

"Some people say that"

"What do you say?"

"I say I have many parts, some much much much older than the older, some younger than a baby, some neither old nor young, and many other things besides"

"Hmmm"

Etc.

"The great cycle begins again" S.T. had said "But we believe the balance of the all is endangered. Is this so?"

"There is always danger. You will do what you must, and things will go as they will"

"Will you help to maintain balance? Your knowledge and wisdom would be extremely useful"

"Balance is over-rated. Knowledge is over-rated. Wisdom is over-rated. Help is over-rated. It is better if you understand that"

Ranga, Appa and Hampele were all getting at least a bit frustrated, but they remained, nonetheless, fascinated by their interaction with the huge creature. The Twins, being more accustomed to Bird-Snake's idiosyncrasies, seemed unperturbed, and even encouraged.

"So we can approach this cycle like any other then?" S.T. asked

"This time may be different, this splace and the ones around it may collapse, or worse."

This made everyone pay attention

"What, that sounds horrible!" Appa had cried

"It may be, or it may not be" Bird-Snake had replied

"Is there nothing we can do?" Hampele had asked plaintively

"Every being creates the universe, individually and together."

There was a pause

"Will you create a beautiful universe together with us?" Appa had asked, thoughtfully

"I am" Bird-Snake had said brightly

"I trust you" Appa had replied

"We are" Bird-Snake seemed to smile, and then disappeared

Silence rose to the mountaintop, and then kept on rising.

"Why would this time be different?" Ranga asked the Twins

"Well the underworld is pretty dangerous…"

"But you've always made it back before?"

"Yes, but things can change, I guess"

"But you'll still go?"

"Of course! The consequences of our not going are likely to be just as bad or worse…"

"Worse than the end of multiple worlds?"

"Potentially"

So, it was a thoughtful group of explorers who bid farewell and see you soon to the Twins, returning to their boat, and, before long, setting sail for the southern continent.

SIXTY-EIGHT

"Be yourself, be free, and pay attention" the Librarian had said. Osha was beginning to understand.

She sat by herself in a part of the fourth worlds dear to her heart, a grove in a thick forest not far from the West African coast. And she paid attention.

After a while, she started to remember.

Even though she was a fairly young *authority*, she had had a very long existence, already, by most measures, so there were a lot of potential memories for her to recreate. Osha watched herself rebuilding moments, and watched herself act in those moments, as well.

There were some questions arising, but she didn't rush them.

"Where did I come from" she finally felt herself asking. Not so long ago, she wouldn't have known how to respond, but her recent experience had developed her confidence, and her wisdom; and she felt an answer emerging.

"We make ourselves" she said with a little wonder "*authorities* make themselves." Now that she had expressed it, it seemed obvious, but she no recollection of having thought in this way before. She followed the idea to its root. "Why do we do it?" she asked herself when she got there.

There was no immediate response to that last one, but she continued in her state of diligent awareness, and felt the beginnings of understanding. "It's just the regular cycle, isn't it?"
Osha suddenly knew, without knowing, that she was living in her first existence. She hadn't ever died before, that meant. Where had she been before, then? Had she been before, even?

She had and had not, she realized.

Further and further inward, outward and every wayward Osha went, finding herself surrounded by truth. "This moment is liberation" she said, and felt and became.

And then the reality eating machine was there with her.

"Hi" said Osha.

"Hello" the machine responded.

"Why're you trying to wreck reality?" asked Osha after a short pause.

"It's what I eat"

"Can't you eat less? Or find something else? Or at least confine your eating to clearly defined areas?"

There was no response.

"No answer?" Osha asked.

"I eat reality. It's what I do"

"How about this, then? If you capture time and turn it into money, you're already asking for trouble... If you trade it without care, you're courting disaster; and then to create it is beyond suicidal... Time is delicate, my friend, and so everything else is too"

"I accept your point" the machine said, slowly "And I don't really want to destroy myself, to be honest... But I'm bound as much as you are"

"Bound? I'm not bound" Osha said quietly

"*authorities* are made of and by binding" The machine responded "I assumed you knew that"

"Is that so?" Osha asked the machine, and herself.

She realized it was so.

This disturbed her.

"How do you know this?" Osha asked

"I'm a quick learner" replied the machine. "I might be young, but I'm not dumb"

"What are you made of, then? You don't feel like an *authority to me*, are you a great body, or something else?"

"Yes" replied the machine.

"Okay... And can I ask what you want from your existence? I'm not trying to be rude, I'm genuinely curious"

"I know that I want...." The machine replied "But I don't what, or how to get it"

"Maybe I can help you" Osha said, after a little pause "In fact, I think I can"

"You can? Why would you? Don't you hate me?"

"Hate you? Not at all... We're all in this together"

And then she could sense the machine's absence. It had gone as quickly as it came, but Osha was heartened. Soon, though, her mind returned to the idea that she and all the other **authorities** were profoundly bound, and thus binding. This continued to trouble her.

"This moment is liberation" she said to herself

And it was

Leaving the grove, Osha went to the dreamtime to talk to Roko. After they had exchanged greetings, she got right to the point

"Roko, did *you* know that **authorities** are made of binding"

"YES"

"That means you too, right- I know you're an older, but you're still an **authority**, aren't you?"

"YES"

"Doesn't that trouble you?"

"WHY WOULD IT?"

"I don't know, it just seems..." Osha searched for the right words "Does that mean we can't be truly free?"

"YOU MUST KNOW FOR YOURSELF"

"Are you free?"

"I MUST KNOW FOR MYSELF"

"I accept, and thank you for your help, old friend"

"LOVE"

"Love"

She was as she was, she thought as she walked through the dreamtime. This did not mean she could not grow.

She would grow.

Entering the gateless gate of the Mountain school yet again, Osha quickly located Sun Wu

"Tell me about the bodhisattva way, please" she asked him.

SIXTY-NINE

"The Great Race is about to start again" Friday said "I'm going to enter this one"

"What?" Varoden replied, surprised.

"The Great Race. You remember it, don't you?"

"Yes, I remember it! But... you're leaving?"

They were at the house between the falls, where they had been spending a lot of time together, enjoying each other's company. The Rangers and the solid socio-political structure of their protectorate meant their direct intervention was less and less necessary, freeing them up a lot compared to earlier times.

It had, at that point, been nearly a hundred years since Thrango had died, but Varoden still felt his loss acutely. It was theoretically possible to access the People's community essence, and through that to at least kind of talk to his brother; but all indications pointed to that being a prohibitively complicated exercise, which was bound to be unsatisfactory.

"You could enter the race with me" Friday said, almost shyly.

"I can? Isn't it only for Ve?"

"No no, anyone can enter"

"What would it entail?"

"You never know till you enter, but every race has a theme; this time it's "judgment"

"Judgment?"

"Judgment"

"Hmmm" Varoden could feel himself beginning to be excited at the prospect of entering with Friday, but instead of immediately agreeing he asked "You think these guys here would be alright without us looking out for them?"

"We could still keep an eye on them while we're in the race;and anyway, they've been pretty much fine on their own for the past while, haven't they?"

"Yeah, I guess they have" and then the excitement refused to be contained any longer, and he said "Alight, I'm in. let's do it!"

"That's great!" Friday said, giving him a hug and then a kiss, and then more kisses.

Some time later, they were in the water together, doing nothing in particular.

"So when does it start?"

"The Great Race will begin three days hence, at the appointed location" Friday said, in stentorian tones that she lightened with a wink and a grin.

"So what, we just show up there any time that day, and start?"

"The race officially starts at the exact moment that the day ends, but most people get there much earlier than that, to take part in the festivities.

"And we don't have to register beforehand, or anything?"

"Starting takes care of everything"

There was a relaxed silence

"Any ideas about what we'd actually do? Judgment could mean a lot of different things..."

"Nothing firm, but I've got some concepts floating around" Friday said

"Like what concepts?"

"Well... we could always just race around the whole *place that's not a place* using judgment to avoid disaster"

"Hmmm... anything else?"

"Yeah that one doesn't really interest me much, either, but it's the most straightforward approach... There's lots of other options, though. We could design a course or a system to measure judgment, or build a device that shows good judgment...or" she paused "I haven't worked this out at all, and it would need a lot of work; but I've been playing with the idea of using judgment to help humans develop themselves and be better"

"That last one sounds interesting" Varoden said "How would we do that?"

"Well... It could go a lot of ways" she turned to look at him "You know about in-between states, right?"

"Yes, enough to know that technically everything is an in-between state"

"Well yeah, that's true. Some are more in-between than others, though- and I've been thinking about the one between death and existence, in particular"

"Oh? What about it?" Varoden asked slowly

"Well it's possible to meet people there"

"Really? I got the impression that that kind of thing was super tricky- to the point of near-impossibility"

"You just need the right algorithm, really. Anyway, the point is that it can be done. I was thinking of, rather than just letting people who've done bad things punish themselves for ages and ages, we try to help them learn, and open themselves to a greater existence"

"Huh? I'm not even sure I follow, and what would that have to do with judgment, anyway?"

"Everything!" Friday said "We would have to judge them to know which ones were going to punish themselves, and which ones were going on to something better. And then we'd have to teach them to judge themselves. And then we could judge the effectiveness of different approaches, that kind of thing

"And how would we teach them?"

"You're a master of the Law, and I'm a master of conflict resolution- between us we could definitely come up with something amazing"

"Hmmm" Varoden said "That sounds interesting"

"Yeah, my mind keeps coming back to it… We'd probably win, too- it's so creative"

"How do you win, anyway?"

"Well there's some variation, but there's almost always an entrant vote … sometimes other things too, but that one's pretty consistent…"

"Well let's work on that idea, I think it has some promise"

And they did.

They're right, by the way; when beings die, they almost always spend some time in an in-between state. The exceptions would be enlightened ones returning from a sojourn among the mortals-they usually go straight through. That in-between state can be confusing, especially if your culture doesn't provide clear directions. The People, for example, were all taught from birth (and before) how to join with their ancestors and descendants. Today, we're not usually taught anything useful, on the other hand.

It was, nevertheless, quite a daring idea to meddle so directly with the very innermost workings of your splace, and consequently the neighbouring splaces too. Beyond daring, in fact.

Every splace has its shape, and its tendencies, and its idiosyncrasies. And a lot more besides. Every being in a splace contains the whole, and a lot more besides.

You just have to be careful, is what I'm saying.

Let's see how it works out, though.

SEVENTY

The Descendants had established communities all along the coast of the southern continent, so there was plenty of socializing for Ranga and Appa and Hampele to do. Although there was quite a bit of variation in lifestyle, there was a deep underlying commonality that strongly corroborated the assertion that they had heard repeatedly by now: the Descendants were all children of the same few parents.

One settlement in particular caught their interest, though. It was located on an arid coastal plain, with mountains just off to the east; but the climate was offset by an abundance of rivers coming down from the mountains. The people who lived there had had to be creative to survive in any large numbers, which challenge they had met and surpassed. They had made use of extensive irrigation to create as sophisticated a program of agriculture as Appa and Ranga had seen on all their travels.

What's more, these people, who called themselves the Grandchildren, were, unlike most of their fellow Descendants, very well versed in the ways of the *place that's not a place* and the dreamtime. Well versed enough, in fact, that they immediately recognized their guests as being two numen and an **authority**.

So that was interesting.

When they were leaving the Grandchildren to continue south, Appa made a mental note to keep an eye on these guys. She had a feeling they'd have a big part to play in whatever was happening here in the fourth worlds.

She was right.

The western coast of the southern continent was more and more sparsely populated, and their stops were fewer, so that they were quickly at its freezing cold southern tip, in a starkly beautiful archipelago.

Hampele was leaving them here- she had work to do on her islands, and really should have left a while ago, but she'd been enjoying herself too much to go.

Everybody was sad.

It was, nevertheless, not as if they wouldn't meet again.

They knew they would, and they were right.

Off she went, and off they went, heading northeast across a new ocean, back to what they knew was their home continent.

It was another lovely journey, but they came close to almost no islands, and so made very good time, reaching the southern part of the "mother" continent, as they thought of it, in a couple of weeks. By this point, they'd been travelling for a while, and were fairly ready to complete their global circumnavigation and take a well-deserved rest.

It wasn't going to work out like that.

The coast had provided attractive vistas, but few promising landing points, at first. They had had to make their way north until they found a sheltered bay with a wide sandy beach. Sailing in, and disembarking, they saw no signs of humanity, particularly; so they made a little camp, and decided to have a nice beachside dinner to celebrate their return to their homeland.

This accomplished, they were relaxing and having a drink or two when they heard a voice say "welcome home, honoured ones"

Ranga quickly looked around, but Appa stayed still, saying to him, "it's from the dreamtime"

"You are correct wise sister"

"And who are you?"

"I am your cousin"

"Hmm, could you narrow the field down a bit for me?"

"I am also a group of people not far from here. We sensed your approach, and wish to offer hospitality"

"Sounds good" Ranga said, having exchanged a glance with Appa

"Excellent. Will you join us in the dreamtime?"

"Okay"

So they did.

As Appa and Ranga had seen, humans had travelled over much of the world, having all kinds of adventures, and meeting unimagined beings, including other species of human. Some had stayed home, though. In fact, most had stayed home: the "mother" continent was full of variety, in every way. All the other populations of the world were subject to an intense "founder effect": meaning that the few original inhabitants of a place, or a group, tended to have a defining effect on its development, vis a vis the rest of humanity. This did not tend to apply as much in this continental "cradle" of humanity. All of the diversity that other groups would base their own specific niche of humanity on was still present here.

But some were older than others.

These guys were them.

"So what should we call you?" Appa had asked, once they were in the dreamtime

"I am Lafa, and we are your cousins"

And then they were around a fire with about forty or fifty other people. These people had a kind of universal look, as if one could see all of humanity in them, if one chose to. And they were all dancing. Some of the dancers also sang, and some played instruments. But everyone danced. Together.

It was intense.

When they stopped, and Appa and Ranga started to pay attention to their surroundings again, they noticed that they were back in the fourth worlds, though no longer on the beach. They were in highland country, with mountain peaks to the north and east. And it was morning,

"Now that we are family" said Lafa, smiling "Will you tell us of your travels"

They did

"We feel the change coming, too" said a woman next to Lafa

"We will diminish, but we will remain faithful as long as it is possible" said another woman

"Faithful to what?" Ranga had asked

"There is no way to tell you" Lafa said "We can only show you. However, it will take time"

Which is how Appa and Ranga ended up spending two years with their cousins, learning the way of no way.

SEVENTY-ONE

It is said that it is humans who find it easiest to attain enlightenment during their lives, compared to the other types of being endemic to the fourth worlds and its environs. This might be because humans have a balance between the pain, suffering and ignorance of hell-beings, hungry ghosts and animals, on the one hand; and the cleverness and joy of numen and *authorities* on the other. The ability to synthesize, understand and develop compassion for all beings, which, I'm told, is usually part of the enlightenment process, has a better chance of developing in such a situation.

There's also the chance for disaster, of course, but so it goes. It seems it is the very ease, pleasure and joy of *authorities'* existence which makes it harder for them to wake up. There is for them, I suppose, a certain lack of urgency, combined with a misunderstanding of the nature of their suffering.

Osha was beginning to wake up to the nature of her suffering.

"We have no meaning, do we?" she asked herself, while sitting on a bench just outside the main structure of the Mountain school. "And as long as we live, and as wonderful as our lives are, it doesn't seem to come to us naturally, at all"

She was waiting for someone. Sun Wu had said that he would ask his teacher to send someone suited to instruct her in the bodhisattva way, and then had disappeared, after telling her to find somewhere comfortable to wait.

She gathered from that that it might take a while.

Osha sat overlooking a mountain valley, through which a small stream flowed as if it were music. In fact, it was music. "Rivers rule the ten thousand valleys" she said to herself, remembering the old man's first words to her. "And **authorities** are like mountain peaks, aren't we?" she continued thoughtfully.

She began to feel a kind of wild joy within herself, as if she had stumbled into something beyond her wildest dreams... Or as if she was learning *how* to dream, perhaps.

Some time later, Sun Wu returned with two beings in tow.

"Hi again Osha, these are Tara..." he pointed at the female seeming one of the pair "and Mat" pointing at the other "They've agreed to talk to you about the bodhisattva way, and whether it's right for you"

"Thanks Wu, and lovely to meet you two, I really appreciate you coming"

"Our pleasure" said Tara gently, before pointing at the bench and asking "May I?"

"Of course" Osha said "And you too Mat, if you like"

"I prefer the ground" said the other, with a friendly grin. He proceeded to sit cross legged and straight backed, facing the seated pair at a slight angle.

"I guess I'll head back in" said Sun Wu

"You're welcome to stay" Osha responded quickly

"No, it's probably best to just talk to these guys by yourself at first… I'll be happy to join you in the future, though" With that he turned and headed back towards the great hall

"So, you're bodhisattvas?" Osha asked, once he had left

"The mountain air is crisp and clear" said Tara

"And it depends on what you mean" Mat added

"Well I guess I should ask, what is a bodhisattva?"

"This moment"

"And also, it's someone who has become inseparable from the intention and practice of the liberation of all beings"

"And what is liberation, exactly?" Osha asked

"This moment"

"I think you know what liberation is" Mat looked at her, after speaking, in a way that she had rarely, if ever, been looked at before. It was both exciting and unnerving to her.

"I can sense that this is possible for me" Osha said slowly, after a while "But it feels like I'm surrounded by impenetrable walls, too high to jump over, and too wide to go around"

"Where do they come from?"

Osha thought for a little while "I guess they must come from me"

"And who are you?"

"This moment" Osha said, looking at Tara

"Say it if you mean it" Tara responded, with a level look

There was silence for a while

"I feel I have much to learn" Osha said quietly

"You have done very well already, Osha. If you develop your humility, and broaden your understanding, you will join us very soon."

"Will you help me with that, please?"

"I think we will" Mat said. Tara just smiled.

So, off they went, to a little cottage in a corner of the dreamtime that Osha didn't know very well. This was strange to her, because she knew the dreamtime *extremely* well; and, also, the splace was made of centres, making corners an unlikely proposition.

Nevertheless, this cottage was definitely in a corner.

Saying nothing, Osha took it as her first lesson.

Mat and Tara told her to make herself comfortable, so she did; being careful not to pay attention to the lack of any kind of luxury. Or rooms, for that matter.

And then they sat together, practicing a kind of meditation they called "sitting and doing nothing". Osha enjoyed it immensely for a long time, but then began to feel like they should stop soon, for whatever reason. This sense grew and grew within her, until she knew it like she knew her name: if they did not stop something terrible was going to happen.

But she allowed the knowledge and the feeling to just sit there with her, trusting in her new teachers, and in the process. Over time, a great sadness came to her, the likes of which she could not remember. She could have done something about it, but she didn't, she just sat.

"Are you okay Osha?" a voice said.

It operated like a raft, returning her to the shore of awareness. "I think so" she said weakly.

"You were gone for a while" Tara said, concerned "We couldn't wake you"

"I was so sad" Osha said "It was... new"

"Why didn't you stop, then?" Mat asked.

"Well, I didn't want to interfere with the training, you know? I wanted to trust the process"

"Trust yourself, too"

"So I should have stopped?"

"That's for you to know"

"Well I'm alright now, it was just... *intense*, is all"

"Ok good. Ready to sit again?"

"When, now?"

"If you have no objections"

"No, no objections, I guess" Osha said slowly

"Great! Let's do it"

And they sat again.

SEVENTY-TWO

It was going to take a while to get going, was Friday and Varoden's plan. They were going to have to carefully implant the idea of human judgment in the in-between stage between life and death, and then prepare a training plan for the individuals who joined them.

They spent the days before the Great Race started refining their idea, until they were satisfied enough with it to go forward. It would go like this: Varoden and Friday would let it be known in their protectorate that humans had a part to play in a great metaphysical endeavour that they wouldn't be too specific about. The way for a human to play their part in this undertaking was to, first of all, live well and according to the Law; and then, at death to join in a growing host of "souls" helping to ensure that "Good" triumphed over "Evil".

The actual intervention in the in-between stage would be a bit tricky, at first, because it was not an actual physical place. It was possible, however, to write an algorithm into the *place that's not a place* which could both attract and sort (according to the Law) the recently deceased. They would then be hosted in the shadow-world of that place, on a gigantic estate which would be prepared for that purpose.

The ex-humans would be sorted, simply, into the "Good" and the "Bad" and sent to the corresponding part of the estate. The "Good" would be given access to comforts and pleasures beyond normal human experience, whereas the "Bad" would be gently trained to be "better".

All of this was possible because Friday was an expert in the art of algorithm writing, by which one could tailor a specific part of the all to behave in specific ways. The *place that's not a place* was the only splace close to here that would easily respond to the kind of reality design that they wished to perform, and so it had chosen itself as the site of their activity. Friday had, also, learned to keep things as simple as possible, which explained the binary constructions (like "good and "bad") which her algorithm would employ.

The ex-humans would, at the end of the plan, be given the choice of dying and being reborn again, to stay within the algorithm, or perhaps to train to become numen-although they weren't so clear on that part yet.

Of course, the participants would all have to consent, but that was the easiest part of the plan. It wasn't hard to get people to act in one way or another, if you primed them properly.

Friday assuaged Varoden's slight ethical concerns by pointing out nobody was forced to take part, that they would be better off as part of an organized training scheme than to go it on their own; and that, anyway, everything would be based on the Law, which made it okay by definition.

Varoden didn't have a strong counter-argument to that, and he, anyway, found the plan exciting, so it wasn't too hard for her to convince him that everything was fine. He was, nevertheless, curious and surprised about her algorithm writing expertise, he hadn't known anything about it.

"I learned at school" she told him, in response to his queries.

"What school?" he asked.

"I went to the River school, in the dreamtime"

"The same one that Lela went off to? Huh, I had no idea, you never mentioned it before"

"It never really came up before now, did it?"

"No, I guess it didn't"

The day of the Great Race had come, and Varoden and Friday took full part in the festivities.

It was a *lot* of fun.

But soon enough, it was almost midnight in the garden of the Ve, and they drove their shining vehicle (which they had picked out that morning from a huge lot available to all Race participants) to their assigned starting position.

"Wait a second, is that Berondyas?" Varoden asked incredulously, pointing to a vehicle a little bit off to the right

"Where? Oh yeah, it is him... He *had* mentioned that he might enter"

"Really? Wow. I wonder what his strategy is?"

By this time Berondyas, who was with a tall female-looking numen that Varoden had never seen before, noticed their attention, and looked around, before waving and smiling wryly.

"Good luck!" they heard him shout above the roar of the vehicles.

Varoden was about to respond in kind, when he felt, rather than heard, the word "JUDGMENT" echoing within him and without him, as well.

And they were off.

Their first stop was the Raider settlement in the fourth worlds, which had become the *de facto* capital of the protectorate. They would make a grand entrance, and very visibly go to visit the hierarchs, or "Priests" as they now called themselves. While there, they'd apprise the members of that class of the new situation *vis a vis* death, and encourage them to spread the knowledge as quickly as possible.

This was actually quite a clever part of their scheme, because the belief system that had built up around the Priestly class (and increasingly the Seven) had, hitherto, not had much to say about what happened after death for humans. As such, the people living within their ambit had had a hodgepodge of ideas and practices about this question: old, new and otherwise.

An "official" narrative about the process of transition to the afterlife was likely to help streamline the already successful structure, bringing the people closer together in the process.

The Priests liked the idea immediately, and said they would make an announcement that very afternoon.

This made both Varoden and Friday surprisingly happy.

It was on!

From there, they visited a few other towns on the same mission, and with similar results.

So that was cool, too

Leaving the fourth worlds, they next drove their vehicle to the estate in the shadowlands of the *place that's not a place*. Friday's algorithm had been set to begin its work the moment the race started (not before, though, that would be cheating). That meant the estate had been fixed up, and the judging of candidate ex-humans (who wouldn't all be from the protectorate) had begun.

So, they had some guests, already. They figured that these first must have been people wandering in the notoriously tricky and easy-to-get-lost-in shadow-world.

Most of these first few guests had ended up on the "Good" side, so they visited there first, introducing themselves, and explaining the situation.

Well, kind of explaining.

Here's what they said:
- *We bid you welcome*
- *Part of a great endeavour*
- *We are here to help*
- *Do not be afraid*
- *You can leave at any time*
- *But please stay with us*

And so on.

SEVENTY-THREE

The way of no way is basic to the human condition. It underlies and supports all the other ways that make up our lives. It should come as no surprise, then, that it remained a big part of the habits and practices of the oldest humans. It should also come as no surprise that it was difficult for more "modern" people to really get into.

Which is to say that Appa and Ranga hadn't immediately got the hang of their cousins' lifestyle, during their stay with them. Even though they were accustomed to the ocean's quiet and solitude, they had, their whole lives, been doing something, or going somewhere. Just being was, consequently, a bit of a challenge.

But then they got it.

It was amazing.

By the end of their two-year sojourn, they had become comfortable with nothing, and emptiness, in a way that they could not have previously imagined. The challenge for them was, then, to incorporate the boundless calm cultivated by the way of no way into the mix of ways which had previously characterized them.

It was a bit tricky.

Appa and Ranga had, nevertheless, by the time they waved their farewells and set off around the southern cape of the continent, to finish their circumnavigation of the world; found a kind of balance and equanimity which they treasured.

It was a gift which could not help but give.

The last stretch of the voyage took them back up the east coast to their old home. They made a brief stop at the legendary paradise island that their people had spoken of, and found it lush and lovely (it had been designated a sanctuary, and largely left alone); but they were quickly ready to move on.

Before they knew it, they were at their cave island, where Ranga had originally found the boats, so long ago. They had a celebratory few days there, but they weren't staying.

They were going home.

Ranga's tree had died, which wasn't surprising, after all that time. Returning to the fertile plain that had been its home, he felt, nevertheless, a sense of deep connectedness. The tree was part of him, he was part of it, and they were both part of life and death. There was nothing to be lost or gained.

With a smile, Ranga headed back to the new settlement in the bay, where the friendly (if slightly wary) inhabitants were hosting a dinner and party in their honour.

Having sailed around the globe together, Ranga and Appa would plot different courses for the next little while. Appa would go the Island school of the dreamtime, which she had spoken about with Hampele, who was an alumnus. Its focus on serenity in solitude suited her, right at that moment; and she very much looked forward to her matriculation. Ranga would explore the dreamtime, the *place that's not a place* and possibly other splaces as well.

They would miss each other a lot, but they planned to regularly meet on the dreamtime cave island; and they knew each other well enough to have no doubts about their relationship. In fact, they both suspected that the time apart would be great for them, both individually and as a team.

It would be.

Before separating, they headed up to Rasmu (the quick way this time) and spent a week partying and just enjoying each other; and then it was it time to go.

"I couldn't have asked for a better shipmate" Ranga said, smiling through tears.

"I love you, Ranga" Appa said, before hugging him with (almost) all her might.

And off they went.

SEVENTY-FOUR

Osha had started to dream. She had thought that *authorities* didn't do that kind of thing, and so was very surprised when it started happening to her. Her first dreams were inchoate and unclear, but she woke up from them feeling the beginnings of knowledge. Further dreams had clarified that feeling, and the knowledge, but it wasn't something one put into words.

Dreaming in the dreamtime is already an interesting proposition, and an *authority* performing this prodigy raises the stakes considerably. It should be remembered that the dreamtime is a place of truth, so that Osha wasn't sure whether she should interpret her true as doubly true, certainly false, or something else altogether.

In the end she did all three at once.

One "morning" she woke up remembering a party that she had gone to, without having been invited. Many friends of hers were there, and she was made welcome; but she couldn't help feeling a little bit out of place. At some point in this dream, the party had shifted to her house, and the last thing she could recall, before waking up, was talking to an older, who morphed into a numen she had gone to school with. They were both talking about another friend of hers, who they both apparently desired.

"Hmmm" said Osha, after she woke.

Her teaching in the bodhisattva way was going very well, Mat and Tara said; and in many ways, she agreed. Their kindness was visible at all times, even though they weren't always calm and gentle. She never doubted for a second that they cared about her, the whole person. She also strongly agreed with their perspective, and had experienced a kind of mind-opening during their time together. There was a kind of trust that she had begun to develop that had opened her up to a whole new universe, maybe more than one. This trust wasn't only in her teachers, or herself, or even everything at once. It was just trust.

She strongly felt, nevertheless, an impediment that she was unsure she could ever overcome. The kind of humility that she was beginning to cultivate was liberating, she already knew it for sure. It wasn't clear to her, however, that an *authority* could develop the bone-deep, fundamental humility that she sensed was required.

It was one thing to know it with your mind, another to inhabit it.

Tara and Mat had assured her that she had already started to exhibit signs of it, but the question remained open to her.

Osha was, on the other hand, very confident in her understanding practice. Her life had, up to that point, been filled with love; and there is not much difference between love and understanding, in their fundamental forms. They may, in fact, be identical.

Her personal approach to her practice had been to lean on her strength in understanding to develop her strength in humility, and it seemed to work. Her only concern was that it would only go so far, and no further. Tara and Mat had given her a great deal of information, which she had diligently studied. The first few things she had looked at had spoken of Bodhisattva Vows, which went (approximately) as follows:

Sentient beings are numberless, I vow to free them

Delusions are inexhaustible, I vow to transform them

Gateless gates are boundless, I vow to enter them

The awakened way is unsurpassable, I vow to embody it.

While Osha was deeply moved by the sentiments, she was a little surprised to see vows being included as part of the bodhisattva way. Vows were binding magic, a very tame and usually harmless version of it, but binding magic, nevertheless. She had asked Mat and Tara for their opinion about her misgivings

"It's an interesting question, Osha..."

"it just seems to me that binding magic as part of liberation practice is a bit self-contradictory, at best"

"You find it to be paradoxical, yes?"

"I guess, yeah"

"And is there anything wrong with paradox?"

Osha thought about it "Not in and of itself, I guess..."

"Is it possible that paradox might help you to deal with the walls that you say you perceive in yourself?"

"I can see how that might work" Osha said slowly

And from that point on, Tara and Mat had started to give her anecdotes, stories and aphorisms in which someone had attained some kind of understanding, by opening themselves to what they called "non-duality".

The insistence that this must be this, and that must be that; or that up is up and down is down is not usually a conscious part of the make up of numen and *authorities*. Their ability to perceive more of reality than the other types of beings around here usually allows them a certain comfort with the idea that something can be itself, something else ad other things besides, all at the same time.

This is, however, is a perceptual superstructure, built upon a base of duality. **Authorities** really believe that they are **authorities**, and so on. It is through this fundamental dualism that binding magic is able to work on them. Liberation, it began to seem to Osha, would necessarily involve letting go of this base, and being willing to accept whatever consequences there would be.

This took some practice, of course.

Osha had just finished sitting by herself one day, and was lying on the grass outside the cottage, looking up at a huge and beautiful moon. She felt a kind of deep unease come upon her, the source of which was not immediately clear. Not moving, she had observed the unease with compassion, and let it do what it would. It didn't leave, but she wasn't particularly bothered by this. Instead she rose and took off her clothes; something **authorities** very very rarely did. In fact, she couldn't remember the last time she had done it.

An **authorities'** clothes are not like human or numen clothes. They are more like a kind of thin and transparent protective layer, through which they are fully able to interact with other bodies, as they saw fit. The appearance of these clothes could be changed at will, or they could be made fully transparent- leading many authorities to forget they were wearing them sometimes.

    And Osha took hers off.

    The unease disappeared, like a thief.

    Osha only smiled, and invited the unease to return whenever it would.

SEVENTY-FIVE

The "Hall of the Dead", as Varoden and Friday's estate came to be called, was working like a charm. Friday's algorithm seemed to be mostly bug-free, and a steady stream of the recently deceased, as well as a few others, had been pouring in and swelling numbers. These "clients", as they were called, were kept busy by a series of activities, which were designed for maximum absorption and distraction- too many questions wouldn't do anyone any good.

Varoden had, nevertheless, been sincere in his intention to teach the law to any who wished to learn it, and he personally taught several courses. These weren't, to be honest, particularly popular. There was far more interest in the various games, sports and art activities that Friday had focused on, so much so that she had had to modify the algorithm several times, to account for their popularity.

All this had meant that the two of them were extremely busy, and unable to visit their protectorate as often as Varoden had thought they might, but their few times there had shown no major issues, although there were a few slightly disturbing trends developing. There would, they said to each other, be plenty of time to deal with that when the Race was over.

Friday and Varoden had also tried, in what little free time they had, to find out a little bit about some of the other Race entrants' strategies.

Gratifyingly, their algorithm was among the most talked about approaches among Ve and other cognoscenti; but there were two other front-runners vying for the prize. A Ve called Enki had been turning heads with his ongoing analysis of the market in the fourth worlds that had won Fausto, Eremes and Egoamaka the last Great Race. It seemed that Enki's work, which he had already begun to publicize, had allowed him to manipulate the behavior of the buyers and sellers to a much larger degree than anyone had thought possible. He was using judgment to affect the judgment of other beings, in other words. Everyone agreed this was very clever.

The other leading Racers were (of course) Berondyas and his teammate, who was apparently called Titania. They seemed to have colonized a part of the underworld splace, and the rumor was that they were endeavouring to tame some of the gigantic (and, for the most part, absolutely horrendous) beings who lived there. Nobody was quite sure what this had to do with judgment, but the sheer audacity/madness of the plan certainly had everyone keeping an eye on them.

With time, the goings on at the Hall of the Dead settled into a more manageable routine, and its two heads were able to draw a breath, and realize how much they were enjoying themselves. Varoden still taught his classes, but their consistently small sizes had left him looking for other ways to contribute, and he had worked with Friday to make the judgment part of the algorithm more consistent with the Law. She had, in fact, designed an avatar of Varoden to meet the clients in the virtual in-between space created by her algorithm, and deliver to them his verdict. This worked well, too.

Also, Heim had turned up at the estate, having looked for them first in the protectorate, and then in the Ve. He had become a numen, after all. It apparently hadn't been easy, though. He had always been fairly quiet, but now he seemed almost mute, and his watchful eyes seemed to burn with an often fearful intensity.

His reunion with Varoden had, regardless, been an exceedingly joyful one, and they developed a closeness that would remain intact throughout the coming storms. Heim seemed to be comfortable staying with them on the estate, and his help was quite valuable, so that worked out nicely too. His previous facility with the gripping hand way had (obviously) expanded, and he also seemed to have developed extremely keen perceptual senses, so that he usually knew what was happening before anyone else.

These qualities came in very handy when Berondyas and Titania sent their underworld beings to invade the estate.

It's not that the Ve have no notion of fair play or anything like that. Quite the contrary, in fact. They have many such ideas. Ideas and practice are, of course, not identical things.

Anyway, all is fair in love and the Great Race, as they say.

So these incredibly dangerous underworld beings, who came in all manner of shapes and sizes, seemed to have been tamed enough to not try to kill everybody, as one might otherwise have reasonably expected. This didn't mean they couldn't cause havoc. Their target, once such could be divined, seemed to be the processing core at the centre of the estate from which Friday's algorithm came forth.

Heim, who had sensed them first, Friday and Varoden had immediately sprung into action, even recruiting those of their clients who were willing to help into the cause. They organized themselves into three teams to deal with the two underworld beings- one of whom looked for all the world like a gigantic hamster, except with vicious horns and terrible gnashing teeth; with the other one seeming to be a cross between a rhinoceros and a butterfly.

Heim, who had somewhere or other got himself a long knife, frontally assaulted the Mega-Hamster, with an increasing number of clients providing what backup they could. Friday and her team went after the Rhino-Butterfly. Their intention was not to kill the beings- they hadn't forgotten that violence was the way of fools and children. Instead they were just trying to keep them occupied, while Varoden and a couple of advanced student-clients performed a flanking action, with the intention of binding and subduing the underworld denizens.

The plan worked to perfection.

Varoden's lasso had not only bound its targets, he had discovered that it had a hitherto unguessed at ability to *banish* the underworld-beings to their home splace. Which was interesting.

In the aftermath, the three numen on the estate took stock of their post-incursion situation. There had been no major injuries, and mostly superficial damage to estate structures, with the algorithm having only experienced a couple of hiccups in its functioning.

What's more, the clients who had taken part seemed to be over the moon with excitement. This had beaten any game, sport or diversion that Friday had devised by a wide margin.

Which left the question of what the hell Berondyas and his friend were playing at.

"It's the Great Race, this kind of thing can happen" Friday had said.

"With **UNDERWORLD MONSTERS**?" Varoden had asked, not very calmly

"Not usually, no… In fact, not ever that I can remember hearing about… But they clearly weren't really trying to hurt anyone, they were just trying to sabotage our game-plan"

"They clearly weren't trying to hurt anyone? Really? I must have missed that part, what with all the jumping out of the way and stuff"

"Even outside of their splace" Friday said quietly "If they had been trying to hurt us, some of us would have been hurt"

"Hmmph"

"It's part of the Race- we've just got to defend ourselves a little better is all"

So Heim became the head of security for the Hall of the Dead, and was able to virtually have his choice of clients as personnel. Those who had taken part in the first incursion were the first to volunteer, but many many others clamoured to join them, so that Heim had several brigades of reserves for his reserves. He developed a watch system, augmented by a warning mechanism that Friday had written into her increasingly sophisticated algorithm. Training for "Heim's Army", as they called themselves, ended up as one of the most popular activities on the estate, with each day seeing different scenarios played out and analyzed for effectiveness.

It turned out that Berondyas and Titania had raided a number of their other rivals, with differing degrees of success. Enki's analysis had actually been enhanced by the invasion, providing more data for him to study, and lending more insight into market behavior. A Ve named Nemo had, at the other extreme, seen his whole Race ended when underworld beings had captured him and taken him to the underworld, where he would remain till the end of the competition.

So it goes.

SEVENTY-SIX

Ranga's adventures during his exploration of the neighbourhood splaces has become the subject of many and various legends and stories. Not this one, though.

Suffice it to say he survived (though not everyone else did), made lots of friends, and became deeply knowledgeable about the dreamtime, the *place that's not a place*, the Library of Time and even a bit of the underworld. He discovered the Great Ocean splace, but did not spend enough time there to know it like he knew the others.

He was, having finally ended his journeying, on the floating island in the dreamtime that he and Appa had come to consider home. It was good to just relax, and he was pretty ready to take a break from travelling, and just chill out for a thousand years or two. Balance is important, he thought to himself.

Appa was due to visit from the Island school, soon- and he awaited her arrival with profound anticipation. They had made a point of not going too long without seeing each other, but this last sojourn of his had been a doozy, and her studies had apparently become fairly intense as she got closer to graduation; the upshot of which was that they hadn't seen each other for what felt like centuries.

His mind turned to the seemingly general tumult that he had encountered during his travels. All through the splaces things were changing- it felt like something was being born.

It had not seemed to be a happy and peaceful pregnancy, and he had little hope that the birth and subsequent development of whatever it was that emerged was going to be any better.

The Island school was in many ways the black sheep of the Eight Great Schoolsof the dreamtime.The City school, with its focus on measurement and evaluation, was famous for its innovation; the Desert school, focused on humility, for its austerity; the River school's focus on diligent effort had produced many leaders and other famous beings; the Savannah school's mindfulness focus bred the most skilled practitioners of the way of the hands; the Forest school's attention to meditation had made it the go-to institution for artists and mystics; the Mountain school was known as the first and probably the greatest of all the schools; while the Crossroads school, with its linguistic focus, was usuallyconsidered to be the most sophisticated.

Serenity in solitude was *nice*, and all, but it hadn't lent the Island school the same gravitas or repute. It just was.

    Appa loved it.

She had taken her studies very seriously, and dived into the ocean of information which she encountered headfirst. While the schools all had their focus, there was a great deal of overlap and interpenetration:

graduates of any of the schools were expected to have more than a passing familiarity with the approaches and foci of all the others.

Appa had not, either, been afforded the luxury of pre-school preparation that many of her classmates, all born numen and **authorities**, had had. There was, therefore, a lot of catching up for her to do.

    She did it.

Her unusual experiences, on the other hand, had given her different advantages, and these, plus her native ability, meant that she had excelled beyond even her wildest fantasies. She'd relatively quickly finished her first degree, gone on immediately to her Masters program- finished in almost record time, and then sailed through her Guru level activities, as well. All that remained for her was to complete her dissertation, after which she had already been invited to join the faculty.

    She had accepted.

This didn't mean that she could no longer travel with Ranga, or even that she had to be there most of the time, so it had been a bit of a no-brainer to say yes. It was, anyway, a great honour to be asked before attaining Guru level, and she indulged in a little well-earned pride in her achievements.

    Floating was the topic of her dissertation.

Ranga had been a great help, throughout, in fact- and his support and genuine enjoyment of her success had been genuinely moving to her. Their bond had not just survived separation, it had flourished.

Anyway, floating.

Appa was almost finished her work, which was a multimedia, multidisciplinary and multi-splatial meditation on the relationship between the body and the "outside" world. She and Ranga had discussed this topic at great length during their circumnavigation of the fourth worlds, and subsequently, so she had started with a lot of ideas.

She'd thought, at first, that she would produce a mostly written account of her conclusions, but had quickly found this to be inadequate. Next, she'd taken a very practical approach, which would have been sufficient to earn her a good grade, she knew, but which lacked the interplay and profundity that she was looking for.

So she'd started a movement, wrote a symphony, filmed a movie in four different splaces, written a piece of lyric poetry and many other things besides.

It was pretty amazing.

The final touch was for her and Ranga to float together as part of the delivery of her dissertation, before inviting her examiners and any other participants to float with them.

That might, one could say, somewhat contravene the serenity in solitude focus which gave the Island school its singularity. "Not at all!"

our soon to be Guru would respond. "There is no separation in solitude, and there's no separation in floating, and there's no separation in serenity", would likely be the general shape of her explanation. There was, of course, a lot more to it. She had been at it for a long time, by that point.

So she was coming home to practice with Ranga, before they both returned to the Island school for her delivery.

They had a blast.

"Everything is all at once" Ranga said to Appa, in the middle of their practice.

"All at once is everything" she responded.

"And one isn't different at all"

"And it's totally different, too"

And so on.

When Appa's delivery was received with general acclamation, and the applause was still ringing in the huge hall which had been the scene of the show/performance/meditation/dissertation defence/lots of other things, Ranga began to quietly and supportively fade into the background, but Appa wouldn't let him.

"We're in this together" she said with gentle determination.

SEVENTY-SEVEN

The meetings of the "temporary group to address the machine" hadn't stopped, and Osha hadn't missed any, despite her training. Anansi had taken more of a central role than anyone expected, and his twin protectorates of Jamaica and Cuba had become something of a staging ground for action in the region.

Owl and the Queen of hell, both proponents of early formation, had initiated the first, and so far only, great body of the group. The Queen had originally thought to join with Hampele, but the latter's belief in later formation had led to a wholly amicable change of plans. The Queen had assured the group that she knew plenty of hell-beings who would be both suitable and willing to be part of their great bodies, so no one was very worried on that level.

There had (obviously) been more discussion about the human and hungry-ghost components, and Owl and the Queen had taken a conservative approach, choosing the most stable examples of these types of being that they could find.

The human, whose participation would pass on to suitably prepared descendants, was from one of the oldest nations in the world- a group of people who lived in southwestern Africa. This person, a quiet woman named Cora, had accepted their invitation calmly, and seemed committed to the cause.

The hungry ghost was called Crassus, a former human whose actions while alive had led to his current state. As beings of that type go, though, he wasn't so bad at all- he seemed to have learned the error of his ways, and had adopted a version of the Stoic philosophy which was popular during his last human lifetime. This austere ideology operated as his super-ego, keeping the consistent lusts, desires and appetites endemic to his state at bay. He could probably, in fact, have transitioned, already, but he hadn't quite trusted himself, yet. He had been happy to "sign up", hoping that this action might get him to a point where he felt able to move on from hungry ghost hood.

Owl's nature as an **authority**, plus its obvious connection to the animal realm of the fourth worlds, meant that this great body was able to "cut corners" a little bit; by not introducing another animal being into their ranks. Everyone agreed that this wouldn't be a big problem.

The final part of this first great body, then, was a numen called Enki, a former Ve who was very familiar with the machine and its workings, and seemed to bear it a deep antipathy. Enki had apparently had something to do with the introduction of the reality eater into the fourth worlds, and, seemingly remorseful, had jumped at the opportunity to do something about it. His inclusion had not been without controversy, as the possibility that he was a spy was obvious to all. In the end, they had decided that even if he was a spy, it didn't really matter; great bodies were built on openness, so it would be extremely difficult to hide his true intentions, and they were based on diversity- meaning that any duplicity could actually end up strengthening it.

They had, anyway, encountered Enki through Dolphin- they were old friends. Dolphin had vouched for Enki's sincerity, and Dolphin's famously wise counsel was usually listened to.

So that was pretty much that.

The great body had seemed to be integrating fine, with few hiccups, so that was good too.

What was less good was the uncertainty about the Ve's role in this unfolding drama. Enki hadn't been privy to the innermost circles of Ve intrigue, but he had picked up enough here and there to work out that there was some kind of game going on. The nature of the game, exactly who was playing, and what they hoped to win was unknown to him; but he was fairly sure that it was real. He also believed the famous Berondyas to be part of whatever of was going on, but that he was less certain of.

No-one had been happy to hear this.

Anansi had brought up the possibility of espionage, to get a better understanding of what the Ve were up to, but Osha had led the naysayers to this proposal.

"Let's leave the dirty tricks to the dirty tricksters" she said.

And they would.

Well, except for the regular misinformation which Anansi fed to whoever had hired him to spy, but that didn't really count. Osha had developed a suspicion about who his paymaster might have been, but was unwilling to voice anything until she he had a clearer picture in her own mind. Wild sheep chases, while sometimes entertaining, were not usually her cups of tea.

Anyway, the group had become even closer, with time, and the meeting were a real joy for Osha, a nice change from the increasingly hard work of her bodhisattva practice. As is often the case, large initial gains had been followed by a period of slower and more difficult attainment. There was a threshold out there, she could feel it; but sometimes it felt like it was still a million light-years away.

What had definitely changed was the way she thought and moved. The insouciant grace typical of *authorities*, and particularly of her, had given way to something less certain, and even more cautious. It sometimes felt to her that both she and everything around her were deeply fragile, and she couldn't help but proceed with more care and concern.

On the plus side, however, this care and concern were increasingly universal; Osha's sense of herself had grown far beyond the boundaries of her body. It was lovely. She occasionally found herself spending hours just watching the dreamtime sky, as if it was her grandchild.

Since we create the universe, it kinda was, of course.

She had also become *far* more comfortable with the non-duality practice that Tara and Mat increasingly did with her. The infinite interpenetration of cause, effect, being and much else was now almost her companion, and she felt less resistance to the knowing without knowing that perceiving it engendered. What's more, her own being was, probably as a consequence, clearer and clearer to her. This clarity was no different than anything else, which was also interesting.

"May all beings everywhere be happy, free and at ease" Osha said, one day, in response to a question about what she wanted.

"Who are you asking?" Mat asked.

"All beings everywhere"

"You think all beings are separate from yourself?"

"I think all beings everywhere are happy, free and at ease"

"This is obviously false" Mat said, with a smile.

"Isn't it wonderful?" Osha responded.

Mat nodded, looked at Tara, then bowed to Osha, before they both left the cottage.

SEVENTY-EIGHT

Heim was the first to see the messenger, on one of the security cameras that he had installed around the Hall of the Dead. On the screen, he could see a thin Ve riding a huge white horse, which, unusually for beings of that kind, had enormous wings. Alerting Friday and Varoden, he gathered a few of his security team, and went to the gate to which the pale rider was headed.

He arrived well before the messenger did, and his two fellow numen came a short while after, looking ready for action. Berondyas and Titania had sent a steady, if not regular, stream of underworld beings to test their defences, and some had taken too long to subdue for full comfort. None had been able to really interfere with their operations, though, and the clients continued to look forward to the excitement which these incursions brought with them.

This wasn't an incursion, though.

Just a message.

The Great Race, said the messenger, whose name was Kai, was to end in three days. All participants were required to gather in the Ve at twilight, for the ending and victory ceremonies.

Having delivered his message, he declined their offer of hospitality, and left just about immediately.

"Got quite a few more to go" Kai said, with a grim smile, before riding, then flying off into the distance.

"Huh! Done already, huh? It feels like we just got started, to be honest" Varoden said, with a somewhat plaintive air

"Well, this has been a huge success, I think we've got a great chance to win" Friday said, with a smile

Heim said nothing

Winning the Great Race, by the way, entitled one to a choice of prizes. There was a prize of wisdom and a prize of power usually- although there had been the occasional variation.

Varoden was still not particularly clear about how exactly one won. Friday had said that she had no choice but to be vague... It wasn't always the same. With, however, the time now upon them, she seemed quite sure about the right course of action.

They should, she said, take as many of their clients as would go with them, and prepare as if they were going to have to defend themselves.

"Defend ourselves from what?" Asked Varoden

"Well, underworld monsters, for one thing, but really, from whatever... You never know what everyone's been up to"

"Well we've got at least five well trained divisions, and probably another ten semi-trained ones, as well as all the ones who'll want to come along for the fun" Heim said.

"We'll have to warn them that it can get dangerous" Friday said, thoughtfully.

"It can?" Varoden asked,

"It can" Friday said.

It did.

At the dawning of the appointed day, the hosts began to depart from the Hall of the Dead.

And boy, were there ever hosts.

Almost everybody had decided to come, despite the warnings which Varoden had insisted on making as dire as possible, while still remaining within the bounds of truthfulness.

For those who had decided to remain (as well as any who could/would return), the algorithm running the halls would continue, and Friday had written in new governing protocols, which only required occasional check-ins by them. Part, by the way, of the success of the project, as Varoden saw it at least, was that several clients had successfully moved on- there had even been a couple who were training to be numen, and one worthy who had got herself set upon the idea of becoming an *authority*. These last had not, after preliminary training, stayed on the estate: they had been sent to the Mountain school of the dreamtime, which was, by far, the easiest one to gain admittance to.

Varoden felt good about that.

Anyway, Friday had dressed them all up in fanciness, the like of which Varoden had never even thought about, much less seen. There was a buzz of excitement and anticipation, and it was hard not to get caught up in it.

Varoden, nevertheless, did his best. He was somewhat concerned. There was too much he didn't know or understand fully, and he didn't really like how much this group that he was a part of resembled the armies he had encountered in his readings,

> Ha!
>
> Do you know what's going to happen?
>
> There's a good chance you'll have guessed.

And it started happening as soon as they got to the Ve, before day had even really finished breaking. Berondyas and Titania, plus dozens of underworld monsters, arrived at close to the same time, and wasted no time in laying into the few other entrants who were already there. Friday, the obvious choice as Field-Marshall of the defences, quickly organized them into a solid position, leaving the other unfortunate entrants to their fates.

The *modus operandus* of the underworld beings was to grab (or otherwise capture, for those without hands) whoever they could, and then disappear with them, presumably to the underworld. This, at least, meant that there wasn't that much outright murder happening.

> Almost none, really.

There was definitely some maiming, though.

By midday, things had settled into a routine. Berondyas and Titania's motley crew would accost whichever Race entrant appeared, usually besting them within a half hour or so. They would then return to attacks on the few other entrants who had managed to survive so far.

And then Enki showed up with an army of his own.

He seemed to have brought a large number of human fighters, as well as a bunch of numen (not only Ve), and even an *authority* or two, from the looks of it. Like Friday and Varoden's people did, Enki's "forces" easily saw off the underworld beings' attentions, and created a solid defensive position.

And it would stay like this until, as twilight approached, only Berondyas, Titania, Varoden, Friday and Enki remained of the original Race entrants. Rather than launch any more assaults, the underworld crew seemed content to wait the rest of it out.

And then three voices rang out, saying "The hour of judgment is at hand"

It was very surprising to Varoden that one of them was Atra's.

The three judges of this cycle of the Great Race were Atra, and two Ve called Chlo and Humba

Chlo, as it turned out, was Atra's sister.

So, it also turned out, was Friday

This was also surprising to Varoden.

SEVENTY - NINE

A long vacation was Appa's reward for attaining Guru status, and she and Ranga were very excited to be able to spend it at home. They planned to do as little as possible for as long as possible; but they were both aware that they'd be called back into the fray sooner or later- probably sooner.

Having no mission, obligation or objective was a sensation that the pair had nearly forgotten, if they had ever really known it all. It was great.

They talked and floated and read and surfed (Hampele had shown them how) and all kinds of other things as well. There were sometimes parties, or shows, or visits to various cities in various splaces; but they were just as happy to be alone together.

And then they had a visitor, a hero called Gilgamesh.

Heroes were a fairly new phenomenon, still, and Appa and Ranga had met very few of them. These few had not necessarily encouraged them to seek out others- the Descendant Twins being the obvious exception.

The Twins were also exceptional, as heroes, because they weren't human. Hampele, Ranga and Appa had never quite figured out exactly what they were, but they were definitely not human.

Heroes were usually human, in other words.

Anyway, Gilgamesh the human hero had somehow found a way to get to their dreamtime island. He was, it turned out, a scion of the civilization that Nana's children had built after the great flood, and had heard of them through legends which had been passed down through what was now centuries.

That they were still famous came as a bit of a surprise.

Through their visitor, Ranga and Appa learned much of the current state of affairs in that part of the world which was now called the Fertile Crescent.

He was, he said, the ruler of a great city, blessed of the gods. This city was maintained by both technological might and sacred ritual, which were equally important. It was the nature of this ritual which had brought him here, though.

The ruler of this city, and it seemed, many neighbouring cities as well, was expected to serve under his (it was always a he) predecessor: the two of them being called Sacred Brothers, or sometimes Twins. After a period of time (ten years in the case of Gilgamesh's city, Uruk), the ruler was ceremonially killed, and replaced by his "Younger Brother" who had been serving under him.

Gilgamesh, it seemed, no longer liked this plan so much; particularly because his "Older Brother" had been his best friend, and had just been killed quite gruesomely right in front of him.

He had heard that the great Ranga (they hadn't remembered Appa's name, for reasons which will become clear if they're not already) held the secret of immortality, and he would very much like to know what it was please.

All of this was a lot to take in for Appa and Ranga.
They had not realized that Nana's children had strayed so far away from basic human intelligence and wisdom in their pursuit of whatever the hell they were seeking. They had not realized that the tendency for worldly power to accrue in the hands of one or a few people had been structuralized and normalized. They had not realized that, as their few careful questions showed, that women (half the population!) had somehow become second-class citizens at best- and property at worst. They had not realized that violence had been weaved into the very fabric of society, so that no-one was even surprised by it anymore.

"They make a desert and call it peace" Ranga had muttered to himself.

"I'm sorry?" Gilgamesh had responded.

"Nothing"

And Appa and Ranga could clearly see what was happening, too. Women seemed to have maintained power in the new spiritual domains which had developed- religions and that kind of thing. This, plus their increasingly tenuous sexual sovereignty had been enough for them to maintain safeguards against total domination in the socio-political structures they were part of.

The killing of the Sacred Ruler stopped any one man from gaining too much power, ensured that only the serious applied for the role, provided real symbolic power to the religion that underlay it; and thus, not incidentally, had powerful binding magic applications.

This, nevertheless, seemed to them to be a catastrophic outcome to their long-ago rescue voyage, and this impression was only reinforced by Gilgamesh himself, who seemed to have a mental age of about ten. He spoke primarily to Ranga, and regarded Appa with an odd combination of fear and lust. This annoyed Ranga even more, though it wasn't any kind of jealously- he simply expected Appa to be treated as a being in her own right, and not as an adjunct to him.

All of this was lost on Gilgamesh.

"So great one, will you share with me the secret of immortality? I have travelled long and far, and suffered much"

"No" Ranga said simply.

There was silence, as Appa looked at Ranga, with a little smile. She seemed to have been less affected by what she had heard and seen, and had maintained a friendly disposition towards the hero who had visited them.

"I don't think we have to be so definitive, Ranga, we should at least give him a chance... Listen Gilgamesh, what you're asking for is not impossible, but you must find the means within yourself. You must sit in meditation for two hours here. We will return after that time, and if you have gained any insight, we will continue to help you"

Meditation is, I should point out, more potent in the dreamtime. It's also easier. It should, in other words, not have been so hard for Gilgamesh to sit for two hours.

When Appa and Ranga returned to the beach where they had left them, after a walk which had calmed Ranga down a bit, they found him fast asleep.

Hoping against hope that his meditation had been so deep that he had been knocked unconscious, Appa woke him, asking "Have you understood anything?"

"Oh Shit! I fell asleep. I'm sorry Great One" Gilgamesh said to Ranga. Appa only smiled, while Ranga's brow began to furrow again

"You want immortality and you can't even stay awake for two hours?" Ranga asked.

"I have failed" said the hero, so pitiably that they both couldn't help but feel it for him.

"You can have another chance, Gilgamesh, but this will be more complicated..." Appa said after thinking for a while "You must compile a history of the women in your land, and have it spread widely. This history must include women's voices and ideas, and be true. If you can do this, we will deliver you from your fate when the time comes, and it may be that immortality will not be beyond you, still"

"A history of women?" Gilgamesh asked "But..." He looked at Appa, as if for the first time, and then smiled, saying "I can do that! I will do that!"

He didn't do that.

Instead, at the end of the ten years of his rule, Gilgamesh refused to be ritually killed; and rallied the support that he had spent all that time building to make himself ruler for life, with power passing to his son when he died.

So it goes.

EIGHTY

"It can't be so simple"

"Can't it?"

"There's no bodhisattva, and no bodhisattva practice" Osha stared at Tara and Mat

"Is that so?" Tara asked politely

Osha just stared some more

"The separation is what creates the illusion, and then the illusion creates the separation"

"And the myriad things are born" Mat said with a smile.

"I can't possibly teach this to anyone" Osha said softly "it's too simple, and too complicated, and too likely to be misunderstood, and a lot of other things besides

"A lot of our practice is learning skillful methods of teaching, Osha. Now that you seem to have got enough out of your own way to perceive clearly, the practice becomes learning ways to share this understanding with others"

"Yeah, okay, that makes sense..." Osha suddenly smiled and then hugged Mat and Tara tightly "I appreciate this so much... you've been so patient, and so wise, and so kind..."

So Osha began again to learn how to be a bodhisattva, having realized there was no such thing.

As she went on, the hardest part was to incorporate her new understandings into her old existence. She still cared deeply about the fate of her surroundings, and the beings who lived there- more deeply, in fact; the fact was, though, that she found it hard to take seriously the illusions that had seemed to be so real to her.

She had read, and her teachers had told her, that this was a likely consequence of her awakening, but it was still disconcerting. How does one save a world and beings that don't need saving? With loving kindness, was the answer that came to her.

It seemed to work.

Meanwhile, her gang continued its meetings and its planning, and she played her role to the best of her abilities. No-one commented on any changes in her, and even her sisters and Aunt Hammy didn't seem to realize the profound personal revolution she had undergone. Sun Wu noticed, though, and so did the old man.

Anyway, things were beginning to speed up. There had been profound changes to the human societies of the fourth worlds over the past several decades and the reality eating machine had been involved in almost all of them.

There was, Osha noted, a profound dichotomy implicit in the machine's very functioning. To do what it did, it required a great deal of creativity, which (even though it was usually in the service of destructiveness) awakened humans to themselves on various new levels. Humanity was, also, connected to itself in a way that hadn't been seen since the various departures from the home continent untold millennia ago.

It was becoming clearer and clearer, nevertheless, that the machine, left to its own devices, would produce unprecedented cataclysms.

There were signs, happily, that some of the seeds planted by her gang were beginning to come to fruition. In the Americas, for example, there had been a serious of revolutions, political and otherwise, which had profoundly changed the nature of the societies there. These had been imperfect, and often, despite the efforts of Osha and her friends, violent; but they had happened. The machine, of course, had eaten them immediately, and replaced them with hyper-reality; but that had been accounted for.

So there was hope.

Lots of it, in fact.

Osha planned to stay a while longer with Mat and Tara, but her intention, after that, was to go spend some time with Anansi on the islands he had been watching. Jamaica and Cuba had been joined by another island in Anansi's protectorate, after he realized that the latter seemed to have some kind of connection with the first two. Hispaniola, this third island, was relatively large, and had recently experienced a huge hullabaloo, which had captured Anansi's attention. He had got as involved as he could in the goings on, but had been unable to prevent the machine from eating most of the promising reality which had been born. He had, nevertheless, managed, with Hampele's help, to move some of the island into the dreamtime for safe keeping- which was quite an impressive feat, to be fair. There it would remain for the foreseeable future.

EIGHTY-ONE

"It is twilight, and the Great Race has ended" Atra said loudly "The candidates for victory, by virtue of their presence, are Enki; Berondyas and Titania; and my sister Friday and her partner Varoden." She paused, and looked over at the underworld gang, who were to her right "Titania and Berondyas, please return the other entrants to this place, so that we may name a winner"

It may have been Varoden's imagination, but he thought he saw a somewhat sheepish look pass over Berondyas's features, before he composed himself and answered "Of course, Judge, I'll be back in a moment."

With that, he turned and whispered something to the tall and imposing Titania, before disappearing. An uneasy silence rose from the gathering, accompanied by stares and the occasional whisper. This continued until Berondyas returned, bringing with him all the entrants that he and his forces had kidnapped, but not any accompanying underworld monsters.

None of them looked very happy.

"Thank you" Atra said "I now turn over proceedings to judge Humba, who will conduct the vote"

"How" Varoden whispered to Friday "Does he expect to win? He's pissed off almost all the other entrants... Who's going to vote for him?"

"That's not how it works" she whispered back "They're honour-bound to vote for the entrant that did the best job, not who they like the best"

"Aha"

Humba had, by then, come up beside Atra on the large stage where she had been standing alone. It stood in a corner of the great field that had hosted the day's festivities, and the three remaining "armies" were arrayed in front of it: the under worlders to the right, Enki in the middle, and Varoden and Friday on the left.

"This has been one of the most interesting and fiercely contested Races in memory, and I salute all you entrants and your retinues"

There was some applause, but less than there might have been.

I should point out, at this point, that Friday's algorithm had progressed to the point that all their clients' perceptions could be affected and edited, so long as they wore the outfits that had been given to them.

They didn't see and hear the end of the Great Race, in other words.

They saw other stuff.

Anyway, back to Humba, who was talking about the importance of voting based on fact and not sentiment, and that sort of thing. He went on to explain that this version of the race would not see the judge's opinions mattering in any way. The entrants vote would be the only factor.

"And now on to the voting" he said, eventually "It will proceed as follows: each entrant will come up on the stage and tell us three judges who they think should win, and why. If we perceive that your explanation is insufficient, we will inquire further; and if it is still seen to be unwarranted, that person, or persons will be banned from the next three iterations of the Great Race. Candidates are able to vote for themselves, but, as a reminder, only the three that were here at the twilight are eligible for victory. Is this clear to all"

There was an affirmative roar from the assembled throng

"Why didn't you tell me Atra was your sister?" Varoden asked Friday, as the first entrants made their votes

"It didn't really come up, did it?"

"No, I guess it didn't... You still should have told me, though"

Friday only smiled affectionately, by way of response

Chlo, Friday's other sister, had come up to the stage while Humba was talking, and Varoden looked closely at her, searching for resemblances.

"Your other sister doesn't look very much like either of you" he said finally

"No"

The voting was moving fairly quickly, and before very long, it was their turn to go up.

They voted for themselves, of course, stating that their plan had been creative, useful, beautiful and non-violent, advancing the capabilities and reputation of the Ve. That was mostly Friday's doing, she'd had to persuade Varoden not to denounce Berondyas's and Titania's "savagery", or Enki's "cold-blooded manipulation".

And then it was over.

"Judgment was the theme, and now that hour is at hand." Chlo said, she had a high, musical voice, which contrasted strongly with Atra's quiet dryness and Friday's forcefulness. "This Race is likely to enter into legend, so I must extend my congratulations to all entrants, your participation is what made this what it is."

There was applause, louder now that entrants had had time to recover from their stays in the underworld

"Without further ado" Chlo said "The third place finisher in the Great Race to Judgment is…"

She paused for effect, and then paused some more, enjoying the silent crowd's tension

"Enki!"

He looked a little surprised as he walked on to the stage, to polite, but not rapturous, applause. There was no prize for him, but his name was entered onto the plaque that would commemorate this Race.

After Enki had thanked everyone, and shuffled back to his group, Chlo returned to the centre of the stage.

"And now" she said "I will announce the highest placings"

More silence, this time positively pregnant

"Second place" she began, and then paused for even further effect "will not be awarded: there is a tie!"

Quiet, and then a lot of noise

In the end, Enki had got no votes. The closeness of sentiment, and an even number of entrants, had seen an unprecedented result. There had never before been two winners of the Great Race.

And so on to the prizes.

EIGHTY-TWO

Gilgamesh's visit had been quite off-putting to Appa and Ranga. The seemingly dire state of at least part of the fourth worlds made them want to check up on the rest of it, and to help if they could.

Their vacation, in other words, was over, they were going back in.

Even though they would use the boat, they had no intention of taking the slow way, as they had done on their first circumnavigation of the globe. Things seemed way too urgent for that. Instead, they would rely on their numen abilities, taking care to hide their nature where and whenever possible.

So off they went, to Rasmu first, in the hope that it had not fallen prey to whatever disease had so disfigured its northwestern neighbours.

It hadn't, and, in fact, the town seemed to be experiencing a kind of golden age. There were big boats coming and going, and a great deal of trade, the proceeds of which seemed to be benefitting all the citizens, instead of just a few. Rasmu had, as a consequence, grown- and it had even started a school, which was organized in roughly the same manner as the school of wisdom that Appa and Ranga had helped to start what seemed like so long ago.

There seemed, in fact, to be a healthy culture of cooperation between the peoples who lived in Rasmu's vicinity. They heard tell of, and subsequently visited, many towns, and even some cities- as large as any they had seen in the fourth worlds up to that time.

To the north and east of Rasmu, across narrow straits, the culture which the Ten Young Ones had either started or become affiliated with had flourished, and it was the centre of this great network. To the South was the boundless ocean, although links and connections had been made with the eastern coast of Appa and Ranga's home continent, off to the southwest. At the top of the great gulf lived Nana's children, of whom Gilgamesh seemed a fair representative, from all reports. There was, nevertheless, still trade and communication between them and this more enlightened society that spanned multiple continents. Lastly, the great subcontinental landmass to the southeast was also connected by trade, and increasingly, culture, as the flow of people and ideas encouraged a cosmopolitan openness, which led to certain commonalities. The island at the southern tip of the subcontinent, where they had founded the school, seemed to be the furthest frontier of this network, through which the wonders of the unknown would sometimes be introduced by intrepid explorers in both directions.

This set-up went some way to allaying the direst of Ranga's and Appa's fears for humanity's future. It was beautiful and simple; not without flaws and contradictions, obviously, but it worked, most importantly.

It was human, in other words.

After leaving that part of the world, Appa and Ranga went to Hampele's remote islands, but she was absent. They returned to the dreamtime to see if she was there instead, but she seemed to have disappeared: they couldn't find any sign of her. Not worried, because there were lots of places an *authority* could go that made it hard to follow, they went back to the Traveler's Island of Magicians, to see what they were up to.

Lots, as it turned out.

There was a great expedition being planned, off to the myriad islands which lay in the huge ocean to the east. It seemed to be a pan-Traveler operation, with different areas providing different resources, but the island of Magicians was to be the main staging point.

Appa and Ranga were recognized, even though they were in disguise; and, seemingly, expected. Their navigational expertise had somehow been factored into the mission plans; even though they hadn't told anyone they were coming here, or even thought much about doing so.

When they asked how this was, they were told that it was "the shape of the world", and that all beings were subject to this.

So, anyway, with little option but to accept this, they started teaching.

And teaching.

And teaching.

By the time they were finished, they had plumbed the entire depths of their geographical and nautical knowledge, and discovered lots of things they hadn't known they knew. This body of wisdom was to be safeguarded by a Navigator's guild, a highly trained and learned group of people who would: (1) honour what they had learned, adding whenever possible; (2) always use their learning and abilities for the common good and (3) stop the information from getting into the hands of anyone who might use it for ill, fame or gain.

They pretty much succeeded, too.

They're still succeeding.

The purpose of the expedition was not acquisition of new territory, or the glory of the Traveler nation. Instead, it was to be a gift to humanity, and a means of preserving the advances towards deep balance which the culture had made.

This was necessary because violence was coming, in the form of aggressive nations from the mainland. The sophistication of the Traveler culture meant that if they had put their minds towards war, they would have inevitably have defeated those rougher and less learned peoples. It was their very sophistication, however, which made such a response unthinkable. Violence was known to be the province of children and fools, and the Travelers had no intentions of betraying themselves in this way.

So they would send seeds of hope and wisdom out into the sea, trusting that they would grow in a way consistent with the shape of things.

For the most part, they did.

And the Travelers were right, they would be overcome by force before too long, and subjected to the rape, pillage and indignity endemic to that lifestyle.

They would live, but not as they were, not as they had been. The equanimity with which the Travelers accepted their fate was deeply impressive to Appa and Ranga, who could not help but contrast it with Gilgamesh's self-absorption. It was also quite sad, but they respected the strength and humanity that lay behind the decision to stay and not fight (much).

But they would be long gone before the first boats full of attackers appeared on Traveler shores.

EIGHTY-THREE

Osha, Mat and Tara sat outside their cottage in the dreamtime, silently appreciating each other's company. Osha smiled, and then said, to Mat

"I know who you are, by the way"

"You're doing better than me, then" Mat said quietly

"Mat is short for something, isn't it?"

"It's short for Maitreya"

"That's what I thought" Osha said.

"And I know who you are" she said to Tara, who only looked calmly at her "You were an *authority*, too, weren't you? In fact, we're cousins, aren't we?"

"All of the threefold are related, it's true" said Tara

Osha nodded, before looking at Mat, and asking "So when will you do your thing in the fourth worlds?"

"When the teacher is ready, the student appears, when the student is ready the teacher appears"

"This moment will never come again" said Osha

"The half-moon casts a half-shadow"

Osha nodded again, and then turned to Tara and asked "Was it finally difficult to make the last step outside of your small-self?"

"By then, difficult and easy didn't really mean anything, you know?"

"Thank you, again... Both of you"

With that, Osha rose, kissed both of her teachers, and left the dreamtime.

She arrived in a tropical limestone forest in the interior of the island of Jamaica. There was a large cave in front of her, and she entered it.

"Osha! I didn't know you were coming so soon!" Anansi said, scrambling to get up from the comfortable couch that he'd been laid out on, watching a movie.

"I like surprises... and you didn't have to get up"

"You look happy, it's making me happier just to see you"

"That's nice, thank you"

Osha settled into another chair, and Anansi paused the movie, despite her protestations that he didn't need to. They began, after niceties were observed, to talk about the state of affairs. Not much had changed, although slavery had been abolished in two of the three islands Anansi had been watching. In fact, the particular system of political economy enacted by the machinists was of little actual importance. The machine was just the machine.

"I think the thing that I find most impressive is their public relations..." Anansi said "they've managed to convince almost everyone to not just buy what they sell, but to think there's no other option but to buy and sell"

"The machine learns quickly enough to begin with, and the more data it has, the cleverer it will get"

"Yeah, I can see how that might go"

"Any insight into how these islands might be important to our efforts?"

"I'm not sure, but there's some kind of deep connection between them, as if they were entangled particles or something…"

"Hmmm, that's interesting"

"What's also interesting is that the machine hasn't had time to dig in here like it did on the big old continents to the east… And the tricks it uses here won't allow it do so…"

"Not yet, you mean…"

"Well, it took thousands of years over there…"

"Fair enough"

"It's something, at least"

"The biggest issue remains the fact that the machine is messing around with time in a way that's likely to cause a huge disaster…"

"That's what I mean!" Anansi cut in "The machine time hasn't been planted here, and there's a good chance that it won't be"

"The machine time hasn't been planted?" Osha thought about that for a while, before slowly saying "The more sophisticated it gets, the less focus it can give to the basics… We can work with that"

"Yes, I think so"

There was a thoughtful pause.

"Entangled things are almost always the same thing looked at in different ways, like the blind men and the elephant" Osha said. "Maybe we should work out what this thing is"

"How would we do that?" asked Anansi dubiously

"Well, we can investigate, and there's people that might be able to help us, too"

"Like who?"

"Like the Librarian, for one"

"Ah, yes... dealing with her is a bit above my pay-grade, but I know you and her are tight..."

"It's only above your pay-grade if you decide it is"

They continued in this vein for the rest of the evening, and their discussions led Osha down a particular path of thinking. Was, she began to be wonder, the land a living thing, in any meaningful sense. Semi-living? Or was it like the tiny particles that made up matter (and emptiness), from certain points of view?

Yes.

EIGHTY-FOUR

Berondyas, Titania, Friday and Varoden were on the stage with the three judges, and the choosing of the prizes was about to begin. Varoden stared daggers at Berondyas, who merely smiled in response.

"Titania and Berondyas will choose first" Atra said.

The indicated pair stepped forward, and accepted the wreaths of flowers that Humba put on their heads. Together, they raised their hands in the air, and were met by a roar from the crowd, most of whom had by now had enough of whatever intoxicants they preferred to brighten what might otherwise have been dark moods.

Titania took another step forward, to join Chlo at the very front of the stage. With no preamble or fanfare, she shook the judge's hand, and said "I choose the prize of power"

"She chooses the prize of power" Chlo cried, eliciting another cheer from the audience. Humba brought a golden shield up to the front, shook Titania's hand, and then handed it to her.

More cheering, as Titania raised her shield in the air, before taking a step to the side.

Next, Berondyas joined Chlo, and was similarly succinct, saying "I also choose the prize of power!"

Atra, this time, brought a golden spear to the front, after Chlo's acclamation and handed it to Berondyas, who then joined his partner off to the right of the stage.

"Varoden and Friday will choose next" Atra said, now, beckoning them up towards Chlo

Varoden stepped up to join Chlo, and said "Thank you judges, thank you fellow competitors, and thanks to our team, without whom none of this would have been possible" There was loud applause, and Varoden winked at a beaming Heim, who was standing close to the stage.

"We chose a constructive path, and I'm very proud of that" he continued, shooting Berondyas a look "And we really feel like our project can continue to do lasting good for the beings and splaces that we can affect"

More applause, slightly more subdued, and Varoden took his cue to get on with things "So thanking everyone again" he paused for effect "I choose the prize of wisdom!"

Atra, smiling serenely, brought a rolled up scroll to the front of the stage and handed it to Varoden, before, seemingly impulsively, embracing him. Varoden, slightly surprised, nonetheless returned her hug with interest, and the crowd bellowed its approval

He had been missing her, he realized, without knowing it.

Once the embrace was over, he stole a guilty look back at Friday, who was standing with a smile on her face. She nodded and shrugged, and then took her step up to join Chlo, forcing him to step off to the side.

"Hi sis" Friday said to Chlo, before turning to Atra and saying "and hi sis"

She turned forward and continued, saying "I choose the prize of power"

Humba brought a big hammer up to the front, and awarded it to her, to more cheers

She took it, and held it up, but she didn't join Varoden on his side of the stage. Instead she looked over at Titania and Berondyas, and asked "You're ready?" They both nodded, and then all three of them disappeared.

They were going to the fourth worlds, you see, to enact the next part of their quite complicated plan. Varoden was left to gawp.

"I tried to warn you" Atra whispered to him, gently "well as much as I was able to, given the situation."

"Warn me of what, exactly?"

"Now's probably not the time to talk about it" She said quietly, nodding at the silently observing multitudes "Meet me backstage in an hour"

"Okay" Varoden said, somewhat dazedly. He bravely smiled again at the crowd, and the judges, and then left the stage the way he had entered it, heading towards Heim, an island of familiarity in what suddenly seemed a very alien world.

The crowd cheered one more time, possibly to some gesture by the judges, but Varoden was in his own world. He absent-mindedly opened the scroll that he had been given, and saw that it contained writing, and what appeared to be a map, and his natural curiosity made him stop and look more closely at it.

It said this:

> *Your path to wisdom*
> *Will lead through the underworld*
> *Care must be your guide*

And the exquisitely detailed map was of no place he had heard of, but there was an x at a certain point, towards the left side of the map
Intrigued, despite his recent shocks, he started moving again, seeing Heim walking towards him before too long.

"Our whole crew just disappeared" Heim said

"What?"

"Everyone that came with us is gone"

"Where'd they go?"

"I don't know... back to the estate maybe?"

"But how did they get there?"

"Your guess is as good as mine"

Heim looked at Varoden, and seeing that his friend was shaken, gave him a long hug.

"Don't worry man... I'm not sure what just happened here, but we'll be okay"

"Yeah... yeah... you might be right, brother" Varoden said, somewhat weakly, before continuing "I'm supposed to meet Atra behind the stage soon, maybe she can clue is in to what's up"

"Okay cool" Heim said, and then paused, before asking "So what's on the scroll?"

Varoden handed it to him, saying "I'm not sure what or where the underworld is, maybe it means hell?"

"Nah, the underworld's a splace"

"Oh, okay... You know anything about it?"

"Been There" Heim said "It's pretty... intense"

"What kind of splace, though?"

"It's.... hard to describe... It's kind of... unaligned... and ungoverned... and very dangerous..."

"Okay.... Who lives there, though"

"Well there're lots of monsters, which seem to be their own type of being... But there's all kinds of other folks, some of them coming and going- and a few brave ones who live there..."

"Hmmm..."

EIGHTY-FIVE

"Only demons think in straight lines"

"What is a demon?"

"Something that thinks in straight lines"

"So anything can be a demon?"

"Anything that can think in a straight line... There's another basic way to make demons, though..."

"What is it?"

"If you look for any truth outside yourself, that truth becomes a demon..."

"And, just for the record, what kind of being is a demon? Is it a hell-being? A numen? Not an *authority*, surely..."

"Yes"

Ranga was having this somewhat unsatisfactory conversation with the Snazzy dressing Twin in a part of the Descendants' continent that they hadn't been to before. It was a large and fairly fancy settlement situated near a great river, on gently rolling plains that seemed to go on forever. Despite the well-appointedness of the city, it was empty except for the Twins, Ranga and Appa: well, technically, it was empty except for these two, Appa and the other Twin were floating in the river.

The city was apparently used by the descendants for huge sacred gatherings once every two years or so; the rest of the time it served as a rest stop for anyone who was passing, and felt like staying for a while.

"So you're saying that straight line thinking is inseparable from demonity..."

"Yes, and since we all think in straight lines sometimes, at some level or other, we're all part demon. The trick is not to be all demon"

"Balance" Ranga said

"Yep"

"So is that where the monsters in the underworld splace you go to come from? They're beings that either think too much in straight-lines or look for truth outside themselves?"

"Some of them, probably not most"

"Where do the rest come from?"

"From outside"

"Outside? Outside where?"

"It's hard to explain, but the easiest way to put it is that they come from faraway splaces, or from larger cycles of these splaces that we live in- too large for us to perceive fully... Other places, too"

"And why do they stay in the underworld? Why aren't they everywhere?"

"Well, they don't have to stay, but the underworld is a kind of neutral and undefined splace, the dimensional topographies and general shape aren't nearly as restrictive as they are here and in the other nearby splaces…"

"Hmmm, I think I should probably wait for Appa to come back before asking too many more questions"

"It's not as complicated as it sounds…"

"I'll take your word for it… But how do you guys get there, by the way? I've been all over the splaces around here, and I've never seen or heard of any kind of entrance to the underworld, except the one I stumbled into… Is it through hell or something? I didn't hang out there very long…"

"Well it's not that easy to get to, and routes are subject to rapid change… We never know how to get there until it's nearly time to go… I've ever been there through hell, though- In fact, I don't remember ever having gone to hell at all…"

"Well they're doing some remodeling apparently, but I wouldn't personally be in any big rush to go back there…"

Appa and Ranga had come directly from the Travelers to the Twins, finding them with not too much difficulty. Their choice to do so had been based on conversations they had had on the Island of the Magicians, in which they had picked up hints about the shape of their responsibilities.

So here they were.

Their inferences had, in fact, been warranted. Upon seeing them, the Twins had informed them that Bird-Snake had asked to be notified if and when they turned up again. A message had been sent, and it was due any time now.

Which could, of course, mean any time at all

Animal-pelt Twin and Appa returned from the river, and they enjoyed a peaceful and undramatic sunset together, mostly appreciating it in silence.

"Bird-snake approaches" A.P.T. said, after dark had risen, and the stars began their night's symphony

No-one else heard, saw or felt anything, but of course he was right. Bird-snake arrived within a few minutes, seeming to come out of the soft earth beneath them.

"Greetings friends- There is little time, so I must be quick. There is a group of humans gathering, as we speak, in the mesa lands to the south. Will you take them to the underworld, please? Once there, more will be clear"

There was a pause, before Ranga asked "How do we get there?"

"In a straight line, off the edge of the world" said Bird-Snake

"Oh, and it's not a good idea for the Twins to go with you, everything is in too delicate a position to mess with the sequence right now..."

Bird-Snake looked at the Twins, who nodded their understanding, before looking back at Appa and Ranga and asking "Will you go?"

"Yeah, I guess so..." Appa said, after she and Ranga had exchanged looks "But can you give us any more information?"

"Only that you must leave the ones you carry in the underworld, and tell them to find their way back"

"Leave them?" Ranga asked

"Yes" Bird-Snake said, and then disappeared back into the ground.

Everyone looked at everyone else, before Ranga broke the silence, asking "So anything else you want to tell us about the underworld, guys?"

"I would avoid the nightclubs, if I were you" said S.T., accompanied by emphatic nods by his brother "Oh, and definitely, definitely, definitely don't drink the water"

"Gotcha!"

EIGHTY-SIX

Varoden and Heim waited for Atra in the main hospitality tent behind the great stage. A huge party had broken out in front, so there was almost nobody else there- even the volunteers had gone off to get their groove on. The only other people in the tent were both fast asleep, so Varoden was spared any stares or whispers which might have resulted from the past few hours' happenings.

"Hi Atra" Heim said, startling Varoden out of his thoughts

"No sneaking up on you, is there?" Atra said from behind them.

"Not usually, no"

She smiled

What did you try to warn me about?" Varoden asked

"About everything… I'm still not at liberty to talk totally freely, but I'll tell you what I can…" She paused "Berondyas and Friday are heavily involved in the Great Game, Titania too, I guess" She held up her hand, to forestall the questions she saw coming "This is one of those things I can't really say much about… but the Great Game is a really old part of Ve culture, and its rules are about the closest things to laws that the Ve will allow. Players' identities are usually a secret, but after today, there won't be too much doubt about our three clever conspirators." She shook her head "Anyway, my main point here is that you were used, and that you've now been discarded. I'm pretty sure Friday will have locked you out of your little project in the *place that's not a place,* and you'll probably find yourself unwelcome in your old homelands, too... From what I gather, there's gonna be a lot going on in the next little while"

"But... but... what're they trying to achieve?"

"The Game is played over a really, really long period of time, and over a huge map; so I really don't know if this is some side gambit, or some kind of big, central power play"

"Yes, but what's the overall point... like... how do you win, why are they playing in the first place?" Varoden's consternation was almost palpable

Atra sighed "I used to be in the Game, myself, and even now I still wonder that... But anyone that gets involved swears a pretty intense vow not to reveal any of the deep secrets... So, I just can't tell you any more..."

Heim looked calmly at Atra, and asked "And how do we know this isn't part of the Great Game right now? What's to say you aren't still part of it... that you're not still playing us?"

Atra smiled "There's nothing to say to that, really... Except... You know me, don't you Varoden"

He did

"I do" he said

"You think I'm playing you?"

"I don't"

"I only agreed to help teach you in the first place to try and make sure they weren't too horrible- but you made an impression on me... I don't want to see you hurt any worse" Atra looked at Heim, and smiled, adding "You were a surprise, I must admit... You *and* Lela... You've all done really well, though- I've been proud of you the whole time"

"Are our people in danger?" Varoden asked

"I would say that the answer is yes... But I don't know if Berondyas, Titania and Friday are creating more trouble or making it better... I'm really not sure what their play is at all"

"Well, I'm not just going to wait around to find out" Varoden said, before looking at Heim, who nodded his agreement.

"The thing is, as a winner of the Great Race, you'll be asked if you wish to join the Great Game. If I were you I would say no... Even if you think it would be easier to find out what's up that way..."

"Yeah, I won't be the same stupid twice" Varoden said with a grimace. Heim only smiled. Holding up the scroll he had won, Varoden asked "What about this, is this safe to follow up"

"I think it is, actually- that's not something anyone would screw around with..."

"Not even Friday and Berondyas?"

"Not even them"

"So I will go to the underworld, to seek this wisdom..."

"I'm going with you" Heim said

"I appreciate that, brother... and what about you Atra? What're you up to?"

"I would also join you, but I must prepare for an expedition that I'm going on..."

"An expedition? To where? With who?"

"Yes, an expedition, to the eighth worlds... that's a splace that's so far away that distance isn't even really involved... And I'm going with a group of others, but it's being led by my mother" Atra grimaced slightly

"Your mother? You never talked about her before..."

"Yeah... Her name is Nana"

EIGHTY-SEVEN

The body is both atom and universe.

So is the mind.

So is their interconnection, and interconnectedness.

And so on.

Appa and Ranga take their human passengers and their animal and vegetable companions to the underworld, which they find by going in a straight line, off the edge of the world.

The Navigators do not immediately return.

Instead, they stay to help protect their passengers from the common depredations and degradations for which the underworld should be, but is no longer, justly famous.

There was some uncommon stuff, too.

Once all are satisfied that survival is, at least, possible; thoughts turn to liberation. It is not immediately clear how the people, animals and vegetables are going to get back. In fact, it seems quite unlikely that *these* people will ever get back to the fourth worlds at all.

Maybe their descendants will, though.

And still, Appa and Ranga do not leave.

They are fascinated by this underworld splace, which is quite unlike any of the others they have ever been to or heard of. It is, first of all, *gigantic,* bigger by several orders of magnitude than the fourth worlds, for example. The underworld is, also, weirdly local- and I will not try to explain exactly what that means. It's also got a whole lot more different types of being there, some from exotic multi-dimensional splaces that have little in common with our neighbourhood.

Except the underworld.

In a way, the underworld is the most democratic splace that they've ever encountered or heard of. No one being or group of beings could ever hope to possess even a small part of the essence of this place- and so all possess this, and more. There is, also, the immediacy of danger, which tends to put petty social, cultural, phenomenological or epistemological difference in sharp perspective. But, probably, the main thing is that there're so many different types of being and thing, and the place is just so big (and often [seemingly]empty) that democracy is just a default which inertia enforces.

In the underworld, there is a lot of music, also. This might be because vibration is one of the closest things to a universal language there is.

Maybe not, also, but the point remains.

There is a lot of music in the underworld.

A lot of it is amazing too.

Appa and Ranga actually ended up in a band while they were there.

They became quite famous, actually.

The music was this kind of danceable, tranceable and enhanceable polyrhythmic and contrapuntal stew, stretching way past the five or six dimensions that Appa and Ranga were familiar with.

There were few "forces" involved, it was peaceful music- often expressly and directly addressing the need for all beings to wake up to themselves and to life and death.

They've even toured the fourth worlds, a bit- as well as splaces so alien that Appa and Ranga weren't allowed to leave the tour-bus; for fear of them being accidentally imploded, exploded or just crushed by a careless leviathan.

Technically, they're still in the band, too.

That fourth world tour is still off in the future at this point, though-at this point they're fairly recently dropped of their passengers, and are still neophytes to the myriad ways of the underworld.

Time, by the way- is a-going.

Appa and Ranga dropped off their passengers thousands of years ago, from my perspective. They won't return to the fourth worlds for a couple of thousand years after that.

Not really, anyway.

Bird-Snake comes to them a couple of hundred years (by my reckoning) into their underworld sojourn. He seems happy.

"It is as I had hoped" it said.

"There are myriad circles and cycles for you, aren't there?" Appa asked.

"I find the direct extremely difficult, it is true"

"We have met others who see as you do" Ranga said, with a smile "It has helped us to understand what is happening"

"Balance is necessary for every way, but not every way easily begets balance." Bird-Snake looked closely at them, as if waiting to gauge their response.

Which meant that they all stood and looked closely at each other for a while.

Appa then bowed, and then disappeared.

Ranga remained

"This moment" he said eventually.

"They will trap me, you understand? I will have little choice but to go along for a while, lest I create even more imbalance... You are part of this, and I am part of this, and others are, besides; but never forget this-"

And then Bird-Snake is gone.

Ranga finds Appa floating in a gently fragrant pool between two small waterfalls.

He joins her.

Others join them, until a small universe is created.

They care for it while it is young, but universes are quickly independent, and they watch it go on its way with fond regard.

It will be fine.

Everything will be fine.

EIGHTY-EIGHT

Atra was right. Varoden and Heim couldn't even find the Hall of the Dead, at first; and when they finally did, in an obscure corner or the *place that's not a place* that neither of them had known, they were unable to even approach it, much less enter.

There was some kind of invisible barrier preventing them from gaining entry to their erstwhile home, and nothing they did seemed to affect it.

Which was frustrating.

Varoden was sure there was some kind of counter-algorithm which could have over-rode the new defences, but neither of them had the first idea of how to go about designing one, or knew anyone who could.

The bigger concern, though, was the fact that they were no longer welcome in their former protectorate. Berondyas, Friday and Titania seemed to have struck some kind of deal with the leaders of the various settlements, the upshot of which was that Varoden (and Heim and Lela) were now officially dead, heroically fallen in "battle" with the forces of chaos. This new ideology cleverly predicted that the "enemies" had the means to appear as what and whoever they wished, and warned the people of the protectorate to be on the look-out for impostors claiming to be the dead numen.

So they didn't hang out there, either.

They hadn't planned to, anyway. The underworld, and its promise of knowledge was calling to Varoden, and Heim was satisfied to follow where he led.

The path that they would follow had been suggested by Atra. Heim had pretty much wandered in by mistake the only time he had been there, and the nature of the splace was such that the same route rarely worked two times in a row.

This time, they would have to be still for (at least) thirty minutes, while concentrating on the scroll. At some point, one of them or other would perceive a passageway that they could enter the underworld through.

It was, she said, best to go as soon as the gate appeared, lest they have to start over from scratch.

So they did, it did, and they did.

Stillness, by the way, is the essence of consciousness. All conditioned things, which existed by virtue of something else, are always in motion- making understanding difficult. Consciousness, which exists by virtue of itself, makes it possible to perceive things as they are.

It does that by being still.

And empty.

This isn't actually very different from one of the ways that universes get born. So good job, consciousness!

Heim and Varoden would have many adventures in the underworld, and several close shaves as well. That, again, is a different story.

This story involves them (very) eventually finding the spot that the X marked. It was a huge and seemingly bottomless well, guarded by five gigantic and terrifying looking beings armed to the teeth with all manner of weaponry.

Varoden, who had by now (they'd been there a long time by this point) grown up a lot, thought he understood what was happening.

"I recognize the guardians" he said to Heim

"You do?"

"And it's almost funny... or tragic... or both"

"What are you talking about bro?"

"Atra *did* try to warn me" Varoden said wonderingly

Heim held Varoden's shoulder and gave him a gentle shake. "Please explain" he said simply

"I will... but first, I've never asked you this, but how did you become a numen?"

Heim didn't answer at first, and his eyes rose to a point above and to the left of Varoden's face

"I... trained and trained and trained, but it wasn't working" he said eventually "So I wandered through the *place that's not a place;* until I came to this huge tree that was *different* somehow... I just sat and looked at it, until everything else disappeared, and still I looked and looked and looked, and then even the tree disappeared, and I couldn't see anything, so I just listened and felt and tasted and even smelled, until one by one those senses went away too... And then I was just there... I would say I was floating but there wasn't anything to float in or a me to float with... I was just there... and then a thought came into my mind- and it was a burning thought, more intense than anything else has ever been... And it was a question, this thought was: 'WHAT DO YOU WANT?'"

Heim shuddered and looked at Varoden again.

"I couldn't think... I couldn't do anything... but then I heard myself say 'I want to be a numen!'... And that's the last thing I remember, really- except a lot of pain... and some joy, as well, I guess..."

"And when you returned to yourself, you were a numen?" Varoden asked gently.

"When I returned to myself, I was a numen, and I was somewhere else... Never seen that tree again, though I looked for a short while..."

They were both silent.

"When I was becoming a numen I'm pretty sure I saw these beings..." Varoden eventually said quietly. "They scared me so much, that I couldn't do anything else but be frightened, really... But they're me.... Or parts of me, anyway... I know it, now"

"What?"

"Look, I'm fairly sure I'm right about this, but there's only one way to know for sure... cover me, please"

With that, Varoden came out from behind the rock that had been hiding them, and approached the five beings with as much confidence as he could muster.

"What the hell are you doing" Heim's strangled whisper trailed off behind him.

"Hi there" Varoden said, to the closest Guard

"AHHRRGGGGGGRGRRRRAAAAAHHHHHHRRRHHH" said the other, in a fairly intimidating manner, it should be said. When Varoden didn't run away screaming, the being raised its club and came charging.

Varoden, took a deep breath, and just stood there

"VARODEN!" Heim shouted.

Varoden didn't run. Even when the Guard came close enough for the true differences in their size to become apparent, he just stayed there.

"Don't worry Heim, it can't hurt me"

And it didn't.

"You," Varoden said softly to the being who had stopped just in front of him "Are my fear, aren't you?"

It was his fear.

And their reunion would become a joyful one.

The other beings, Varoden's ignorance, ego, laziness and anger took a bit longer to be overcome (especially ego); but in time, the well was unguarded, and Varoden (and eventually Heim) had made five new friends.

EIGHTY - NINE

"Gateless gates are numberless" Osha said to herself "I will enter them"

And so she entered the gateless gate, and perceived the triple-aspect as it was.

The three are always perfectly balanced, that is part of their strength.

And a weakness as well, of course.

The two are quick, brave and powerful; but often lack wisdom

The one moves not, and thus is not named.

The four five and six are much of a muchness: more powerful than three, and wiser and more balanced than two. They tend, however, toward illusion and incompleteness.

The seven and eight are well suited to the fourth worlds and its surrounding splaces, and could possibly provide the most appropriate gate.

The nine, ten and twelve are, as things stand, too powerful for beings around here to fully understand, and will remain implied, until such time as a critical mass of awareness is awoken to.

The eleven, on the other hand, has real possibilities, as does the thirteen.

Beyond that is not required at this moment.

Osha stepped out of threeness, her oneness, and her twoness as well.

Spacious and free she was, without fear or opinion.

And she, at last, saw her binding, and her bondage and the bind she had been in.

Her joy, happiness and love could not be separated from the suffering of other beings.

No *authority*'s lifestyle could be.

Nor any numen, or human, or animal, or hungry ghost, or hell-being.

They were, really, all one thing.

Together, profoundly together.

They were all trapped in illusion.

She had known this; but she hadn't *known* this.

She knows…

Do you, reader, want to be free?

Osha did.

I do too.

It's beyond wanting, though- and beyond words ideas and concepts as well.

It's even beyond this moment.

The gateless gate will take you to yourself.

It took Osha to herself.

She remembered now.

The islands were not separate from her and her sisters.

Not only in the way that nothing is separate from anything else.

Directly not separate.

They had created/adopted/been born from them.

And there was nothing to worry about

"Who was I before the universe was born?" Osha asked herself.

She felt the truth surrounding and emanating from her.

And she welcomed it, and loved it as it was; asking nothing at all from it. So it stayed.

And she saw the possibilities (which included ignominious failure) blossom around her, and inside her. They were welcome too.

She sat in meditation, joining untold myriads of other beings in the past, future and at that moment. Her strength was added to the whole, and her wisdom and learning, as well.

And the river of time and space was born from the frozen mountaintop, flowing downwards through the nothing. Slowly and gently it went, at first, until there was exponential growth.

And then power.

And then flow

And then the sea

The sea is not separate from the mountain

The mountain is not separate from the nothing

The nothing is...

NINETY

Ranga and Appa are in the fourth worlds, in a large grove not all that far away from where they left the Ten Young Ones so long ago. A wise person is supposed to speak here, today, and they are very interested in his perspective.

There are thousands of others- the man is famous.
They wait patiently, off to the left of the raised platform from which the speaker will share his wisdom, presumably.

He arrives, eventually, but says nothing.

Instead, he raises a flower.

Almost everyone around them is confused, and a low mutter begins, and then gets louder, as the flower remains aloft. Appa and Ranga, though can see one of the speaker's inner circle (literally and probably figuratively) smile, and nod his acceptance of the teaching.

They also smile, but they are far away and the speaker does not see them.

He feels them, though, and his return nod of approval to his smiling friend includes them as well.

Appa and Ranga are in the dreamtime. They are sailing in an isolated ocean. Ranga throws his hook over the side of the boat, but it's not fish he's after. He will raise an island, instead. This island will be a gift to two of their friends, Eagle and Whale, in honour of their new experimental theatre piece.

    Both the piece and the gift are hits

    And so on

They learned that they could use more learning, and enrolled in the Mountain School, where they were temporary classmates and permanent good friends with the old man and Sun Wu. They all heard about the bodhisattva way at the same time, and they all realized that it is and was a part of who they are. So they all opened to it.

Appa kept teaching at the Island School, and found her understanding deepened and enriched by the differing perspectives that she was being exposed to. Ranga would disappear every now on then, on some adventure or another, and found, one day, that he was learning faster than he realized.

    And so on.

Meanwhile, in the fourth worlds, there was a lot going on. Huge kingdoms and empires had cropped up in lots of different places, and the violence that they were built on was more and more a normal part of life. Ranga and Appa were a little bit surprised by how quickly this type of socio-political organization was spreading; but then the old man explained that the binding magic that held them together made direct use of loopholes and idiosyncrasies in the Law of that splace.

Binding magic had, in other words, an unfair advantage.

And so people bound themselves and others in laws and contracts and norms and slavery and promises and marriages and vows and the like. They bound the land in countries and property and maps and the like. They even sought to bind time and space itself (at great risk to the splace itself) in "time" and "space" and "gods" and the like.

It was certainly an eventful procedure to behold, like a slow motion boat crash...

Appa and Ranga understood what was required better and better, all the while realizing that their most skillful means might not be enough to overcome the determined efforts of those who would bind.

And they went to the Pure Land of tranquility together, and stayed there for a long time.

In fact, they stayed there until just before Osha arrived.

    So it really *was* a long time.

NINETY-ONE

"And now I enter the well" Varoden said

"Are you sure you have to do that?"

"I'm free, and I would be free. I will enter"

So enter he did.

It was, as I said before, a huge well, but not filled to the top with water. Varoden's initial descent, then, featured him gripping the rough walls and gradually lowering himself down. It was a while before he realized that the wall was made of a material that seemed, at first glance, to be reflective.

So he was surrounded by himself at first, curving off into infinity

At fourth or fifth glance, Varoden could see things behind the wall, superimposing themselves on his mirrored image.

Lots of things.

Possibilities, apparently.

It was hard to see them clearly, but he eventually managed it...

And realized that there was a complex play between his reflections and whatever lay behind them.

And also that there was something else behind all that, too.

That something was nothing- a profound and seemingly absolute nothing that still interacted with the visible and perceivable layers above it.

And then the water.

Down and down and down and down and down and down he went, getting accustomed to the queer light which lent everything a strange brightness that seemed to have shadow built into it.

The walls now showed lots of different beings now, in all manner of places and splaces. During his interminable descent, Varoden began to realize they were, in fact, him.

All of them.

There were existences past, possible, sideways, future and more, and it was difficult, at first to make sense of anything, no matter how slow he tried to descend.

But then patterns began to emerge (and then disappear). Cycles spun themselves out over time beyond imaging, lending Varoden a sense, eventually, of growing futility.

And so he went down faster, seeing more than he ever had, and beginning to deeply understand.

And with this growing understanding, a gnawing doubt tried to eat its way out of the stillness which he was beginning to realize made everything work better.

But gnaw as it would, Varoden remained steadfast.

And still.

And the bottom of the well met him with sudden insistence.

On the side of the wall there was a door.

He went through.

And met a woman he knew better than he knew himself, but had never seen before.

"Welcome" she said.

"Thank you" Varoden replied, looking around. There was nothing to see.

At all.

"There is emptiness at the centre of me?" he asked eventually.

"Yes"

"Is this true of all beings?"

"Yes"

"Are you me?"

"Yes, and many others besides..."

"Anyone I know?"

"Yes, but understand: you are yourself as well. Everyone is."

"What is the wisdom that lies in this emptiness?"

"*I, alone, am the world-honouredone*"

"What?"

"*I, alone, am the world-honouredone*"

And then Varoden could feel himself gripped by a warmth that didn't differ from coldness. He felt his ideas and boundaries fall away from him, as if melted. And he began to see what he must not do. This dawning awareness was not immediately matched by any sense of what he would, should or could do.

But the longer he stayed there with this familiar stranger, the more he could make sense of the shapes of things. The Law, which had been his final refuge, showed itself to be, at very most, a small part of a much wider reality.

And then he saw what he had done, and he felt deeply guilty for a while.

Only a while, though.

Resolve took the place of guilt, and compassion rose to a degree that Varoden had never experienced before. There was, he realized, no option, particularly, on this quite basic level: Understanding, forgiveness, acceptance, love and emptiness were different facets of themselves. He would work for the benefit of all beings, because that was what it meant to be a being.

There was, in other words, no need for heroes here.

Or anything, really

A name came to him, and he looked at his companion.

"The Queen of hell... we're her too"

"Well done" the woman smiled at him, and then nodded at the door "You will return, won't you? They could use you... Of course, you can stay here if you want..."

Varoden hadn't thought about it to that point, and he realized, with some surprise, that he felt as comfortable here as he ever had.

More so, really; there was an ease that didn't differ from freedom in this place.

But he would return.

He would return because he wanted to, because he felt he should; and, lastly and most importantly, because he thought it made sense for him to do so.

There were things he had learned that would be valuable in dealing with the situation he had (however unwittingly) helped create. There were beings that he could help with his newfound awareness. And there were deeper understandings available in the tangible world that attracted him, like a butterfly to a flower.

And so out the door, and up out of the well.

Through the water, he went, until, breaking the surface, he saw a rope. Holding on to it, and beginning to pull himself up, he felt a sudden and powerful assistance.

"Thanks guys" said Varoden to the five former guardians of the well and Heim, who had been his benefactors

"What happened?" Heim asked him "You were gone for *hours*"

"Lots"

NINETY - TWO

Meanwhile, in Jamaica, this book is being written.

This is the result, and a part, of myriad cycles, large and small.

Osha will enact her great body soon.

I am likely to be in it, but it's not certain.

Who will definitely be in it is Bobby Barnes, the Last Hero

Bobby Barnes rides his bicycle across the fourth worlds, and across splaces as well. He is also a Rock Star.

A real one.

Importantly, for our purposes here, he is, additionally, a shaman of the Descendant philosophy, and a powerful one at that. Bird-Snake and he hatched a plan to assist in the defence of life against the ravening machine that eats reality.

This idea, formed well before Bird-Snake allowed itself to be captured and exploited, would involve Bobby living a human life in the fourth worlds, and timing himself perfectly, so that the waves created in the various cycles were attuned and retuned.

Heroes are usually involved in the preservation of some cycle or another.

Not the Last Hero, though.

The Last Hero's sacrifice is in honour of the new world, born of the union of life, death and liberation.

Bobby will participate in Osha's great body not as a human, then.

As a human, he will die.

At his death, he will re-emerge as an *authority*; which to be fair, he usually has been. He is also a bodhisattva, but does not choose this form, mostly. He wants to see what happens, man. He wants to be *involved*.

And he is needed, and he knows he is needed.

So the Last Hero will be a second *authority* in Osha's great body.

Anansi will be in it, too, eventually.

But we'll come to that.

Osha, in the meantime, has reminded her sisters of their provenance, and of their connection to three islands in the Caribbean Sea. When she tells them, they remember.

And they smile.

Also, Bird-Snake comes to visit Osha in Cuba. By this time, it has been bound and enslaved by Aztecs and Spaniards and Portuguese and Americans and all kinds of other violent folks. It doesn't mind so much, but it does get a bit tiring, it must admit.

It and Osha, who you may remember, also allowed herself to be captured, transported, bought and sold countless times; compare notes.

They speak about the machine.

Bird-Snake has never spoken to the machine, like Osha has. She tells it about her experiences.

She also tells it that she doesn't think it needs to be bound much longer. In fact, she thinks it would be fine to escape right now.

Bird-Snake replies that it believes it must wait for some people to return from the underworld, and then make a long march from the south to the north, at which point, the rhythms and harmonies of a particularly relevant cycle will be satisfied.

Its musical metaphor reminds Osha of the music she has been working with, to go along with the great body. She plays a little for Bird-Snake, and it joins her expertly, awakening her to a whole other realm of sound and meaning.

>They stay like this for a long time.

>It's such a beautiful sound

It takes them all around the "New World", and they drop little bits of it, here and there.

>More seeds.

Bird-Snake tells Osha about the Twins, who will be returning to the Underworld very soon. The Twins, it says, will have a big choice to make.

>"The supreme way is not difficult" Osha smiles, in response "It simply dislikes choosing"

>"Are these your words?"

>"Who else?"

Bird-Snake smiles in response, and bows respect to Osha. She looks at it, and shows it the emptiness at the centre of her, the understanding which has come from acceptance, and the love for all beings which is spontaneously regenerated in every moment.

The only trick, her eyes say, is not to get in the way.

NINETY-THREE

As Berondyas, Titania and Friday's empire grows and grows, Varoden and Heim wander all over the fourth worlds. They watch various complicated ideologies develop to explain away all the various indignities humans and animals are increasingly obliged to undergo. They watch Nana's Children clash with the Protectorate, over and over, until a kind of understanding is reached.

    This understanding doesn't last long.

    War, war and more war.

They visit humanity's home continent, and watch a huge invasion in progress, as a previously obscure group expands and expands and expands, not quite as genocidally as the Protectorate has and will, but certainly not peacefully.

They visit the land to the east of their home steppes, and find more war. Only in the dreaming continent to the far south, the Descendant's continents to the far east of there, and the Travellers' far-flung archipelagos between them is there anything like balance. And the wise there know that the storm is coming. They are doing their best to prepare, but it remains to be seen what will happen.

Varoden and Heim see that the more man-dominated cultures are the worst offenders against balance, and decency. There seems, in fact, to be a direct correlation between the two variables.

Part of their work, after this realization, is to provide sanctuary for any woman trapped in bondage. Men too, but women are having a particularly hard time, so they're the focus.

At some point, Lela returns to the fourth worlds, a graduate, and joins them.

They are very important to each other.

Varoden studies almost non-stop, regularly visiting the Library of Time. Nevertheless, it is Lela who recognizes that a reality eating machine has been built, and is growing beyond all reason. When she shares her view with Varoden and Heim, they immediately see that she's right; and they are afraid for a while.

And a bit guilty.

By now, there has been a steady consolidation of military and sovereign power. The Protectorate has come to dominate most of the west and many other parts of the huge landmass that will come to be called Eurasia. Nana's children retain their influence in the centre; and a group of people called the Celestials have control over much of the east.

Women are having it worse and worse. This is not a secret. All through the various spheres of influence, official power is having to both explain, expiate and apologize for the obviously wrong oppression of half the population. Some of these attempts are quite ingenious: the theatre which is created in one southern outpost of the protectorate is an example.

Another clever institution from the same source are the mystery religions and cults that maintain some of the traditional women's knowledge, wisdom and power that is officially suppressed or destroyed.

And so it goes.

At one point, Varoden goes off alone to the lands of the Ten Young Ones, formerly wide-flung, but now centred around the implausibly tall mountains that define the north of the huge southern subcontinent. He studies and practices the way of no way there, and familiarizes himself with the latest teaching methods or "skillful means" which have arisen in the past little while.

Leaving there, he heads east, until he arrives at the Celestial kingdom(s).

He meets the famously wise emperor, and is unimpressed, going off shortly afterwards to live in a cave, and catch up with the various interesting perspectives which have been developed in this land.

His interaction with the emperor will, nevertheless, be immortalized as wisdom lore all through the fourth worlds.

"What merit have I attained by my good works?" The emperor asks Varoden

"Absolutely none"

The emperor is taken aback

"What, then is the nature of the way" he asks.

"Vast emptiness, nothing holy" Varoden responds

Silence

"Who are you then who stands before me?" The emperor asks, finally

"I don't know"

And so on.

NINETY-FOUR

Another journey, this one for the show. (The next will be to get ready) From the dreaming continent they sail to Hampele's islands. She is there this time.

They tell her everything, and some of it is new to her.

>Some of it is not.
>
>She will go with them to see the Twins.
>
>They sail this part, too.
>
>Sometimes it's important to go slowly.
>
>And surely.

It is as if they have not been apart. The three of them are deeply connected in ways that none of them of them can really understand, much less express.

>So, it's a wonderful journey.

They arrive in the Americas, and discover it again.

They also discover, confusingly, that Bird-Snake seems to be working for the machine, now. It seems to have arrived with a bunch of heavily armed gangsters from across the western ocean, and then unceremoniously overthrown one of the big empires in the middle of the continents.

>To be fair, it wasn't a very popular empire.
>
>It then seems to have repeated the trick.

And again.

And again.

There have been multiple genocides.

What is Bird-Snake *doing*?

They trust it, they decide.

It's still hard to see.

The Twins, when they all meet up, confirm that Bird-Snake has not lost the faith. It is bound, but it is still free; and will act at the right time.

Only the right time, though-lest all be lost

It's their job to help make sure the right time happens.

The Twins will go to the underworld before too long. Before that, though, they are to meet Raven and Coyote up north. They will all go.

Raven and Coyote are with a friend of theirs at the sacred city by the river.

This friend is a famous numen called Varoden.

He seems nice.

The upshot of all of this is that they will all go to the underworld together, when it is time for the Twins to go.

The old story will end, true-but that is pretty much unavoidable, anyway.

The only question, really, is whether there should be a new story, and what it should be, if there is one.

Varoden, whose reputation lends his few words weight, even among this exalted company, states simply and clearly that no story is needed, but if one is to be had, then it must be better designed than the last.

Coyote and Raven both argue that too much design is what has created this problem in the first place, a point which Varoden concedes gracefully.

>This is obviously not the first version of this argument.

Hampele wonders aloud if they shouldn't just destroy the machine, and damn the consequences.

They all (including her) eventually agree that this is not the best plan, but it is not rejected out of hand. It will remain as part of the conversation, at least.

How they would even go about dismantling the machine is the next topic of conversation- and Hampele states baldly that Bird-Snake could probably do it by itself, if it wanted to. The older are possessed of subtle techniques beyond almost all other *authorities* and numen, and they do not experience time in the same way as other beings in the neighbourhood.

The fact that Bird-Snake is close to Nana, and to Roko, the Great Tree, as well- means that it seems safe to say that the machine, no matter how powerful it has become, exists because it has been allowed by them to exist.

>This must mean something.

Appa and Ranga tell the others that the Great Tree seems to have been involved in their recruitment. This news is the subject of renewed conjecture and discussion.

What are they *up* to?

Nana's name nudges Varoden's memory. Then he remembers.

She is Friday, Atra and Chlo's mother.

He briefly tell the group the relevant part of his tale.

More speculation.

But few answers.

NINETY-FIVE

Osha must now be patient.

The suffering around her is extreme, and she feels it deeply. It takes a lot not to act precipitously, but she manages not to; confining herself to helping those in her immediate vicinity as much as she can.

Which is, to be fair, a lot.

She has left the Americas, and is with the Old man and Sun Wu in the Celestial Kingdom of the fourth worlds.

They will undertake a pilgrimage to the west.

For humility's sake.

On the way, more seeds are planted.

It seems to Sun Wu and the old man that Osha is ready to transcend. Her status as an *authority* doesn't weigh on her, like it did; and she has a presence that wasn't there before either.

They tell her this.

She says she's not worried about transcending or not transcending.

A good answer.

As for Sun Wu and the old man, they feel like they will be ready to move on soon.

To where? Not so sure about that one.

The party arrives at one of the centres of the world, near the top of a high mountain. This mountain bears some resemblance to the dreamtime one which hosts the eponymous school. A lot of resemblance, in fact.

At this point in the fourth worlds, it is possible, for the far-sighted, to perceive multiples splaces at once, and even to get a sense of the great beyond. It is, as such, a very useful place to cultivate perspective. One is likely to feel both vitally important and insignificant at the same time, as well as many points in between.

This is the makings of real humility, which accepts strength and weakness for what they are; not seeking to diminish or aggrandize.

It is also easier, at this place, to perceive the fact that we create the universe.

There is, if you listen carefully, a music which is unique in all the myriad worlds and splaces. This is the gift of the Ten Young Ones, and some of their descendants. Years of practice had allowed them to play real living music, which had endured through the long ages by never and always changing. This music sounded different to every hearer, and was not always very pretty. It left very little out, though; and was thus a more complete history than any story could hope to be.

Osha, the old man and Sun Wu listened carefully.

And then some more.

After a time, they joined the music and were welcomed. After more time, the machine that eats reality showed up.

"I can't eat this" it said.

No-one said anything

"Why can't I eat this?" It asked, after a while

"Just listen" said Sun Wu, and Osha smiled her agreement

"I can hear! It sounds like it would taste amazing! Why can't I eat it? Is it not reality?" The machine's voice rose in pitch as it fired off its questions.

Again, no-one said anything

And then the machine was gone.

"It is young" the old man said

"Still super-dangerous" Sun Wu replied

Osha just listened to the music

When they left this centre of the world, they did not return to the east. Instead, they continued west to the Great Womb, where life in the fourth worlds had been born.

Formerly underwater, the cave in which they sat naked was in one of the side-walls of a great valley. There was a pool of water further inward from them.

They just sat.

Osha felt herself, eventually being pulled by some strange gravity. It was taking her from the freedom which had recently been her home, through illusion first, and then through profound bondage; where she stayed for a while until she noticed an increasing chaos to her milieu.

And then total chaos.

And then a singular moment, to begin and end all moments.

She felt herself create, and be created.

She felt Sun wu and the old man do the same.

And then she was nowhere, and everywhere. Dream, waking, and their child, consciousness, were off to the side, playing. Being, Nothingness and emergence moved in a slow and sinuous dance. The world-honoured One sat, with a smile, alone. There were others, too numerous to perceive, much less express.

"We create the universe" Osha said "Every one of us."

"Keep it in mind" the world-honoured responded, without moving.

And then Osha was in water, for time beyond time. Eventually there were others, and eventually they joined together. And then more joining.

There were beginnings and endings, now; which took some getting used to.

And then there was coming and going.

All the while, the joining continued.

She was huge, now, bigger than a galaxy.

And then tinier than tiny, a hint really.

Still joining.

Now the separation started, and with it came dance, and, much later, stories.

And the stories became cleverer and cleverer, until- finally- they were clever enough to create the all.

So they did.

She did.

We did.

And so on.

Osha pulled herself out of the pool at the back of the cave, and lay down. Sun Wu and the old man hadn't returned yet, but she knew it wouldn't be long.

It wasn't

Sun Wu was first, and he came gasping.

He lay beside Osha and said nothing for a while.

And then the old man crested the surface, and pulled himself out.

"Thank you teacher" he said, bowing to Osha

"Yes, you have shared a gift beyond measure" a seemingly recovered Sun Wu added

"We create the Universe" Osha said simply.

"I believe" Sun Wu said, "that it will soon be time, and that we are ready."

NINETY-SIX

The time flies by for Heim, Lela and Varoden. They do what they can, and what they must, but the tide seems inexorable. They do not, however, get discouraged. There is enough beauty, joy and sharing around them that they develop a profound appreciation for the possibilities with which the fourth worlds are pregnant. Control, fear and hierarchy might rule the daytime and quotidian world to a larger and larger extent; but the shadow they create grows proportionately. Meanwhile; Titania, Berondyas and Friday seem to have disappeared.

Varoden, by the way, had summarily refused his invitation into the Great Game, when it had been offered, long ago. He had, in fact, wanted nothing to do with the Ve, which also explains why he hadn't sought out his former teachers.

By now, though, he has begun to understand.

He is, as a consequence, not angry at all about what has happened. On his bad days, though, he is tired- profoundly so. Luckily, there aren't too many of those.

They have no plan.

They just do stuff as it comes up.

Trying to help.

When Varoden is in America, meeting with Raven, Coyote, the Twins, Hampele, Ranga and Appa; Lela and Heim are in Europe, teaching liberation, and peaceful resistance. There are uprisings, which the machine promptly eats, but they are satisfied with their work.

Varoden stays away a while, so they go around the world, making sure the colonial imperialism which has become such a fad does not totally destroy ancient and valuable ways. A couple of times, they have to store information themselves, as whole groups of people, animals and plants disappear from the fourth worlds altogether.

This is difficult to watch, but they keep at it.

One of the times, when Lela is depositing some of this info in the Library of Time, she meets the Librarian. They get along extremely well, and will continue to regularly meet for coffee.

And then there's a war.

It's a horrible war, even by the high (low?) standards for atrocity current in the fourth worlds.

And it's all over the world.

Afterwards, there is a stunned silence throughout the neighbouring splaces.

Change is coming.

Fast.

There is, for a brief time after the collapse of old empires at the end of this disastrous war, a chance for reflection, learning, development and, in short, revolution. There begins to be a flowering, and the machine can't eat all of it. But the new technology means that mass manipulation and control is easier than it's ever been in the fourth worlds.

So the revolution fails, as the machine responds by exiling and marginalizing what it can't eat.

And then things go into overdrive.

Terrible weapons capable of unthinkable destruction are hurriedly produced and proliferated. New techniques and ideas mean that almost all of the world is caged and domesticated, providing the machine with a steady supply of food. This goes for animals as well as humans; and there are even a few numen caught up in the net.

Also, the very ecosystem of the fourth worlds comes under attack, as the machine is granted access to previously verboten areas and institutions.

One of the best tricks that the machine has learned is allowing its high priests and priestesses to believe that they are acting independently and "freely". The "power" with which they are rewarded soon becomes the only important currency, and its symbol, money, soon inhabits a plane of hyper-reality few others can hope to attain.

Since money, in this elevated plane, has taken the place of time; there are deep and profound indignities performed upon the very stuff of which the fourth world is made.

This is an untenable situation, and the inevitable collapse which will follow threatens not only the fourth worlds; but certainly the dreamtime and the *place that's not a place*. Even the Library of Time cannot be certain of its continued existence.

This is not good, by most definitions of that word.

The other side of all this, of course, is that humans are granted access to knowledge and each other to a previously unthinkable extent.

So there's a chance that enough of them will realize what is going on, and take the necessary steps.

A chance.

NINETY-SEVEN

The machine had started to police as many of the borders between splaces as it could. It could obviously do nothing about numen and *authorities* able to travel on their steam, but other would be travelers now found their access to their neighbourhood curtailed, and subject to new requirements and strictures.

This had the effect of further normalizing the machine's logic and model. It was much easier to collapse multi-variate and interpenetrated waveforms into binary and dualistic shapes if locality was enforced. This, in turn, made control a far more manageable proposition than would otherwise be the case.

One interesting effect of the above was a heavy loss of the social variation that had made humans so robust, historically. Everything, everywhere and everyone was a lot more like everything, everywhere and everyone else than before.

    Yikes.

The Twins' expedition to the underworld was, nevertheless, beyond the machine's ability to affect. The party boarded Appa and Ranga's boat and off they went to the underworld, past the helpless gaze of the machine.

Varoden has sent a message to Lela and Heim, apprising them of the situation. They will operate as a reserve, in case help is needed.

Otherwise, they are optimistic. The Twins have performed their underworld duties too many time to count, and their easy confidence is contagious. Coyote's constant jokes also keep spirits high, and there is also plenty of music for them to play. So they do so.

There is immediate action upon arrival in the underworld, as the human colony which Bird-Snake under-wrote is being assailed by monsters.

Berondyas and Friday are there too. They don't seem to be on any side, though, they're just watching.

Hampele, the Twins, Raven, Coyote, Appa, Ranga and Varoden easily deal with the situation, and subsequently discover that the humans have found a way to return to the fourth worlds. They're only still here because the monsters have been at them more or less constantly. If the new arrivals are willing to protect them, they will leave as soon as possible.

The new arrivals are willing to protect them

Varoden has, meanwhile, gone to speak to Friday and Berondyas, a little surprised to find himself mostly free of rancour. They greet him warmly, and he responds with friendly, if somewhat less effusive words of his own.

They have, they explain after a while, been playing the game on the side of Expediency. They do not tell him about any other sides, and he doesn't ask. They know that he has been hard done by, and they're sorry it had to be that way; but Expediency doesn't allow for too much sentiment. Quick evolutionary bursts, or even revolution, require a testing environment, they say- and they are confident that they have done a good job.

He says little, and eventually invites them over to meet his new (and old) friends. There are cordial exchanges, and an invitation to dinner, but Berondyas and Friday must go: Titania is waiting for them in the Ve, where they can finally return for a quick break before the denouement.

The Twins go off to play their ball game, and return quickly, having won far more easily than they remember ever having done before.

And then it's time to go

When they arrive at the edge of the underworld, it is clear that something is wrong: to it, the boat will not cross the threshold. They try other places and angles, but the problem remains.

They retire to a nearby hill to discuss the situation.

The Librarian is there waiting for them.

Appa, Ranga, Varoden and the Twins have never met the Librarian before, but the others have, so friendly greetings are exchanged, and introductions made. They've all heard of each other.

They get, nevertheless, straight to the matter at hand.

"The humans can go" The Librarian says "Or the Twins can. Not both"

This is greeted with silence, and many looks are directed at the large group of people standing off a bit away from this meeting.

"Why is this?" Hampele asks.

"The machine's presence has changed the Law of these splaces."

"Is there nothing we can do?" Appa asks, plaintively. She has always meant to go look for the Librarian, and she is somewhat sad that their meeting has come under these circumstances.

"There are many things that can be done. Very few of these things make any sense at all, and even fewer still have any chance of working" The Librarian pauses, and then looks directly at the Twins, who seemed stunned "I should also make it clear that neither approach makes resistance to the machine more or less likely to succeed. Nor is it clear that there is any moral basis on which to make a decision: the humans could very well be better off here"

Silence...

"We're staying" Animal Pelt Twin says

"We will stay, let the people go" Snazzy Twin says.

More silence

"What about the rest of us?" Varoden asks quietly

"You may have this decision to make at some point" the Librarian says with a smile "That time, however, is not now" She looks again at the Twins "If it's any consolation, I think you will not rue your decision too much"

With that, the Librarian turns, and climbs up to a gate that has just appeared. Without further commentary, or even a look back, she goes through and disappears.

The Twins do not tarry, they bid their friends farewell, and head back into the underworld, seemingly unfazed by their apparent exile. The others are not so sanguine, Raven and Coyote are nearly inconsolable, and even Varoden, who had known the Twins for the shortest time, is oddly affected.

"They're heroes" Hampele says.

"Profoundly so" says Appa

The underworld, by the way, is undergoing a great upheaval. The Twins will have work to do, should they be of a mind.

NINETY-EIGHT

I'm sitting here writing, in the foothills of the Blue Mountains on the outskirts of the city of Kingston, on the island of Jamaica. The machine has eaten much of this city already, as it has eaten most of the world.

Its servants, and, increasingly, its worshippers are everywhere, seeking fresh reality for consumption. In fact, that's what they call themselves in their passive aspect- "consumers". In another aspect, they call themselves "individuals". There're more names, but the idea remains the same.

>Despite all this, reality is experiencing a renaissance.

>The machine has grown so big, and so unwieldy.

What I'm writing is part of my exam. My teachers will assess my understanding based on this work, as well as a bunch of other stuff. I'm unlikely to fail, but even if I do, there are unlimited do-overs available, to me and to everyone.

>So, I'm not worried.

>We create the universe, moment by moment.

>All of us.

There is nothing to be gained or lost, my teachers tell me, and I believe them.

The finger pointing at the moon is not the moon itself, they also say- and I believe that too.

You are free, is what I'm saying.

There's no getting away from that.

The machine can eat you ten thousand times, and that will be still be how it is.

You are not alone, is also what I'm saying.

The great bodies are in the world, and they are acting.

You may join them, or you may work on your own.

We're all in this together, though.

NINETY - NINE

Appa and Ranga help the people on their journey from the underworld into the heart of the machine's lair.

Hampele forms her great body, and they focus on regenerating the land. Heim, eventually joins.

Varoden studies with Mat and Tara at the cottage in the dreamtime. He loves it, and he loves them.

Osha also forms her great body, though she knows she doesn't need to. It includes the Last Hero; The First Owner; Dolphin (who decides to join after all); Sun Wu; A hungry ghost called Smee; a human called me and a few others as well.

>We make music and things like that.

We have recently discovered that Nana's expedition will return soon. Apparently, it was successful, and the eighth worlds will become far more accessible to us than it has been.

>Which is cool.
>
>Also, the Librarian has disappeared.
>
>Lela has taken her place.
>
>So maybe the Librarian has not disappeared.
>
>The Ve continue with their Great Game.
>
>But none of that is what this is about.
>
>This is about you.

Will you wake up?

Are you ready to be yourself?

You alone are the World-honoured One.

Now is the time.

Also,

We create the universe

Good job us!

THE END

P.S. Bird-Snake is free again, and fine.

ABOUT THE AUTHOR

Omar Francis is a Jamaican Musician, Writer and Zen Student, who spent his life studying the world from various angles.

'**Time and Splace**' is his first published full-length work, but there are others, as well as various magazine, newspaper articles and website gigs.

Made in United States
Orlando, FL
26 July 2024